86 The Chef

Adam K. Watson

Wooster Street Publishing

For Elizabeth

My perfect partner on this perfect journey

1

Trey Chapman expected an empty refrigerator. The two eggs sitting in a small, porcelain bowl on the top shelf seemed like a mirage. His mind tended to play tricks in the morning. He certainly hadn't bought them and couldn't remember the last time he'd actually cooked in his own kitchen. Trey pulled the bowl out, and the mystery unraveled at the sight of a bright yellow, almost golden, slab of butter next to the eggs. It could have only come from one place.

Scrambled eggs aren't easy to make. Well, good scrambled eggs aren't. Trey learned that early on. As soon as he was big enough to drag a chair across the kitchen, he would stand on it and watch as his father never stopped stirring. Those childhood eggs were velvety, like custard. The trick was to take them on and off the heat to prevent them from drying out. Salt was only added at the very end. Trey never could quite duplicate his old man's, but his were nothing to scoff at. Fresh out of high school, those scrambled eggs would land him his first real job, one outside of the large shadow cast by his father's restaurant.

Chapman's Steakhouse was an institution in Chicago. Inside, it was like nothing had changed in the almost fifty years since it opened. It was classic, with oak-paneled walls and tuxedoed waiters. But to Trey, it was a dinosaur. There was so much more to dining out than a grilled ribeye and baked potato. James Chapman Jr. wanted his first born to take over. But James III had bigger ambitions, and everyone in the family knew that wasn't going to happen when he began introducing himself as Trey.

Culinary school would've been a waste of money and time. Trey grew up in that restaurant kitchen. He was scaling fish while other kids were playing T-Ball. Taking over for his father would've been easy, but the end of the road. Trey wanted an empire. He wanted a line of cookbooks, pans, aprons, and a restaurant in every major city. At age 18, his last name alone could have landed him a job in any kitchen in Chicago, but he wanted to prove himself. There was just one question in that first job interview. It was more of an order, "Make me some eggs." Trey didn't flinch. He didn't ask how the chef wanted them prepared. He just got to work stirring, the same way he was taught.

Trey set the porcelain bowl on the long, cold marble island next to the stove. He fished the butter out and laid it in a small sauté pan as he turned on the burner. It looked like far too much for two eggs. But it wasn't. Trey cracked them into the porcelain bowl and squinted out of the window at the sun rising over Lake Michigan as he whisked. The view was rare, and worth appreciating. The chef's mind just wasn't there though. It was a collage of the dinner hosted in his honor by some investors the night before, the anguish of trying to fall asleep, and the injustice of then waking up in the middle of the night to pee. Twice. That was the first thing that had started to make the 48-year-old bachelor feel old.

The butter at the edge of the pan started to bubble. Trey poured the eggs in and got to work stirring. He adjusted the flame and worked the shiny sauté pan on and off the heat for several minutes.

"Salt?" he said to no one, looking around the kitchen.

Trey turned off the burner and walked to the pantry. The heavy door opened to reveal a space clearly related to the fridge. Just a handful of items dotted the floor-to-ceiling custom shelves. Trey's glance immediately landed on a small glass bottle of hot sauce with his face on it. At least, what he had looked like a long time ago. It was a souvenir from when he would endorse anything. The once bright red liquid had faded to a brownish orange. Trey ran his hand over his cheek as he stared at the picture. The youthful tan that belied a life cooped up in a kitchen had crossed the threshold to leathery. The only thing that hadn't changed was his wavy, blonde hair, that almost seemed in constant motion.

He put the bottle back on the shelf and grabbed a box of Maldon sea salt. The green diamond on the front hinted at the pyramid-shaped flakes inside. As a kid, he would sneak around the expediter at his father's restaurant to snag a handful of the large grains. Then he would disappear and find a quiet spot to place them individually on his tongue and let them slowly dissolve. It was a temptation he still couldn't resist, but as he went to shake some of the fancy salt into his hand, it cascaded out all over the pantry floor. Trey knelt down to clean it up, then remembered the eggs. He raced back to the stove, but knew he was too late even before he slid the spatula under the yellow mounds. The creaminess was gone and they had started to adhere to the pan. To Trey, there was nothing worse than dry eggs. He flipped the pan into the sink, the bottom revealing his last name etched into the metal.

"Some chef," he muttered as he headed to the shower.

***

Biv Trammel grew impatient in the back seat of a hired black sedan idling in front of the most exclusive building in the Gold Coast. He stopped working with musicians and artists because their ideas of punctuality were not anywhere in the ballpark of the definition. Chefs would be different, he told himself. They have a sense of timing- how long to grill a pork chop and how slowly to drizzle melted butter while making hollandaise. That's why he took a chance on a first-time restaurateur almost two decades ago. Trey Chapman was never late, not for a meeting with his business manager, much less a book signing. But things had changed over the years. The celebrity chef spent less time in the kitchen. His internal clock was off and he rarely paid attention to external ones. Biv had taken to lying to Trey about exact start times, and even those buffers were beginning to get taken advantage of.

Trey jumped in the car and immediately noticed the look on Biv's face.

"I know. I know," Trey said as he put his hand up in a preemptive strike. "I'm running a little behind."

"Perpetually," Biv replied.

Only a month from his 55th birthday, the business manager could easily pass for 70, with fluorescent white hair in a tight crew cut and bags under his eyes darker than squid ink.

Biv threw Trey a grease-soaked bag. "Better get your energy up. You've got three hundred cookbooks to sign."

"Three hundred?" Trey said, reluctantly accepting the bag and digging into a barely recognizable breakfast sandwich. "You said two hundred last week."

"Did I? Must've gotten it mixed up with another signing."

Biv opened his briefcase and tried to look busy while Trey ate his breakfast. They played this game all the time. The business manager would under-promote, and the celebrity chef would act surprised and indignant. But it was Biv's job to push his client and keep building the empire, and Trey knew it. He never would've cranked out a dozen cookbooks if it hadn't been for Biv, or done the cooking segments for the morning news. There would be no Chapman line of pots and pans. To be sure, Trey wanted every bit of it, but his expertise was branzino, not business.

"I've got another good opportunity for you," Biv said.

"Good? I'll pass," Trey replied. He was exhausted. Not just from the night before, but from the past two decades. His rise to culinary stardom was a blur. He left Chicago before he was old enough to buy a drink, not that there was any shortage around the kitchens he worked. If a restaurant didn't have at least one Michelin star, he wasn't interested. He staged in New York, France, Tokyo and Chile before returning to the Windy City and opening his namesake, *Trey*. Using his last name was not an option.

Success came at the price of sleep. A twenty-hour day was the norm, with the insomniac chef working on infusions or extractions in the wee hours in his tiny apartment kitchen. It was worth it though. *Trey* and Trey were a hit. But just as the restaurant seemed to be reaching perfection, the enigmatic chef scrapped the menu on the anniversary of its opening.

"Hear me out," the businessman said. "This isn't a line of cocktail napkins. It's signature cutlery."

"Knives?" Trey sighed.

"I'm not talking Ginsu or late-night infomercial crap. The company is German. One of the top guys at Wusthof split and is starting his own thing."

"What's it gonna take from me?" Trey said, knowing not to expect the truth.

"A couple appearances. A few autographs," Biv lied. "I'll bring you the paperwork tomorrow."

Trey didn't say anything. He took the new chef's coat lying on the seat between them out of the plastic packaging and slipped it on as they rode in silence. The sedan pulled up to the back entrance of the last bookstore left on Michigan Avenue. The sausage grease slowly entering his bloodstream seemed to exacerbate Trey's morning fog. Now wasn't the right time to make any big decisions. Fifteen years ago, he would've partied until 4am and been up running by 9.

But now his celebrity had taken its toll. He had to cross a lot of time zones to keep tabs on his empire. He rarely shook off the jet lag before jetting off again. His days had every minute seemingly accounted for and ended in late night obligations. The joy of cocktails and fancy dinners was eroded by the someone sitting next to him who always wanted something.

Trey smiled politely as an overly friendly woman escorted them through the belly of the bookstore. Biv knew he didn't need to say any more about the knives. He had planted the seed and could see the wheels turning in Trey's mind.

A few steps down the hallway, Trey stopped and leaned up against the wall. Biv assumed it was a hangover, but Trey was clutching his chest.

"You alright?" his manager asked.

"It's probably just the breakfast of champions you brought," Trey said, trying to shrug off the pain. He'd been chalking the infrequent bouts to indigestion, certainly no cause for alarm. But this wasn't the lack of sleep or too many bourbons or the subpar breakfast sandwich.

Up ahead there was a steady rumbling that sounded a little like the ocean. It only grew louder as Trey tried to ignore the pain. All he could think of was the pros and cons of another endorsement. Did he need to have his name out there any more than it already was?

Their guide stopped at a set of double doors and told Trey and Biv to wait there. As she opened one and slipped inside, it became clear that the noise they had been following was coming from an enormous crowd. Biv's silence was almost as distracting as the cacophony just a few feet away. They had turned down cutlery companies before, but Biv seemed pretty set on this. How much longer could he really say no?

The chest pain had not gone away, and Trey shrugged his left shoulder as if warming up for a tennis match. It was impossible to miss the grimace on his face.

"I'm making you an appointment with Dr. Nevins," Biv said. This was how the manager operated. He knew when to ask his client and when to direct him. Trey wasn't going to the doctor though. You never get good news from doctors.

The large doors in front of the duo appeared to fly open by themselves and the sight of the celebrity chef worked the room into an instant frenzy. The attention had become like a shot of adrenaline over the years. It seemed to cure all. The throbbing headache and exhaustion were gone, for the moment. Trey had to shout for his business manager to hear him.

"Let's do the knives!"

Biv barely reacted, and Trey Chapman disappeared into the crowd as the adoration crashed over him.

***

Audrey set a plate of bacon, fresh out of the microwave, onto the counter next to some ready-made biscuits and jam. The kitchen looked like something out of a TV show. No splattered oil around the burners. No trail of errant salt grains dribbled across the counter. In essence, no signs of cooking life. The former socialite had never learned the culinary arts, not that she wasn't capable of nuking the occasional breakfast. Her lack of skills was commensurate with the room, which had no table, only a single stool that peeked out from beneath the counter.

An hour earlier, she'd sat there with some yogurt and the morning newspaper. Audrey had the terrible habit of reading her husband's reviews. This time she made it to nearly the third paragraph before she lost her appetite.

The hurried breakfast she was scrambling to leave out was an olive branch. Maybe if she didn't run into him, he wouldn't ask. Maybe just this once, they wouldn't fight over his work.

But Audrey had been playing this game for far too long. Her husband's greatest joy was indirectly responsible for the biggest flaw in their marriage. And twice a week it reared its ugly head.

She looked again at the newspaper and considered throwing it away. But that would only cause a second problem. Her husband never grew old of seeing his work in print. Another copy would show up at some point. And truthfully, he was a talented writer. Unfortunately, he was an equally talented liar.

So Audrey folded the newspaper open to her husband's latest review and put it smack dab in the middle of his plate. There was no missing her intent. But she needed to clear her head with a run before the confrontation. She grabbed her sunglasses and slipped out the door.

Jackson Chapman was still full from dinner when he lifted his paunchy frame onto the old bar stool. His spare tire was a side effect of his craft, and aversion to exercise. With a fuller head of hair, it would be easy to recognize him as James Jr.'s second born. But with every pound gained, he seemed to look older than Trey, despite being two years younger.

With two slices of bacon inhaled almost instantly, Jackson settled in on the biscuits and jam. The breakfast spread, even as modest as it was, captivated his attention. It was a full five minutes before he even realized the paper was opened to his latest restaurant review. He brushed off the crumbs and read around several sticky dots, admiring his detailed description of yet another amazing dinner out on the town.

The basil alone is worth a visit. The leaves are so brilliant green they seem to have been picked just seconds before they land on the plate. Cristiano's highlights the herb in many dishes, but the fresh offerings are the best. Whole leaves simply torn over the Insalata Caprese. Thin ribbons sprinkled over the Pizza Margherita on its way to the table. Pesto with a texture that sings of a grandmother's patience with a mortar and pestle.

Cristiano Antobaldi's attention to detail continues with no less than twelve varieties of pasta, each handmade daily in limited quantities. They *will* run out of the ravioli stuffed with braised Swiss chard and homemade sausage. You'll be lucky to have the last order of Pici with anchovies and bread crumbs. Arriving after 9pm almost guarantees ordering only through the process of elimination.

Moving on to the Secondi, a wave of seafood offerings stands out including whole branzino and grilled prawns. The tonnato sauce accompanying the veal is the highlight of the night however. This Italian surf and turf marries fork-tender meat with the briny, salty punch of anchovies and fresh tuna. The best waiters will deliver a basket of fresh bread seconds before you realize you want to mop the plate clean.

The wine list is small, but Cristiano only serves bottles he's intimately familiar with. The owner relishes relationships with most of the vintners dating back decades, including one producing the only offering of lagrein on the menu, an inky red from the Alto Adige region of Northern Italy. An evening at Cristiano's comes with two guarantees- some of the finest food in the city, and that you'll be making your next reservation as you exit the restaurant.

Three stars.

Extremely satisfied, Jackson lowered the paper to find Audrey back from her run. She'd been standing there for several minutes, but apparently even the clinking of ice cubes into a glass wasn't enough to snap the master from his work. He set the paper down and re-centered himself on the stool.

"Did you already go for a run?" he asked, barely getting the words out before finishing the last piece of bacon.

Audrey nodded, but her dark brown hair barely moved as the sweat had started to dry it to the corners of her face.

"How was your breakfast?" she said, eager to get it over with.

"Good," Jackson replied, wiping the crumbs off himself before standing.

"Good like Cristiano's?" his wife asked.

Jackson wasn't oblivious, but he never seemed prepared for these situations. The writer constantly sought approval, but never realized the ramifications. They were on two separate pages anyway. Her qualm was the veracity, while he was more concerned with how the sentences moved and flowed across the page.

Jackson was a great reviewer, but a terrible critic.

"What's that supposed to mean?" he asked, more inquisitive than defensive.

"Cristiano's was terrible," she attacked. "They nearly made you sick. The shrimp looked like library paste and the tuna sauce smelled like fishy garbage."

"I disagree. We've eaten there several times, and my review is a sum of those experiences. Besides, the pasta was divine. And you can't say one word about the basil."

"I'll be sure to find out who grew it and thank them," Audrey said, not quite ready to let things go. "Come on, Jackson. According to you, there's not a bad dish in the city."

"You know Cristiano is a family friend," he pleaded.

"Cristiano is a friend of your father," she clarified.

Therein laid the issue. Jackson owed his start to his old man. His last name was a password to soft launches, friends and family dinners, and cold openings tightly sealed from the public. Jackson got the jump. The Tribune had little choice but to hire him as their critic. He kept the job due to his access and talent with words. He kept the access thanks to an ability to turn those words into glowing recommendations. Over the years, Jackson had developed an unconscious way of romanticizing the meals he consumed in the hours between when he ate and when he wrote. What got printed was more of an account of what could have been instead of what was, and that's what never ceased to upset his dining and life companion.

"The best reviewers aren't well liked, but they're well respected," Audrey said.

They are also typically anonymous. While their names may be known, their identity is well-cloaked. That, of course, was never an option for Jackson.

"What do you want me to do? I'm not taking money out of a guy's pocket because the pasta was a little overcooked."

Some couples number their arguments in an attempt to head them off at the start. When fighting about money, one person will say, "Number four." Or if it's about the kids, "Number six." The simple recognition causes a momentary smile, brief enough for both to realize they are in old territory. If Audrey and Jackson were to number their disagreements, this would be their one and only. They didn't have kids and money was never an issue. Their relationship was so strong that they almost blocked out these weekly exchanges. The confrontations never went too far.

"I just wish you'd be a little more ...honest. That's all," Audrey concluded, as she had so many times before.

Jackson nodded, and lovingly spread a little jam on his remaining bite of biscuit before feeding it to his wife.

Everything in their relationship started and stopped with food. They were an unlikely pair, not just because of the five-year age difference. He was the Renaissance man; a twenty-something when they met with an encyclopedic knowledge of the culinary world, but without pretension. It was the osmotic byproduct of a childhood running through a restaurant kitchen, but with no desire to pick up a knife. She was the debutante, who didn't know caviar from camembert. She seemed to never be without a glass of champagne, holding the delicate flutes at impossible angles as she floated through cocktail party after cocktail party. Jackson taught as he wooed. There was something about a man who could tell her exactly how the bubbles would feel on her tongue before he had popped the cork.

That trick had not lost its effect. Audrey was still impressed whenever her husband could simply look at a label and tell whether the effervescence would come fast and hard like a can of soda or roll slowly up her glass.

She also never tired of being fed. Jackson had opened up an unadventurous palate with his trusting hands bite by bite. Food was a literal connection.

The tiny morsel of biscuit and jam that Jackson had put to his wife's lips was greater than the sum of its parts. On the surface there was nothing extraordinary about it. But Audrey knew the gesture meant more than her husband could say. He would give everything to please her, down to his very last bite.

***

Patrick Schuler was one of the hottest young names in the Chicago culinary scene, despite not having a brick-and-mortar restaurant to work out of. His popularity stemmed from a series of underground dinners, a trend that had grown in popularity across the nation. What set the not quite 30-year-old chef apart was that his followers were cult in more than one sense of the word. Not only were his dinners exclusive, but he catered to an adventurous, yet admittedly dark subset of diners. People weren't paying hundreds of dollars a plate for coq au vin or any other chicken dish for that matter. They wanted the bizarre and the macabre, and that's why Schuler was doing some of his shopping behind a packing warehouse dumpster.

The chef's tattooed arms could easily be mistaken for a guy working one of the many loading docks nearby. Any sign of nervousness was less about the authorities and more about getting the product that had caused a near-instant sellout of available spots for his upcoming dinner.

An old Mercedes rounded the corner and came to an abrupt halt just a few feet from the anxious chef. This had to be his contact, although the windows were tinted so darkly, he couldn't see inside. Not that that would've helped since the two men had never met before. After an uncomfortable minute, the door opened and a short guy in skater shoes, an oversized flannel shirt, and a poor attempt at a mustache stepped out. Schuler looked perplexed.

"You Merlin?" he asked.

"Yeah," the driver said, noticing the chef's odd gaze. "What'd you expect? A pointy hat or something?"

"I don't really know," Schuler said.

The nickname was a mix-up, one that Joey Chapman liked the moment he heard it. As the youngest of James Jr.'s sons, he had the toughest job living up to the family name. Growing up, Trey was the rising culinary star, and Jackson was the food almanac, which didn't leave much room for the littlest brother to gain his father's attention. He became a jack of all trades around the restaurant, never excelling in any role. He did a little cooking and some cleaning, but the only time he received praise was coming through in a crisis. On a busy Saturday night, Chapman's Steakhouse would invariably run out of something, and James would send his third born on a mission to beg and borrow from nearby restaurants. Whether they felt sorry for the kid or didn't want to disappoint knowing who it was for, Joey always came through and was rewarded by a pat on the head from his father.

Over the years, Joey got to know just about everyone around the city. Out of chanterelle mushrooms? He knew a guy. Need fresh horseradish at 9:30 on a Tuesday night? He could get it. After high school, Joey took odd jobs here and there. It was his father's idea to travel around and see the world while he was young, helping when he could with a job or place to stay. Joey's Rolodex grew, as did the list of what he could procure. He always smuggled back an exotic item or two, and word spread.

One of his first clandestine meetings was with a not so bright chef who wanted horse meat for a private party. He was aware that it was illegal in the U.S. and was willing to pay a high premium for Joey to get it smuggled into the country. Joey agreed, for two reasons. One, horse meat is eaten all over the world, so he didn't have any problem of conscience. Two, it would be extremely easy to get. He knew a guy in Texas who worked at a horse slaughterhouse. All the meat processed there had to be sold overseas, but no one would miss a few pounds. Joey profited handsomely and got his nickname in the process. When explaining to the chef that he didn't have a 9-5 job and mostly sourced things, he referred to himself as a sourcer. The dull chef confused it with sorcerer and replied, "Like Merlin?" Joey held back a laugh and nodded. Word spread that Merlin could make things appear and so it went.

The requests got more and more difficult over the years, but Joey always came through. When Chicago outlawed foie gras in 2006, he supplied everyone's habit for the fattened goose liver until the ban was lifted two years later. It was his golden age, and although business had slowed, his services were still needed from time to time. That's precisely why the 42-year-old had a wheel of cheese full of maggots in the trunk of his car.

"Did you get it?" chef Schuler asked, wracked with anticipation.

"Of course."

Joey walked slowly to the back of his car and popped the trunk. It was filled to the brim with boxes.

"Decoys," Joey explained.

He selected a medium-sized package and pulled out a knife. He carefully cut the tape and stepped away. Chef Schuler was almost knocked back by the pungent smell before the box was completely opened. Inside was a pristine specimen of casu marzu- Sardinian for "rotting cheese."

The chef lifted the top from the wheel of pecorino to reveal the creamy maggot-eaten center, still writhing with its passengers.

"You have to tell me how you got this," the now giddy chef requested.

"You have to pay me," Joey responded.

The chef pulled a thick wad of cash out of his back pocket and handed it to Joey, who didn't bother counting it. No one ripped Merlin off. And even though casu marzu is illegal, even in its country of origin, he was dealing with chefs, not criminals. They always played fair.

Joey closed the trunk and opened his car door.

"Wait, you've got to try some with me," the chef insisted.

"No, thanks. I've had it before. Took two days and three bottles of Mirto to get the taste out of my mouth," Joey said, referring to the traditional Sardinian liqueur. "But knock yourself out."

Chef Schuler shrugged and scooped up a small amount of the almost liquid cheese with his finger. He inspected it closely, watching a single maggot squirm for a moment before he raised it to his mouth.

"Don't forget to chew," Joey warned.

The chef licked his finger clean and took his time before swallowing the putrid mash. The horrified look on his face quickly turned to a grin.

"You actually like that crap?" Joey asked, getting into his car.

"It's stronger than I thought," Schuler said, his eyes watering a little. "Almost spicy. But the funk. Man, it's like blue cheese that got left in an old hockey bag."

Joey shut the door and rolled down the window. "Don't forget to put the lid back on. Those little bastards can crawl. Oh, and no pictures at your dinner."

"No pictures?"

"Yeah, it's illegal, remember? That's why we're meeting behind a dumpster."

Joey waited for Schuler to nod before he sped away.

***

Biv was long gone by the time Trey weaved his way through the belly of the bookstore and into the waiting black sedan. On the road, the business manager wouldn't leave the chef's side, but at home there was no reason to hang around. Trey was used to collapsing into the backseat and heading back to his condo alone.

As the car pulled out of the garage, Trey clenched and unclenched his right hand trying to get some feeling back. He never kept count, but that seemed like a lot more than three hundred cookbooks. His autograph had devolved with time. How he cherished signing copies of his first book. Biv had gotten him an Italian fountain pen to sign the first few. It took weeks of practice to learn how to use it properly. Trey lovingly blew onto the paper to ensure the ink was dry before closing every cover. Now his signature was unrecognizable- nothing more than an uppercase "T" and "C" followed by a squiggle.

The pain in the aftermath of one of these signings was much worse than any 18-hour day gripping a knife. The adrenaline usually wore off after the first hundred fans or so. The remaining hour of each appearance was practically unbearable. It would take the better part of a week to return to normal. But they were a necessary evil for the celebrity chef. People don't buy books anymore. They download them if you're lucky. And with millions of recipes available for free online, the sales trump card was getting to meet the author for twenty or thirty seconds and watch the chicken scratch in person.

Trey learned this lesson the hard way. After traveling so much for his first two cookbooks, he informed his business manager that he would not do any signings for his next project. He couldn't be away from his restaurant. The budding celebrity chef believed his name was enough to sell his latest work. Biv disagreed, but didn't put up a fight. He knew it was a terrible idea, but the result would make his job with the stubborn client easier from then on out. "Back for Thirds" was a failure as far as circulation went, with most copies collecting dust on the shelf. The publisher was outraged and dropped Trey two months after the release. Biv, rarely one to worry, reminded his client whose idea it was to become a famous chef, and within days had a new publisher on the hook for book number four.

As much as his hand throbbed, Trey never said a word. Not that there was anyone to complain to presently. All he could do was look out the window and try to focus on something else. After a rainy August, it was nice to see the city under sunny skies again. September was Trey's favorite month in Chicago as cooler weather started to set in. Not that he usually got to enjoy much of it. He spent just ten nights in his high-rise condo the same month the year before. As soon as his attention was back on the buildings going by, Trey realized that the black sedan was headed in the wrong direction.

"Hey!" Trey shouted at the driver. "You're going the wrong way!"

There was no response from behind the partition, and the car continued its path, which only enraged the already irritable passenger. Trey leaned forward and beat on the divider, completely forgetting how much pain his crippled hand was in. He let out a scream and collapsed to the floor cursing for several minutes before he could right himself. Trey started pounding again, this time with his left hand.

"I know you can hear me! You're going the wrong way!" he yelled, not letting up on the thumping.

This went on for several minutes, but the driver simply ignored it and continued to his alternative destination. When the car finally came to a stop, Trey had only a momentary sigh of relief. The second he looked out the window, it all made sense. They were parked outside the offices of Trinity Medical- the private practice of Dr. Richard Nevins.

Biv had learned that, especially lately, Trey not putting up a fight at one of his directives didn't mean he would go along quietly. This was the game of chess that their relationship had turned into. And having long dealt with his client's phobias, Biv knew getting Trey to the doctor would require more than an appointment. He also didn't want to be present for any showdown. So, the wily business manager had paid the driver to take Trey to the doctor, warning (and tipping) him in advance about the scene that would unfold.

"I'm not going in," Trey said, throwing himself backwards like a petulant child. So, they sat.

As the minutes ticked by, it became clear that Trey would not win the standoff. "Fine. I'll just get out and take a cab home," Trey bluffed, but he had no money and hadn't carried a wallet in some time. As his career took off, he drove less and less, always being chauffeured. It was more to ensure he was punctual than because he was a diva. So that took care of the need for a license. And every meal he'd eaten since birth seemed to be free between his family's restaurant, dad's friends, and everyone wanting to send out their best for the famous Trey Chapman. So that eliminated the need for cash, and his lone credit card remained tucked into his suitcase for trips. Biv was, of course, aware of this tidbit of information, and made sure the driver was too.

Trey continued to pout while trying to decide how long it would take to walk home.

Halfway through mapping the route in his head, he gave up and exited the car. After slamming the door with as much violence as he could muster, Trey stormed into the Trinity Medical office.

2

Trey refused to sit on the paper-lined table in the examining room. It was too close to what most cuts of meat come wrapped in from the butcher, and he needed no crinkly reminder of the poking and prodding he was about to endure. Instead, he sat on the small rolling stool normally reserved for the doctor. If there was any benefit to his celebrity it was that he never had to sit in the waiting room. He believed the receptionists respected his privacy so no one would tip off any paparazzi or sell some false story about him having ringworm or crabs. Really, the team in the front office had simply tired of his theatrics. The suave celebrity chef who could charm a room and make women swoon, was reduced to a nervous mess at the sight of a white coat, so they'd taken to immediately escorting him down the hallway.

Trey had gained a reputation among the rest of the staff as well. Despite having only been to see Dr. Nevins a handful of times in the last decade, there wasn't a nurse who would go near him at this point. Anyone who had attempted to draw blood or so much as take his pulse had to deal with Trey's hysterics. Word gets around quickly in a doctor's office, especially when it involves a celebrity who pretends to faint at the sight of a stethoscope.

Time seems to stand still in an examining room. Any relief of finally getting separated from the masses evaporated quickly while sitting alone staring at posters of the human body and pamphlets about various diseases. Trey had the bad habit of searching through the drawers, trying to hide his fear behind curiosity. He was busy removing the tops from the jars of cotton balls and tongue depressors when Dr. Nevins finally made his entrance. Already in an excited state, Trey flung the metal lids to the ground as the door opened. His diving attempt to save them sent the pamphlet stand flying, covering the doctor in a tornado of trifolds.

"Sorry," Trey said, sheepishly picking a pamphlet about gout from Dr. Nevin's shoulder.

"Is it safe to assume that no one has taken your blood pressure or so much as weighed you?"

"Yes," Trey replied, sitting back on the stool.

"Will you please get out of my seat?" Dr. Nevins ordered as nicely as could a man whose day had been intruded upon by a forceful business manager and his client.

Trey shot up and reluctantly sat on the butcher paper, shifting back and forth as it rustled below him.

"Okay, what seems to be the problem?" Trey asked.

"What? You tell me," the doctor replied incredulously.

"I don't know. Biv set this up."

"Yes, he said you haven't been eating or sleeping well, and today you were having chest pains. Would you care to elaborate?"

"Well last night wasn't my fault," Trey began protesting. "There was this function, and Biv was the one who brought me that breakfast this morning, so it's pretty rich that he'd say I wasn't eating well..."

The chef droned on and on, trying to explain away symptoms or attach the problem to someone else, while the doctor picked out the tiny clues within. He made notes and let the patient come to a full and complete stop before saying anything.

"Sounds like you're the picture of health then," Dr. Nevins said, closing his chart and heading towards the door. Trey smiled, probably the first time he'd ever done so in a doctor's office, but it was wiped from his face the instant the doctor turned around.

"But," he began, lingering for effect, "maybe we should run a few tests just to be sure."

Trey lowered himself onto the exam table, fully believing he was about to pass out, but unfortunately for both men, that didn't happen. Dr. Nevins gathered the instruments he needed from the drawers and started with the blood pressure cuff.

"180 over 110. That's pretty high" he said, releasing the pressure with a hiss.

"Did you ever consider," Trey said shooting upright, "that it might be high because on the way here I thought I was being kidnapped!?"

"No. You're right. We'll take it a few more times, Mr. Chapman."

Trey went horizontal again, and for the first time in his career, Dr. Richard Nevins felt underpaid.

***

Jackson and his wife, Audrey, had worked up quite an appetite with an afternoon of marital activities, none of which occurred outside of their bedroom. It couldn't really be tabbed as "make-up" because it was the norm. They fought like adults, but loved like teenagers. Calorie depleted, they got dolled up for a night on the town, but with one quick pit stop on the way.

"I can have them whip up a couple of shrimp cocktails to tide us over," Jackson said, pulling into the near empty parking lot of his father's restaurant.

"No, I'll be okay. We're not staying long, right?" Audrey asked.

"I don't think so. Dad said he had an idea he wanted to run past me really quick."

The happy couple got out of the car and made their way to the front door. Jackson noticed how run-down the restaurant looked. The paint had begun to crack here and there, just a little too much for it to pass as character on the old facade.

Inside Chapman's Steakhouse, Benito Perez stood behind the host stand, his head barely tall enough to see over the massive walnut fixture between the coat rack and front doors. If it weren't for a tremendous, ink black mustache, he could be mistaken for a child. Benny, as he liked to be called, was a new addition to the restaurant. With dwindling profits, James had convinced a professor friend over at DePaul University to create an internship with course credit for manning the front of the house. Anyone enrolled in the hospitality leadership program was eligible, and a new student rotated through every semester. Word got around among the school that the post at Chapman's Steakhouse, while not very educational, was laid back and basically provided a quiet environment to study. Benny's attention was fixed on his tablet and a lesson on catering when Jackson and Audrey came in. They, of course, bypassed the stand and headed straight to the bar.

"Excuse me, do you have a reservation?" Benny said, leaning over the bulky piece of furniture.

"We're not eating," Jackson said, making a very temporary pause in his stride.

"But this is a restaurant."

"I'm Jackson Chapman."

Benny looked down at the reservation list. "I don't see you on here."

Jackson walked back to the host stand and pointed to his last name on the stack of menus, and promptly walked off.

"You must be new," Audrey said, extending her hand.

"Benito," he said, shaking it. "Benny."

"Nice to meet you, Benny. I'm Audrey," she said, and went to catch up with her husband.

James Chapman Jr. sat at the very last stool, staring deeply into a nearly empty glass of rye as Frank Sinatra's voice slid out of a speaker in the ceiling. The owner, who once floated through the packed house passing out free drinks and comping desserts, still dressed the part of a time his restaurant had long forgotten. James wore a suit and matching hat that cast a shadow over his pale,

Victorian complexion. He examined a new age spot on his thumb as he downed the last of his drink, then turned to see Jackson and Audrey mere steps away.

"How long have you been standing there?" James asked, shooting off his stool. "You could give a guy a heart attack."

"Hi, Dad," Jackson said, extending a hand. "Good to see you."

"Hi, James," Audrey echoed.

No matter who the other two boys married, if they ever managed to do so, Audrey would always be James' favorite. His boy had over-achieved in marriage, much like his old man. To see the two of them together made his heart swell.

"Audrey, my dear," James began, taking her hand and pressing it gently to his lips. "You look lovely this evening."

"Thank you."

"Why don't you have a glass of champagne and let me steal Jackson for a minute?"

Audrey smiled and headed to the other end of the bar as James led his son to a table in the corner.

"I saw your review this morning," James said. "Cristiano was very pleased. You could've maybe played up the seafood a little more though."

Jackson said nothing, but gave a slight nod.

"So where are you and Audrey headed this evening?" James asked.

"Just out to grab a bite," Jackson said, still not quite sure what his father's agenda was.

"Why don't you eat here?"

James Chapman Jr. was anything but subtle. Jackson didn't need to scan the restaurant to see how empty it was. It felt empty. And he feared that his father was one question away from putting him into an awkward position.

"Dad, I can't review your restaurant."

"Who said anything about a review?" James protested, too proud to ask the question himself. "You and your lovely wife just have a nice dinner. I'll give you the quiet booth in the back."

"Dad..." Jackson started, but didn't get very far.

"I know how much you love the porterhouse. And I'll send out a tray of those oysters that Audrey can't get enough of."

"I can't write a review of my father's restaurant. There's no chance they'd even run it if I did," Jackson tried to reason.

James Chapman Jr. was not going to beg his son. He was too proud. But he was not above guilt.

"I'm just saying we could use a little help around here," James said, motioning to the lifeless restaurant. He got up and walked back over to Audrey, kissing her on the cheek before grabbing his glass and heading into the kitchen.

Jackson wasn't far behind and took his wife's hand, leading her out of the restaurant.

"Everything okay?" she asked.

"Yeah," he lied. "Dad wanted to know if I'd seen Joey or could get a hold of him."

"That's nice. What is your brother up to these days?" Audrey asked as they got into the car.

"I haven't the faintest clue," Jackson said, unaware that Joey was speeding past the restaurant that very minute.

***

The hours of signing books and being worked over at the doctor's had left Trey exhausted. He could barely keep his eyes open on the ride home and collapsed into a deep sleep back in his own bedroom. After what felt like a short four hours, Trey awoke in darkness. Even after he'd flipped on the kitchen light, he remained disoriented. With no purpose in opening the fridge, he filled a glass with water from the sink.

Trey didn't ever go to the grocery store anymore. Outside of being mobbed in public, he didn't see the point. He was never around, and when he was, he wasn't planning on it. Trey often wondered if he'd forgotten how to cook some days. His eyes would roll back as he mentally walked through recipe after recipe in his head to try and calm his fears. The biggest irony of becoming a celebrity chef was getting farther and farther away from food.

Having eaten nothing since the breakfast sandwich, Trey was running on empty. His best bet for sustenance came in the form of an opened package of crackers he discovered while cleaning up the salt in his pantry. But after a single stale bite, he threw them away. The calendar on the fridge confirmed his fear-tonight the chef was on his own. There was no dinner to attend or cocktail party to glad-hand through. If the stale crumbs sticking to the inside of his cheeks were any indication, Trey was going to go hungry. Normal households have a drawer full of take-out menus or refrigerator magnets pointing weary masses towards provisions at times like these. But not his.

On his way up, Trey had promised his friends and loved ones that he wouldn't turn into some helpless, vapid celebrity. James Jr. never lost sight of who he was and where he came from, and his sons never forgot it. They watched their dad help unload every side of beef and box of lettuce at Chapman's Steakhouse. He was never too big for any job- not mopping the bathrooms, not cleaning the windows, not even jury duty. That's what Trey strived to be. But he was failing. Having someone coordinate his every minute, do his shopping, and pick up his dry cleaning?

Too Hollywood. He could keep track of his meetings. What was so hard about that? Eventually the travel, dinners and appearances took over and crowded out the backyard barbecues and Cubs games. He could only manage his professional life or personal life, and since he chose the former, he didn't have the latter. There were plenty of contacts in his phone, but few he could call friends, and even fewer he could call at times like this. As he scrolled through the names, Trey realized he was just as lonely as he was hungry. There was only one person he could call.

And as he listened to the phone ring, he wondered if that was only because she was paid to answer.

"It's me," he said, turning the lights on in the living room and flopping down on the couch.

"Home alone?" the woman on the other end of the phone asked.

"I think you know the answer to that."

"Then can I assume you're calling for the usual?"

"You make it sound so dirty," Trey said, sounding far more alluring than he currently looked with his bedhead, and legs splayed wide across a wooden coffee table with a blue river of resin running through the middle.

"You know how busy I am. Man, if I told anyone around here I was talking to you the place would go nuts," she said.

"You wouldn't," he replied, sounding somewhere in between a threat and begging.

"Guess you'll find out depending on which rings first, your cell phone or doorbell," she said, and hung up abruptly.

Trey was used to people pandering to him, so there was something refreshing about such a conversation, as blunt as it was. The only thing he could do now was wait.

***

Joey made a quick turn down an alley and into the almost hidden parking lot of the equally almost hidden bar where he always celebrated his latest cash infusion by spending it. He wasn't necessarily bad with money, just not great with it either. He always put away a few dollars for a rainy day, but didn't see the point in squirreling away everything. Joey had enough for an emergency, with some to spare. But he wasn't saving for a house or fancy car. He didn't live dangerously but wanted to think that if it did all end tomorrow, he had treated himself on the ride.

The back door to the bar, which was the only door, would keep most people away. More paint had fallen off than remained, making it resemble a rusty Rorschach test. The mat at the base read "unwelcome" to really drive home the point. This kept the clientele exclusive, albeit seedy. The proprietor, who was also the bartender, custodian and security guard, once hired Joey to procure several bottles of absinthe. This was before the nearly century-long U.S. ban on the "green fairy" was lifted in 2007. During his travels across Europe, Joey gained an affinity for the spirit and its psychedelic effects. He found a distiller that used real wormwood, which contains thujone, the chemical said to be responsible for the mind-altering state. On every trip, he would smuggle a bottle or two home. Word eventually got back to Crete, the imposing owner of the nameless bar. Joey never got a straight answer on the origin of the name. Some said it was because she was Greek. Others said it was short for concrete, referring to her massive, immovable size. It didn't really matter to Joey though, since he went by a similar nom de guerre.

Merlin came through as he always did, and Crete was pleased with the absinthe. The transient sourcer and gruff owner forged as loose a friendship as possible while still being able to use the word. Whenever Joey was around, he stopped in for a drink. On nights after a score, though, he settled in for more than his fair share. This was one of those nights.

Joey got out of his car, not bothering to lock it because there wasn't any need. The parking lot, if you could call it that, was a 40-foot gravel square with high brick walls on three sides, and just a narrow alley connecting it to the street. It was a place that looked like crimes had already been committed there. Anyone who knew of it, knew enough to stay away. And anyone dumb enough to venture back there ended up on the black and white television underneath the bar fed from the hidden security camera. Crete always kept an eye on the TV, for two reasons. One, she was lazy and didn't want to walk from the bar to the door. Second, there was no knock or secret password to get in. You were recognized or you stood outside until you realized you weren't going to be.

Joey didn't have to break stride as the door buzzed.

The bar was cleaner and brighter than its exterior would suggest. Crete nodded as the door closed behind Joey. A few regulars were well into their evening pours, but otherwise the place was empty. Quiet too. Music was hard to talk over, and many of the conversations that took place required a whisper. The bartender was the only person whose voice carried around the room.

"Appetizer or Entrée, Merlin?" Crete asked.

Joey pulled out the wad of cash chef Schuler had given him hours earlier for the wheel of maggot-ridden cheese, minus what he'd stashed away. He peeled off a handful of bills and set them on the bar.

"Entrée."

The nameless bar was also priceless. There was no menu and none of the drinks had any set value. It was like a clandestine country club. The patrons paid dues of sorts. Money wasn't necessarily exchanged on a nightly basis, but everyone made sure they were square with Crete.

Joey only dropped such a large amount after a job, which also meant he was planning to tie one on. Because of his restaurant and food background, Crete had started referring to these nights as appetizers or entrees. It was all or nothing. A single bourbon or a cab ride home near dawn, and it was rarely a single bourbon.

"So, what'd you pull off this time?" Crete asked, filling a rocks glass with a brown liquid from a very old bottle with much of its label missing.

"How's your stomach?" Joey asked, getting nothing in return but a stare. "Okay, but don't say I didn't warn you. It was a wheel of cheese crawling with maggots."

"Fucking disgusting."

"The cheese isn't bad actually, but good luck getting the taste out of your mouth," Joey said.

"You ate maggots?" Crete asked, loudly enough for everyone in the bar to hear.

Joey wasn't fazed though. He was an oddity in a room full of oddities.

"Yeah," he shrugged and finished his drink, offering the empty glass back to the bartender.

Crete poured another two fingers.

"Speaking of weird shit, I have a job for you," she said, then moved to the end of the bar to refresh another patron's glass.

Joey was left to wonder. Besides the absinthe, he occasionally procured various other items for the owner of the nameless bar. Over the years, it became clear that Crete was a middle woman for various enterprises- legal and illegal. Joey never met any of the actual buyers and it was unclear whether that was a matter of privacy or simply the bartender wanting her cut.

Crete walked back over to Joey and leaned in close. "I need something daring," she whispered.

"Okaaay," Joey said, dragging out the word.

"What do you think?"

"Can you be a little more specific?" Joey asked, as confused as ever. He was used to Crete conducting business almost inaudibly, but the bartender was never this vague. Her instructions were usually explicit, to the point of being annoying. Now, though, she was having the opposite problem.

"Some people want something... unique," she said, raising her eyebrows as if that helped explain things.

"I have no idea what you're talking about," Joey confessed.

"Doesn't have to be crazy, just something that'll impress some foodie snobs," Crete said. "Your choice. I need it by next week."

"Okay. Just so we're clear," Joey said, gesturing with his drink, but Crete cut him off.

"We're clear," she said, and that was enough for Joey. It had to be enough, because Crete wouldn't bring it up again.

Joey nodded ever so subtly and finished his drink. He pushed the glass forward for the bartender to refill, a cycle that would repeat itself for several more hours.

***

The knock at the door stirred Trey from his second nap of the day. He flipped on a few lights as he stumbled down the hallway, using his fingers to comb his hair back into some sort of order. Through the peephole, he saw a familiar brown takeout bag. But he failed to notice that the woman holding it was growing impatient and had to scramble to get away from the door as she knocked again. His head rang as he opened it. That's when Trey noticed the outfit.

"Never seen a black woman wear a pencil dress before?" she asked.

"Pencil dress?" Trey said, stepping out of the way to let her in.

Erica Tomlin was easily two decades younger than her boss, if you could call Trey that. He not only thought of having a younger, attractive assistant as cliche, but he hadn't wanted one in the first place. Biv Trammel hired her anyway and paid out of his own pocket- a clever move by the wily businessman. That made Erica impossible to fire. But still confident he could handle his own affairs; the celebrity chef gave her nothing to do. Erica became a permanent fixture at *Trey*, mostly holed up in his office. She used her free time to learn and befriend everyone around the namesake restaurant. She phoned in orders for Maurice, the head chef and kitchen boss in Trey's absence. She worked out the server's schedule for Edward, the restaurant manager. She even tended bar on occasion. And since no one knew exactly what she did or why she was there, no one bothered her.

"I was this close to leaving," Erica said, taking the to-go boxes out of the bag and sliding them onto the counter.

"Sorry, I fell asleep again," he said. "Thanks for the eggs, by the way."

"And the butter."

"And the butter," he echoed. "What'd you bring me?"

"I managed to get you some of the sous vide pork loin and Brussels sprout pesto."

"What about the purple potatoes and wilted arugula?" Trey said, sounding more whiny than he had intended.

"Did you want everyone to know you're here sleeping off a hangover while they do 240 covers?"

"240? That's pretty good for a weekday," Trey said, missing the point. "And I'm not hungover."

Erica opened the cabinet and took out a plate, dumping the food on it. Having gone through this ritual every couple months, she knew the territory well. A weakened Trey would implore the assistant he never wanted to rescue him from hunger and boredom. He liked the food, it was his after all, but the company was better. If crowds of fans were his adrenaline, isolation was his kryptonite.

Erica grabbed a fork and carried the plate to the living room, leading Trey to the couch.

Trey ate slowly. Painfully slowly. He figured Erica wouldn't let him eat alone and the longer it took, the longer she stayed. But the truth was Erica really liked Trey. She enjoyed his charm and wit. She also knew how many women would love to get the call and nurse the great Trey Chapman back to health, so although it didn't always seem like it, Erica relished being his Florence Nightingale.

"So, the outfit?" Trey asked, gesturing with his fork.

"I hostessed tonight," she said.

"Is Tiffany sick or something?"

"Tiffany was fired two weeks ago," Erica said.

"Really?" Trey wasn't really asking, and he wasn't surprised to know he'd lost touch with his restaurant and employees. "They hate me, don't they?"

"Yep," Erica said, without any sugar coating.

"Am I a terrible boss?"

"They hate you because you're not stuck in that hundred-degree kitchen. Because you're not picking the silks off 200 ears of corn or clarifying ten gallons of veal stock. You made it out. You've got what they want."

"I don't want it," Trey said. "I mean, I do. I used to…"

Trey trailed off and went back to his plate. He stabbed at a piece of pork, but accidentally knocked it to the floor. Erica picked it up and walked it over to the trash can.

"I don't think you're in any condition to make big, life-altering decisions right now," she said. "Let's see what's on."

Erica grabbed the remote and turned on the television. Trey took one more bite of the pesto.

"Tell Maurice there's too much pec in this."

"You tell him," Erica said, flipping through the channels, not really looking for anything in particular.

3

Lisle, IL sits twenty-five miles due west of Chicago. It was once ranked among Money Magazine's "Best Places for the Rich and Single." Ken Nakara was neither. He was a happy suburbanite who enjoyed helping his wife get their two daughters off to school each morning before heading into work. His office was inside a large, z-shaped building visible from the highway, made of concrete and glass.

Nakara was going through his usual morning ritual- a cup of tea and a moment to center himself before turning on his computer. As the old desktop warmed up, he walked to the break room to wash his mug and spoon. He often got strange looks for microwaving the communal sponge, but there just wasn't any way to know what it had been used on and how many strains of bacteria were hiding in the pores.

With his day now ready to begin, Nakara settled into his rolling chair, snuggled it close to the desk and locked the wheels in place. His email routine was as particular as everything else in his life. While most people tried to achieve "inbox zero" going in order, Nakara had devised a system of sender hierarchy. *Always start with the boss* was his motto. Today would be no different. Except that the first email had an attached image that propelled Nakara's tea back out and into the wastebasket.

***

All evidence of the previous night was long gone. The to-go containers were taken out, along with the trash. The plate and silverware were cleaned and put away. Trey couldn't remember Erica leaving or him falling asleep. He wasn't even sure they happened in that order. For a second, he wondered if he'd dreamt the whole encounter, but then he remembered the black dress. He couldn't have made that up.

Trey looked around for a note, not really expecting one. He went to the printed-out calendar taped to his fridge. Just one item on the schedule- a cooking demo on the Channel 2 midday news. That meant Biv in another chauffeured Sedan outside in a matter of hours. As Trey headed off to the shower, his phone rang. He took two more steps, contemplating not answering it, but finally gave in.

"Hello."

"Mr. Chapman, this is Dr. Nevins. I need you to come in today to discuss the results of your tests."

"I've got a busy day; can you tell me over the phone?" Trey pleaded, not wanting to set foot in that doctor's office again anytime soon.

"I would really prefer to see you in person," Dr. Nevins said.

"Is something wrong?" Trey recognized the uneasy tone in the doctor's voice and was starting to become panicked.

"You really can't come in?" the doctor implored.

"No."

"Okay. Your LDL cholesterol and triglycerides are extremely over range. And your blood pressure is high. Considering the stress and poor sleep habits you mentioned, you're at elevated risk for some diseases," Dr. Nevins explained.

"Am I going to die!?" Trey yelled as he threw himself over the arm of the couch.

"You know I can't say for sure, but I think we need to try some changes to reduce the possibility of things like a heart attack or stroke."

"I don't understand. I'm still the same size I was in high school."

Trey poked at his waistline and was shocked to be able to grab a small love handle.

"I'm going to have my office send over some information on ways we can start tackling this," the doctor said, moving the conversation along. "But you can start today by reducing your salt, fat and alcohol intake."

"Anything else?" Trey asked sarcastically.

"Sure, exercise and get at least 8 hours of sleep every night. Look, you need to take this seriously, Mr. Chapman. We can also consider medication to control some of this, but there are side effects to consider."

Trey felt his chest tightening up. He pulled at his shirt, almost ripping the collar. "Side effects!? What am I supposed to do, quit everything?"

"Come back in six months," Dr. Nevins ordered. "We'll run some more tests and see how you're doing."

"Oh, you'd love that, wouldn't you?"

"Yes, it's such a joy seeing you," Dr. Nevins said dryly.

The reality of the situation suddenly hit Trey. He dropped the phone and began pacing back and forth across his condo. Still feeling tight in his chest, he took his shirt off and flung it to the ground. A high pitch scream seemed to come out of nowhere, startling Trey even though he was the one who made it. The panic had fully set in. He needed air. Trey sprinted over to the window and opened it. As he took deep breaths, he could hear Dr. Nevins' muffled voice calling from the phone. After another minute of hyperventilating, Trey rushed back over to the couch.

"I think I'm having a heart attack," he panted.

"Calm down," Dr. Nevins said, more annoyed than worried. "It's probably a panic attack."

"Am I going to die?" Trey whispered.

"Not from a panic attack. But I want you to take this very seriously. And please read what we send over later today."

Trey's fears were confirmed. The bouts of chest pain over the past few months were finally explained. His lifestyle- the lifestyle that he worked so hard to achieve- was killing him.

Trey hung up on Dr. Nevins and remained motionless on the couch for a few minutes, not knowing what to do. When the strange thoughts passing through his head turned to his own funeral, Trey sat bolt upright and shook off the mini depression. He could get through this. He could figure it out. But the first order of business was the TV cooking demo that was rapidly approaching. As Trey got off the couch and turned to his bedroom, he nearly ran into Joey coming down the hall.

"Ahhhhhh!!!" Trey screamed, grasping his chest. "What the fuck, Joey?"

"I figured you were on your world tour," Joey said, trying to massage the hangover out of his head.

"How'd you get in here?"

"I have a key," Joey said.

"No, you don't," Trey countered.

"Were you screaming earlier, or did I dream that?"

"That was me," the older brother admitted. "My doctor basically said I have to quit everything, or my heart is going to explode."

"No shit?" Joey said, with as much concern as his throbbing headache would allow.

"Yeah, I don't know what to do."

Joey thought for a moment as he opened Trey's fridge.

"Don't you have anything to eat or drink in this place? Some O.J.?"

"I'm dying and all you can ask about is orange juice?" Trey asked, starting to get worked up again.

After a long night at the nameless bar, Joey wasn't in any condition to deal with the problem at hand. He must've gone through a full bottle at Crete's. Or was it two? The only good decision he made last night was not driving home. As he stumbled out of the alley, he planned on hailing a cab but couldn't find one. After a few minutes, Joey realized he wasn't far from his brother's place, which he was well accustomed to gaining entry to. And now, after a few hours of drunk sleep, he couldn't find any worldly wisdom to calm Trey.

"You should just tell Biv. Take a few months off," Joey reasoned.

"That's only a temporary fix. In no time, I'd be right back to all the book signings and appearances."

"So, walk away. You've got enough money, right?" Joey asked, settling for a glass of water from the sink.

"I think so."

"You don't know how much money you have?"

"No, do you?" Trey asked, but Joey jumped in before he'd even gotten the question out.

"$67,432," Joey said plainly. Then he remembered the cash in his pocket and counted it out. "Sixty-seven thousand, six hundred thirty seven dollars. And fifty cents."

"Wow. I don't even know what bank I use," Trey said.

"How is that even possible?"

"Biv handles everything. But look I can't just quit. I have contracts that I have to fulfill."

Joey got another glass of water. There had to be a way. This was his chance to help his big brother, who never seemed to need anyone's help. They were six years apart, but it might as well have been ten or even twenty. Since he didn't want to live in Trey's shadow like Jackson, he led an almost underground existence. Very few people even knew there was a third Chapman son, and Joey kept it that way with the help of his pseudonym. Merlin had his own celebrity status among his circle, and that was enough for him. He was the man who could get anything. Well, anything in the culinary world. If he could figure out how to get maggot-ridden cheese into the U.S., he could figure out a way to help Trey.

"What if you got fired?" Joey asked, just thinking out loud.

"What? I can't get fired."

"No, like what if the sponsors left you? What if people stopped buying your cookbooks? All we have to do is get everyone to leave *you*," Joey said, starting to figure out a plan.

"No one's going to leave me."

His younger brother ignored the arrogance, as he had done for almost his whole life.

"Let me put this in terms you understand, chef. We need to 86 your celebrity status," Joey said, referring to the restaurant saying for a menu item no longer being available.

"You can't just stop being a celebrity," Trey said.

"You want out, right? You *need* to get out."

Trey's priorities had changed drastically over the years. He started out as the driven chef, not content just to have a restaurant, but the best in Chicago. After he conquered the Windy City, he made a list of five other markets to put his stamp on. *Trey* opened in New York, then Los Angeles. Within two years, there were outposts in Vegas, Miami and San Francisco. The next challenge was *Trey Chic*- several smaller, quick service restaurants across the country. Trey cranked out about a cookbook a year and added endorsements along the way. The signature cookware was first and most prominent, but he had his name on aprons and other kitchen accessories as well. The meteoric rise took its toll over the past few years and Trey had stopped pushing. The cookbooks felt like a chore. He didn't have any new recipes because he was never in a kitchen anymore. He had pined, secretly and even out loud, to Biv for a small restaurant to hide away in. A place to get back to food. A place where he could do the shopping and set the menu daily. With each passing day, that seemed like an impossibility. But Joey's budding plan, as crazy as it sounded, gave Trey a glimmer of hope.

"Yeah, I want out," he said, almost instantly feeling the weight fall from his shoulders.

"Cool. This should be fun. You ready to ruin your reputation?"

"Do we have to ruin it?"

"Oh yeah," Joey said with a wide grin. "This has to be drastic. Your sponsors, fans- everyone has to hate you."

Trey wasn't so convinced. He stared at his brother, hoping the pep talk would continue and it would eventually make sense, but Joey was busy at the faucet rehydrating.

"I guess I really don't have much of a choice. This is my health we're talking about here," Trey said.

"Exactly. Oh, and we can't tell anyone about this," Joey said. "Not even Jackson. He'd tell Audrey or Dad, and if anyone finds out about this it won't work."

"Well, since I'm still not really sure what I'm doing, that will be pretty easy," Trey said, getting up and walking towards his bedroom. "Look, I have to do my cooking demo on Channel 2. Biv is going to be downstairs in a little bit."

Joey's eyes lit up. "Great. I'll come with you."

***

Jackson Chapman sat at his computer trying to figure out which restaurant he should review next. His office, technically a converted bedroom, was filled with stacks of books and magazines. He subscribed to every recipe and cooking journal known to man and never threw them out. Shelves lined three walls, and the rows of cookbooks and other food tomes were sometimes piled two deep.

The room was an extension of Jackson's mind. It was a doctoral class in the culinary world without hope or want of graduation. He spent hours in the office reading as much as he could and seemingly absorbing the rest. Jackson refused to part ways with any of the collection, much to the dismay of his wife. He insisted that it was a necessary reference section for his work, pointing out the myriad colored sticky notes that peeked from the pages in pile after pile. After bringing up what she saw as clutter a half dozen times, Audrey capitulated, allowing

Jackson to work in whatever atmosphere he wanted if it didn't spill over to the rest of the house. It was one of only a few compromises needed to make their marriage work.

He stared at the latest *Bon Appetite* magazine and wanted so desperately to crack the cover, but instead had to sort through the dozens of emails in his inbox. Jackson was old school, preferring tactile experiences to digital ones. He hated flashing internet ads and webpages that blared noise at you. It was all a distraction and the main reason he would never leave print.

Jackson knew newspapers were a dying business, but he wanted to write in a space with some decorum. He liked being able to hold his reviews and even enjoyed the smudge of ink that rubbed off the edges of the page. Clicking with a mouse was like nails on a chalkboard.

Still, Jackson had a job to do. He wrote two reviews a week- usually one casual and one fine-dining. The problem was not in finding 100 restaurants annually for his column, there were thousands in Chicago and the surrounding suburbs to choose from. The problem was keeping everyone in his life happy with the choices. What would Audrey think? Would his father be happy? What would his editor say?

Martin Easley was the bane of Jackson's professional existence. The editor hated the transparent nepotism practiced in the food column and set out to change it when he took over the Food & Dining section of the Tribune five years prior. For several months, he refused to print any reviews that had the slightest whiff of James Chapman Jr. or his connections. Instead, he pushed a steady diet of new restaurants on his writer. Had either man not been so stubborn and head strong, they would've gotten along brilliantly. Jackson certainly wanted to branch out to more exciting places, but Easley's dictums rubbed him the wrong way. He didn't ask. He demanded.

Given the choice between the bully boss and his dad's friends, Jackson chose family, refusing to give in. As weeks passed with no restaurant reviews being printed, Jackson's inbox swelled with an outpouring from his readers wondering what was going on. It was the first time the internet had come in handy. Originally the editor-in-chief of the paper had told the two to work it out on their own but armed with a stack of emails and some outside pressure, Jackson won the standoff. The direction of the column was his domain again. That didn't stop Easley from bombarding him with places to review though.

Of the three dozen or so emails that arrived since he'd stopped working the previous day, Easley seemed to be the sender of every other one. Jackson, for the most part, ignored them. On occasion, he would review a restaurant suggested by Easley, but often months after the request. The rest of the emails were reader responses, which he equally hated. But connecting with the paper's readership was part of his contract. It was this or social media, which Jackson considered neither social nor a form of media. So, he spent a painful hour or two every day clearing his inbox.

Thankfully Jackson had finished for the day and was onto the topic of dinner. Every night seemed like an impossible choice. He envied the working families that ping ponged between the two most prevalent delivery staples- pizza and Chinese. Chicago was his oyster. Money was no object as the paper paid for all his meals out. And there was no master list being narrowed down as new openings seemed to happen nightly around the city. Plus, his review could drive thousands of diners and be the difference between a restaurant thriving or closing. It was a lot of pressure and power. That made the daily decision take longer than the meal.

After an hour of pouring over menus, Jackson had just a handful of dinner contenders remaining. Unfortunately, at one time or another, they were all suggested by Easley, which left a bad taste in his mouth before even opening it. As he flipped back and forth, his phone rang.

"Jackson Chapman." He always answered with his full name.

"Hey, Jackson. It's Dave Talmidge. How's it going?"

"Fine, Mr. Talmidge. How are you?" You could almost hear Jackson rolling his eyes.

"How many times have I told you to call me Dave? I wanted to tell you about some new things we're doing at The Portobello Grille."

This was no courtesy call. Talmidge was a friend of James Chapman Jr., and ever since he had gotten the job, the requests for a review had come in steadily. The problem, other than the connection to his father, was that The Portobello Grille wasn't that good. Not wanting to cause a scene, Jackson had Audrey pick up dinner from there not long after it opened, but the takeout was disappointing. So, he politely declined both his father's and Talmidge's requests to review the restaurant, which came like clockwork.

"We've scrapped the old menu for the most part, and we're going more farm to table. Got a couple of dishes that will be available all the time, but a handful will be new every night. It's exciting stuff."

"Sounds like it," Jackson said, almost convincingly.

"I'd love to get you down here to check it out. Tonight's the big debut, and we're not inviting just anyone. We're going to knock your socks off," Talmidge said.

Jackson looked down at the restaurants he was considering for dinner. They seemed to blur together. The ding from his computer snapped him out of it. It was yet another email from his editor.

"Table for two then," Jackson said with a smile, knowing how much a review of The Portobello Grille would likely anger his boss.

"Fantastic! You won't be disappointed. The re-launch is at eight but come in early for cocktails. See you tonight," Talmidge squealed.

"Great," Jackson said, hanging up.

Easley might not be happy, but there was no way he could complain to the higher ups at the paper. This was a semi-private invite that would give the Tribune the first look. The exclusivity trumped the family ties and restaurant's mediocre history.

But there was one other person who wouldn't be happy, so Jackson set about a plan on how to tell his wife.

***

Ken Nakara couldn't look at the picture of maggot-filled cheese any longer. But as a Supervisory Special Agent with the Food and Drug Administration Office of Criminal Investigations, he knew this was just the beginning.

The FDA was well known. The OCI was not. Nakara often described himself as sort of a federal health inspector with a gun. Founded in 1991 in the wake of a generic drug scandal, the OCI was tasked with protecting FDA-regulated products from theft, counterfeiting, fraud, tampering and false advertising. In his nine years there, Nakara had helped bring to justice illegal online pharmacies, counterfeit energy drink makers, and even a pair of farmers selling bacteria-ridden cantaloupes. But this creepy, crawly cheese was a first.

"Supervisory Special Agent Ken Nakara," he said, answering his phone.

"Did you vomit?" asked the woman on the other end.

"Yes, Deputy Director."

"That photo is going around social media from some underground dinner in Chicago. I need you to work with your old ICE buddies to figure out how it got there," she said, referring to his time with Immigration and Customs Enforcement.

"Do we know who posted it?"

"No. Apparently it's a screenshot from one of those apps where the messages disappear."

"I'm familiar," Nakara said. "Teenage girls at home."

"Well, get a move on. It's only a matter of time before this gets on the news, and we need to have a response ready.

"Yes, Ma'am."

***

"What a...surprise," Biv said.

Surprised didn't begin to describe Biv Trammel's reaction as Joey Chapman climbed into the hired black sedan waiting outside of the Gold Coast high-rise condo. Biv hadn't seen him in close to two years, and figured he was off living in Siena or Cabo or Phuket. The fact that he was back in Chicago was news to the business manager. In fact, Trey rarely mentioned his brothers, something that had always struck Biv as odd. They had similar occupations, and now apparently all were back in the same city, yet there was very little interaction as far as he could tell.

Joey sized up the car for a moment, which had ample space for the normal payload, but was cramped with three full grown men across the backseat. He squeezed closer to Biv as Trey got into the car and shut the door.

"You guys can't afford a limo?" Joey asked, speaking to no one in particular.

"Can't afford a cab, Joey?" Biv replied.

"Why would I take a cab?"

"Why would you?" Biv said under his breath. "Where should I tell the driver you're going?"

"He's coming with us," Trey said.

He leaned forward and smiled reassuringly, but the business manager was not pleased. Biv was immediately suspicious. Joey had never once accompanied Trey during any of his appearances over the years, of which there had been plenty of opportunities in Chicago alone. His sudden desire to tag along didn't sit right.

"Oh, really?" Biv asked.

"Yep," Joey replied.

He knew Biv was probing for more of an explanation, but he wasn't providing one. There wasn't any sense in making up some elaborate reason for the impromptu visit. He had learned that the longer someone talked, the less truth was coming out. Joey didn't have much of a plan anyway. The wheels had spun as he showered back at Trey's condo, but he hadn't come up with much. The idea was simple though- help his brother lose the endorsements and obligations that monopolized his life. Joey had a couple hours to figure out what Trey should do on the cooking spot. It was only local TV, but as good a place to start as any. Joey closed his eyes to brainstorm as the trio rode in silence.

One seat away, Biv Trammel was unsettled. The usual routine with his client was completely thrown out of whack. Normally, they'd go over what the celebrity chef was cooking one more time. Trey never had any input in the matter- at least he hadn't in years. The TV demo was huge in the beginning and something Trey used to look forward to. But now, he was just going through the motions. Biv always selected a recipe from the latest cookbook and coordinated the ingredients with a producer over at the news station. He made sure it was simple and, despite Trey's steadily building rust in actual restaurant cooking, something he could execute without any trouble. Still, Biv needed the time in the car to focus his client, and Joey's presence was disturbing that.

As Biv shifted, trying to get comfortable, he nearly crushed the breakfast sandwich he always brought for Trey.

"I almost forgot," Biv said, offering the bag over.

Joey heard the crinkling and could smell the sandwich as it passed in front of him. He opened his eyes and snagged the fast food away from his brother.

"What are you doing?" Trey and Biv asked simultaneously.

"You can't eat this crap," Joey said, unwrapping the sandwich and inspecting its contents. "Do you have any idea what goes into this mass-produced sausage? This shit will kill you."

He made sure to look his older brother right in the eye on those last words.

Trey got the message. "I'm good. I already ate. Thanks though."

Joey stuffed the sandwich back into the bag and tossed it in Biv's lap. It was all the business manager could do to keep from exploding. This is just a one-time thing he told himself. All Biv had to do was get through the cooking demo and he probably wouldn't run into Joey for another year at best. He took a deep breath and put the fast-food bag on the floor near his feet.

That bag was part of the problem, and in Joey's mind, an extension of the true cause of his brother's ills- Biv Trammel. He was the one who bought the heart-clogging food. He set the crazy schedule that caused Trey to fly from one city to the next. It was the business manager's constant pushing that was killing the great Trey Chapman. Joey's plan now had a focus; protect his older brother from Biv. He closed his eyes again and went back to brainstorming about the cooking demo.

"What am I making again?" Trey asked.

Biv took a long look at Joey and hoped he would stay in his meditative state long enough to go over the plan.

"The seared beef salad with Thai dressing," he said, handing over a copy of the recipe. "The ribeye will already be cooked. Basically, all you'll need to do is slice it, make the dressing and assemble the salad."

"Easy," Trey replied, not even looking at the cheat sheet.

"Go easy on the chili flakes," Biv reminded him. "Joan hates spicy."

"Won't everything be pre-measured?" Trey asked.

"You've made this a million times. I didn't think you needed it."

Trey shrugged and sat back. He had made the dish at least a dozen times in the last few months alone on the latest cookbook tour, but there really wasn't any cooking involved. He cut some steak, stirred a little, and voila. That was the magic of having people prep these demos for him. He didn't even have to think. The irony was that he'd spent countless hours in the kitchen measuring the dressing ingredients down to the drop. The balance of sweet, sour, salty and bitter was paramount to him, especially in Asian-inspired dishes. During the testing phase, he'd experimented with seven types of limes and dozens of chilies. Trey called the best fish sauce producer in Bangkok to understand the nuances of traditional *nam pla*. He nearly made himself sick testing various sweeteners one afternoon and refused to eat desserts for a month afterwards.

Trey had lost a zeal for a lot of things over the last few draining years, but one of them wasn't flavor. He could go the rest of his life without signing a cookbook or doing a TV demo, but he was still a 23-year-old trying to prove himself when it came to inventing recipes. Perfecting recipes was more like it. And the thought of going on even the local news and not getting a dish exactly right terrified Trey. But even if he could execute the beef salad blindfolded, it wouldn't matter. Joey had overheard the last exchange with Biv and was cooking up an idea of his own.

***

The sound of Audrey making her way up the steps seemed slow and labored. Jackson reached into his desk drawer and produced a small square box just as she appeared in his office doorway. He took one look at his wife's red swollen feet and handed it to her.

"A sercy?" she asked.

Jackson had read about the southern tradition of giving a gift for no reason and introduced it into their relationship even before they were married. He loved the gesture and the mystery behind it. Neither the origin nor the spelling of sercy could be agreed upon. But both he and Audrey loved the sense of surprise it created in their relationship and the feeling that they were constantly on each other's minds.

She opened the lid and removed a beautiful piece of jade in the shape of a "T." He could tell by the way his wife inspected the light green stone that she wasn't entirely sure of the purpose, so he grabbed her hand and pulled her onto his lap. Jackson began slowly rubbing the stone along the arch of her foot.

"That feels amazing."

Audrey considered herself a career volunteer. Most of her time went to organizations that helped single mothers throughout the city. She rarely spoke of her work as a shoe fit model.

"What was it today?" Jackson asked.

"Maricella is designing a pair of slingback heels, but she might as well call them sling blades. The strap across the ankle was so thin it literally cut into my skin."

"That sounds just awful," he replied, not really knowing what any of it meant.

Audrey loved it though and had been doing it since her last growth spurt at age 15 when her feet stopped at a perfect size seven. The days were sometimes long and uncomfortable, but her opinion was valued, and she appreciated being a small part of the design process. Payment was more than fair, and occasionally she took it in the form of shoes, but it was the sporadic nature of the work that she enjoyed the most. Sometimes it was several days in a row, and sometimes she wouldn't get the call for weeks. It left Audrey enough time to be fulfilled with more meaningful activities.

Jackson switched to the other foot, and his wife leaned back farther into his arms.

"Where are we going for dinner tonight?" she asked, expecting to be titillated.

"Got an invite to a relaunch. The Portobello Grille," Jackson said, almost swallowing the name. "They're going farm to table."

"The Portobello Grille?"

"Yeah, I know it wasn't great the first time we tried it," Jackson said, attempting to get ahead of what he knew was coming, "but to be fair that was takeout, and nothing holds up well in plastic containers. Besides, they've scrapped the old menu. Who knows what they'll serve tonight."

Audrey sat straight up, not happy. She had a memory of her own and saw right through her husband's attempt at revisionist history. To-go containers or not, the food was bad. Jackson even said so at the time. They had tried four dishes that night. The least offensive was a beet salad, which may have been palatable at one point, but judging by the deep purple color staining the goat cheese and greens, had been put together days before. They ordered an appetizer of oven-roasted tomato dip, which seemed to be nothing more than reduced, canned marinara. It was cloying sweet and thick enough to grout tile. One of the entrees they split was so bland it was instantly forgettable. The other was the restaurant's signature grilled portabella cap stuffed with mashed potatoes and topped with a braised short rib gravy. One bite of the potatoes and it would've been clear to even the dullest of palates that they were once dehydrated potato flakes. The mushroom was charred beyond recognition and the meat more akin to jerky.

The meal stuck out in Audrey's mind because they barely made it through one bite of each dish before dumping them in the trash and hightailing it to their favorite pizza place around the corner. They nearly ate an entire sausage deep dish pie themselves, so happy to be tasting something delicious. They laughed and moaned on the uncomfortably full walk home. It was just one of thousands of experiences where they had bonded over food- the terrible takeout experience salvaged by an impromptu pizza feast. To eat at The Portobello Grill seemed like Jackson was forgetting the highs and lows of that evening.

He could see the consternation on his wife's face though and knew her well enough to save the moment.

"I'll have a large Chicago classic standing by," Jackson said. "Extra sausage."

Audrey blushed a little. She sometimes forgot how much of a romantic her husband was, and that when it came to food, he had the memory of an elephant.

She leaned back and kissed him.

"If I see a single spoonful of that tomato dip, we're out of there!" he said.

***

Local television is the worst. It's often staffed by eager recent graduates that will work for cheap. They treat any brush with fame like a visit from the Pope. Trey dreaded those appearances because he spent all but the few minutes on-camera surrounded by a crowd of autograph-seeking underlings. If he sold a cookbook for every Facebook picture he appeared in, Trey would never fall off the Bestseller list. There wasn't the sense of boundaries during those local TV spots like there was at The Today Show. The green rooms, which are guarded like Fort Knox at most national outlets, might as well not have doors in places like Wichita Falls and Montgomery. Biv could only do so much on those tours, and Trey was left drained on a nightly basis.

The Channel 2 appearances were different though. They started with the same frenzy of excitement, but it was mutual. Trey Chapman was just as eager to get on television as the crew was to meet the chef of the city's hottest restaurant. They stocked the green room with a wide array that would've fed a rapper's entourage. The first couple years, Trey looked forward to the cooking segment and prepared for it as if the whole world, not just Chicago, was watching. He developed a rapport with the staff and knew many of them by name. But the marriage had gotten dull over the years. Everyone at the station had become used to his presence, eroding any level of professionalism. The green room at Channel 2 was now a waste land. The once-bountiful spread had slowly been reduced to a couple stale bagels and a coffee pod machine.

Trey usually sat in silence as he waited for a producer to ferry him into make-up and then onto the set. Like all his other local appearances, Biv accompanied his client to the studio, but pretty much let him fly solo, as was the chef's wish from the very beginning. Trey badly wanted to be the anti-celebrity during his rise. He didn't need a posse. But the more time passed, he realized the army of assistants that so many of the famous employed weren't so much to take over the simple details of everyday life, but to serve as a layer of insulation from a demanding world.

Trey wasn't alone for his latest appearance though. Joey was a few feet away in the green room working on a scheme, in his mind, to save his brother's life. And the business manager seemed equally focused trying to figure out what the youngest Chapman was thinking. Joey paced back and forth in front of the bagels. He picked one up and tapped it on the table. The thud was unsettling.

"There's got to be something edible around this place," Joey said, throwing the bagel in the garbage and leaving.

Biv took the opportunity to focus his client. "Feel good, Trey?"

The answer was no. And it had been for a long time. Maybe years. Maybe since he was just Jackson Chapman III. The past few hours of thinking about ruining everything he had worked for had Trey's head spinning. It didn't make sense, but neither did staying the course. There must be some reasonable way to get his life and health back.

"I've changed my mind on the knives."

"No can do. We're already off and running."

Trey was confused. "But we just said yes."

"Knives were like the last big thing on your empire wish list. This is the top of the mountain," Biv said, very pleased with himself.

"So, there's no way to shut it down?"

"I'll double check the contract when I get back to my office," Biv lied. "And hey, I know they'd love it if you mentioned the knives on the appearance today. Pre-sales would go through the roof."

Trey ran his fingers through his hair and closed his eyes. Biv was just doing what he always did, but this time it felt different. How could he get the man who had worked so hard to make this all possible understand that it wasn't what he wanted anymore? That it needed to end. That it *had* to end. The tightness in Trey's chest had returned. Figuring out how to sabotage this cooking demo would have to wait. Right now, he had to stifle the panic attack that was about to pounce. Across the tv station, though, Joey had stumbled onto a solution.

Joan Jones had been a fixture at Channel 2 for nearly two decades and could read a teleprompter better than anyone in the Midwest. Her hair and personality seemed to have grown at the same rate during her career in the Windy City. Her blond bouffant was distractingly high, as was her opinion of herself. Joan incorrectly believed that her celebrity around town was as big as any of her guests. She liked to say that she was the first person to put the great Trey

Chapman on TV, something that annoyed Biv Trammel to no end, and part of the reason the business manager liked to hide away in the green room during these appearances.

Joan was on her way back from makeup when she noticed someone in the prep kitchen stuffing his face.

"Who are you?" she asked with great authority as she walked up behind him.

"This is the type of spread you should have in the green room," Joey said, helping himself to another bite of steak.

"Put that down! That's for our cooking segment with Trey Chapman," Joan said, shooing him away.

"Oh, then he won't mind," Joey said, trying to reach around and grab another bite. "That's my brother."

"Well, you're not supposed to be in here," Joan said. "All of this has been pre-measured and laid out for the segment."

Joey saw the bowl of chili flakes and remembered what Biv had said in the car about Joan's dislike of spicy food. But there was no way he could add a little extra kick with her standing there. He would have to come back.

"You must be Joan. Trey says how much he loves going on with you," Joey said, laying it on thick. "I'm a little turned around. Can you show me back to the green room?"

Joey extended his elbow towards Joan, and her ego now properly inflated, looped her arm in and walked him out of the prep kitchen.

The not so dirty secret to most cooking demonstrations on television is that there actually isn't any cooking done. Trey learned that right out of the gate. His first demo was choreographed by a segment producer who walked him through the three steps to every successful on-air appearance.

Step 1: Explain the recipe while pointing at a beautiful display of all the raw ingredients.

Step 2: Dump some pre-measured ingredients into waiting bowls or pans.

Step 3: Move over to the already cooked ingredients and plate the dish for the host to try.

What was not explained to Trey on his inaugural cooking segment with Joan Jones all those years ago was that the allotted 5 minutes would go by at the speed of light. All the polite, Midwest host with the big hair could do was try to pull the stammering young chef along. Eight minutes in, she finally walked over to the semi-final product, took a bite, gave the camera a thumbs up, which allowed a frenzied control room to cut to a commercial.

Trey's return to Channel 2 to promote his next cookbook came with several stipulations, including a large red countdown clock next to the camera. It was distracting, but efficient. Trey never went over his time again, but it took quite a while for his character and charm to find their way into the demos. Now he was stuck wondering how he could not only make this one go poorly, but make it look unintentional to boot.

With the weather segment almost over, a producer came to escort Trey to the studio.

"You coming?" Trey asked Biv, knowing the answer.

"I will," Joey said, popping up. "It'll be fun to see you in action all up close."

The producer shrugged and led the Chapman brothers down the hall. Biv remained motionless on the couch, more worried than ever.

"Wait here," the producer said, stopping at the studio door. He pointed at the flashing red light above it, made the universal sign to be quiet, and disappeared inside.

"I'm freaking out, Joey," Trey said, tugging at his shirt.

"All you have to do is go heavy on the chili flakes," Joey said reassuringly. "If this thing goes viral, you're free and clear by dinner time."

"I can't do that to Joan!"

"It's a little hot pepper, not rat poison. You do this right and you never have to do another cooking demo with her or anyone."

The door opened and the producer motioned them inside. The Channel 2 studio was a maze of cameras, lights and wires. The frantic motion behind the scenes, though, reminded Trey of the dance in the kitchen during the dinner rush. Everyone knew what everyone else was supposed to do, and trusted that they would do it. Trey had learned to stay close to his escort all the way to the makeshift kitchen far off to the side of the main anchor desk. He knew not to speak until the stage manager called "Clear!" indicating the three-minute commercial break that led into his segment. It was the same routine in every city. The only thing that changed was the host. And the one he had known longest and was now supposed to dose with capsaicin was headed his way.

"You must have more cookbooks by now than Minnesota's got lakes," Joan said, pausing just long enough for the hair and makeup team to touch her up.

The same producer that had ferried the Chapman brothers to the set handed Joan a stack of note cards. They included information about the chef, recipe, and potential questions to ask about the book.

"We don't need these, do we Trey?" she said, handing them back.

"Ninety!" the stage manager called out. With that, the producer ushered Joey over behind the cameras.

"Cat got your tongue, Chapman?" Joan asked, eyeing him awkwardly.

Trey had already started to sweat through his makeup. The lights seemed brighter than usual. The whole thing felt wrong. He was sure there was a better solution; he just needed time and a clear head to figure it out. Five minutes, he thought to himself, focusing on the red countdown clock next to the camera. Trey took a deep breath and managed a hint of a smile.

"Any excuse to see you, Joan."

"Let's have some fun then," she said, as the stage manager counted them back from commercial.

Biv was also sweating as he watched from the Channel 2 green room. He had seen his client shake off hangovers, exhaustion, and one time even a kidney stone before turning into a culinary Bradley Cooper in front of the cameras. But Trey was clearly not himself. There was no flirty banter with Joan. No mention of other recipes to tease the audience and get them to buy the book. And most troubling to Biv, there was no mention of the new knives.

"Next up is the Thai dressing," Trey said, racing through the demo.

"Let's go back to the steak for a second. Is that a *New York* strip?" Joan asked, putting extra emphasis on the city.

"No, it's a ribeye."

"Good. Wouldn't want to offend all the fine Chicagoans watching at home," Joan said, winking at the camera. But Trey didn't get it. He was too focused on the bowl of chili flakes. His hands shook as he lifted it. Joey watched eagerly from just behind the camera. Biv was just as dialed in from the green room.

"The nice thing about this dish is that you can make it as spicy as you like. Or," Trey said, putting the bowl down, "you can omit the chili flakes all together."

Biv breathed a sigh of relief. At least his client had gotten one thing right. Trey and Joan stepped to the far end of the makeshift kitchen in front of all the finished elements of the dish. The business manager relaxed as Trey sliced the steak, tossed it with the premade dressing and perfectly plated the cookbook's signature salad. As she had done so many times before, Joan offered her forkful to the camera before happily bringing it back to her own mouth. Trey waited for her well-rehearsed moans of enjoyment, but they didn't come. Instead, there was instant panic on the polite, Midwestern anchor's face. She grabbed a bottle of water beneath the counter and chugged it as Trey stood by helplessly.

"We'll be right back," Joan gasped, waiting until the red light above the camera had turned off before exploding into a coughing, expletive-spewing tornado. "Someone get me some fucking milk!"

Trey started to apologize, but was whisked off set by the producer, who motioned for Joey to follow them out of the studio.

"I didn't put them in," Trey said, baffled.

"I knew you wouldn't," Joey said, winking at his older brother.

"What did you do!?" Trey whispered angrily.

"I'm trying to help you."

Trey was about to blow up, but as they arrived back at the green room, his business manager beat him to it.

"What did I say about the chili flakes!?" Biv screamed.

"You saw the demo," Joey said, rushing to his brother's defense. "He didn't use them."

"You taste everything! How many years have we been doing this? You don't trust some intern to follow your recipes," Biv said, running his hands through his hair. "How could you be so careless!?"

Trey was coiled with anger. He could still feel the pain in his right hand from the cookbook signing. The tightness in his chest made each breath a struggle. The warning from Dr. Nevins was all he could think about. And the one person who should have his back was berating him about something that wasn't even his fault. Trey sucked in as much air as he could, preparing to unload on Biv, but stopped when Joan Jones popped up on the green room tv.

"Welcome back," she said, no longer red in the face. "I just want to apologize to Chef Chapman. Don't let me getting a little pepper caught in the back of my throat scare you away from his new book. It's filled with incredible recipes. Trey, we hope to see you back here at Channel 2 real soon."

Biv let out a sigh of relief. "Thank goodness."

"A little warning now for our viewers," Joan continued on the television. "The next image is not for anyone with a fragile stomach."

Up popped the viral screenshot of the maggot-filled cheese.

"You may have seen this photo across your social media feed. It appears to be a type of cheese filled with fly larvae called casu marzu. Not only is it disgusting, it's illegal in the United States. I, along with many people online, are wondering how it got into our fair city," Joan questioned. "Channel 2 has requests out to several government agencies for comment. No word on if anyone has been sickened from eating it."

Joey was frozen, the blood drained from his face, and all he could think about was how long it would take for this to come back on him.

"You look a little queasy," Trey said. "Do you need to sit down?"

"I need to go. I'll call you later, Trey," Joey said, hurrying out. He had another chef to see.

Trey didn't have the energy to fight with Biv anymore. "Let's go," he said to his longtime business manager. "Please look into that knife contract. I can't keep this up."

Biv nodded and motioned for his client to exit the green room first. The hired black sedan was waiting outside. It would be a long, silent ride back to the empty high-rise condo. The only thing waiting for Trey was the calendar on his fridge telling him where to go next.

4

Portobello translates to "beautiful door," something Dave Talmidge's restaurant no longer had. The once rich mahogany, tortured by sunlight for decades, had faded to mauve. Jackson ran his hand across the dried-out grain as he opened the door for Audrey. It wouldn't take much, he thought. Some steel wool. A beeswax conditioner. New stain. Once inside, Jackson realized how futile that restoration would be. The Portobello Grille may have a new menu, but the decor hadn't been updated since the 90s, coincidentally the last time anyone was excited by the oversized fungus.

"Same brown tablecloths and beige curtains that were here when we got takeout," Audrey said. "It's like we're inside a mushroom."

It wasn't meant as a joke, but Jackson couldn't help but smile at his wife.

As he looked around the drab restaurant, he noticed it was empty except for a handful of people at the bar. At 6' 7", Dave Talmidge was hard to miss. But it was the man standing on his left that made Audrey furious.

"Is that your father!?"

It was. But before Jackson could say anything, Dave spotted his guest of honor by the door.

"Jackson!" he shouted, waving them over with his ridiculously long arms.

As they walked to the bar, Audrey expressed her growing displeasure by squeezing the life out of Jackson's hand.

"I didn't know you were going to be here, Dad," the middle son said.

"Just came to toast Dave on the big day," James Chapman Jr. said, raising his glass. "I'm not staying though."

Audrey was, above all else, polite. She forced a smile for her father-in-law even though his presence confirmed her fears about why they were really there.

"Thank you all for coming," Dave said. "I hope you're hungry."

Audrey wasn't.

"The new beet salad sounds like a real winner," James said, finishing his drink. He kissed Audrey on the cheek and patted Jackson on the shoulder. "Good to see you, son."

Dave escorted Jackson and Audrey to a table in the front window.

"I'm just going to have the chef send out some dishes and you all yell 'Uncle!' when you've had enough," he said, and headed for the kitchen.

"Thanks, Mr. Talmidge," Jackson said.

"It's Dave!" he called out, not breaking stride.

"Does this look like a relaunch to you?" Audrey asked, not waiting for a reply. "Because it looks to me like your dad was cashing in on some free drinks for getting his son to review his friend's restaurant. And to put us right here in the window! It would be more subtle to put your name on the sign out front."

Jackson let her finish, and even waited an extra beat to make sure she had gotten it all out before speaking.

"You're absolutely right," he said, sliding his hands across the table as a peace offering. "I feel ambushed too. This isn't what I...we signed up for."

Audrey may have let her husband off the hook that easy in the past, but her tightly crossed arms told Jackson he would need to work much harder.

"I've got a bottle of Lambrusco stashed away in the back of the fridge. It's screaming for pizza. The bubbles are as faint as the sweetness. It's a perfect foil for spicy sausage. Just say the word, my love."

Any other night, that combination would make for a wonderful evening. She could picture them laid out on a blanket in front of the fireplace. The temperature outside never mattered when they were in a mood for a fire. Full and happy, they would entertain themselves by tearing pieces from the box top and tossing them into the flames. Jackson would disappear and return with an inky bottle of primitivo, her favorite. The failings of the beginning of the night would fade away.

As Audrey contemplated her options, a waiter dropped off the first wave of food. She took one look at the fluorescent purple stained goat cheese on the beet salad, and abruptly stood up. Jackson slid his chair back from the table.

"No," she said, putting a heavy hand on his shoulder. "I'll see you at home."

Audrey did not rush out. She calmly walked to the old mahogany door and gracefully pushed it open.

As Jackson watched his wife disappear onto the street, Dave Talmidge came rushing over.

"Everything okay?"

"She's been fighting something all day," Jackson said. "Hopefully a little rest will do the trick."

"You know, I thought she looked a little sick when you guys walked in, but I didn't want to say anything," Dave said, not helping the situation. "More for you, I guess!"

Jackson Chapman managed a smile as he placed his napkin in his lap. As a restaurant critic, he had trained his eyes to take in every visual nuance of a dish so that he could recreate the plate in words. He believed this set his reviews apart from those who simply described flavors.

He wanted to transfer his experience into the minds of his readers like it was a memory of their own. But as he lifted his fork, all he could think about was the empty chair across the table.

***

"How long on the rattlesnake?" Patrick Schuler asked, using a prep towel to wipe the sweat from his forehead. After hosting so many underground dinners in places like auto body garages, church basements, and once even a Spirit Halloween store, he was ecstatic to return to an actual kitchen. But it was tight quarters in the back of the recently closed King Falafel.

"Three minutes," the lone assistant said, standing over the fryer.

Chef Schuler placed a drop of the sauce he was stirring onto the back of his hand, then tasted it. Cayenne pepper and vinegar were the backbone, and the sorghum syrup he used instead of molasses added a sour note while keeping the consistency thin. There was no doubt in his mind that his Nashville Hot Rattlesnake would be a hit.

The 25 spots available at the dinner sold out in less than a minute. The process had evolved tremendously over the years and now all the enigmatic, young chef had to do was send a mass text with a link. To add to the secrecy, the location wasn't revealed until an hour before the meal. He didn't even include a menu anymore, only a theme. The Nashville Hot Rattlesnake was the second course for "Crawl, Slither, Run."

"Was I right?" Chef Schuler asked as two servers came in from clearing the starter.

"There was some plate licking," one begrudgingly admitted.

"Some!?" the chef exclaimed. "Those look like they could go straight back in the box."

"Snails in pepper," the server shuddered, tossing the plates into the sink. "Disgusting."

"Cacio e pepe escargot. You forgot the cheese," Schuler corrected.

The diners paying $200 each believed that their host had graduated from one of the top culinary schools in the world and been trained under a sky of Michelin stars. But Patrick Schuler had never left the Midwest, much less studied at Le Cordon Bleu in Paris. He knew the rumors and knew they were good for business, so he did nothing to quell them. Joey Chapman was not fooled though. It had taken just two phone calls to figure out who the guy trying to get his hands on an illegal Sardinian cheese really was.

Merlin's business, if it could be called that, was entirely referral-based. You had to know someone who knew someone that could get your request in front of the sourcer. The process from there was always the same, starting with a fresh burner phone. The first calls were to vet the new client. Joey was always worried about being set up. He honestly didn't know what would happen if he got caught, so he made sure that was never a possibility. Patrick Schuler, he learned, wasn't a concern.

"Captain D's?" Joey said, staring at the flip phone.

"Captain D's," the voice on the other end said. "After that, it was some soul food cafe. We did the lunch shift together at P.F. Chang's for about six months. I heard he worked at one of the Mexican joints Rick Bayless owns after that, but not sure if it's true."

"Real rags to riches," Joey said. "Thanks. I owe you one."

Patrick Schuler had cooked at nine different restaurants over the past seven years. For a guy with no high school diploma and a sketchy work history, he had climbed surprisingly high up the culinary ladder. But he was stuck and didn't want to make twenty bucks an hour for the rest of his life. Schuler heard about some pop-up dinners in Los Angeles where chefs were making good money without a restaurant of their own. The inspiration for his first attempt came on a drunken walk home. As he devoured a plate of street tacos, Schuler heard the group of twenty somethings next to him talking about getting dumplings. He realized that other than a large collection of tattoos, he had amassed the knowledge to make food from just about everywhere in the world. His gamble that people would pay to eat around the globe in one stop was right. But it wasn't until he served a grasshopper taco that he realized the draw of the bizarre.

The Nashville Hot Rattlesnake was so good that the crowd of twenty five diners chanted the chef's name until he finally popped out of the kitchen.

"Thank you. Thank you. You ready to *Run?*" he asked, igniting an even louder cheer. "The final course is a take on Sichuan-style lamb with cumin. But

I'm going to do it with a 700-pound Asian antelope. Anyone here ever eaten Nilgai?"

No hands went up, as the chef expected. What he did not expect was the man waiting for him on the other side of the kitchen door.

"No pictures!" Joey yelled.

"Merlin?" Patrick Schuler froze.

"Why is my cheese on the news?"

"I took everyone's cell phone. Someone must have snuck in a camera or something," Schuler pleaded.

"Has anyone asked about me?" Joey said, inching closer.

"No. I swear! Hey, where's Luis?" the chef asked, noticing his assistant was missing. "Did you kill him!?"

"Short, Hispanic guy?" Joey asked. "He was having a smoke when I drove up."

"Look, what do you want?"

"It's only a matter of time before someone figures out that picture was from one of your dinners. What are you going to say when they ask you where you got the cheese?"

"I hadn't really thought about it," Schuler said.

"Well, then let's think about it," Joey said, sitting on the counter.

"Look man, I'm in the middle of service here. Can we do this later?"

One of the servers poked his head through the door. "Hey Chef, someone's asking where the Nilgai is from again?"

"India," Schuler replied, and the server disappeared.

"Bullshit. That butterfly," Joey said, pointing to a symbol on a piece of plastic wrap in the garbage, "is the logo for Mariposa Ranch. In south Texas. Not India."

"How in the hell?" Schuler questioned.

"Don't worry, I'm not going to tell any of your diners. And you're not going to tell anyone about me. Got it?"

Schuler nodded. It was all the assurance Joey was going to get. He walked through the back door past Luis who was wrapping up his cigarette break. Joey got into his car and started to drive away, but stopped. He rolled down the window.

"You know your boss worked at Captain D's, right?" he said, then sped off toward downtown.

***

Trey stared at the calendar on his fridge. His night was free. But he needed a drink to figure out what to do with it. He opened the door to the left of the sink which contained four rocks glasses and a half empty bottle of A.H. Hirsch Reserve. Trey poured three fingers of the bourbon and walked to the couch.

The right thing to do, he thought, was go to his restaurant. But after the fiasco at Channel 2, he was mentally exhausted. The decision not to go to his namesake made him feel guilty. The bourbon helped, but it also made him hungry. Trey realized that after refusing the fast food from Biv in the back of the hired black sedan that morning, he hadn't eaten anything. Calling his assistant, Erica, was out of the question. He was perfectly capable of getting his own dinner. Wasn't he? The celebrity chef finished his drink and walked to the bedroom to fish his credit card out of his suitcase.

The cool, fresh air on Lake Shore Drive perked him up. Not having a particular destination, he decided to head south. Trey stared over at Lake Michigan as he walked along. The water was peaceful. Simple. His stomach rumbled, bringing purpose back to the stroll. He was looking for something fast; something he could take back to his condo, but the only restaurants that could afford the surrounding real estate were fine dining. He was beginning to rethink calling Erica, that's when he heard someone scream.

72

"Trey Chapman!" a woman yelled, running towards the chef. She waved her three girlfriends over. "I told you it was him! Can we take a picture with you, Chef?"

Trey forced a smile. He used to love this. The first time he was recognized on the street he talked with the fan for 20 minutes and even recorded a new voice-mail message for her. Now the encounters felt more like intrusions, especially this one. Couldn't he just walk around his city to get a bite to eat without being bothered?

The photo op had attracted the attention of a nearby tourist group. Before Trey knew it, he was swarmed. His name was being shouted from every direction, and his view and path were both blocked by a wall of phones taking pictures. The crowd was starting to press against him. Trey felt his chest tighten. With panic setting in, he put his head down and pushed through the mob. As soon as his feet were free, the celebrity chef sprinted back to the safety of his high-rise condo.

Joey Chapman was already inside, enjoying a glass of the bourbon that was left out on the counter, when Trey burst through the door out of breath.

"Fuck!" Trey yelled, clutching his chest. "How'd you get in here, Joey?"

"I told you. I have a key."

"No, you don't," Trey insisted, collapsing to the ground.

"You go for a jog?" Joey asked.

"No. I was trying to get some food," Trey said, extending his arms and legs onto the floor like a snow angel.

"Ever hear of Uber Eats? GrubHub? DoorDash?"

Honestly, Trey hadn't.

"I'm gonna get us some gyros," Joey said, pulling out his phone. "Hope you don't mind, but I helped myself to some of your Hirsch."

"That's fine," Trey said, finally catching his breath.

"I knew you were rich, but a $9,000 bottle of bourbon?"

"That bottle is nine grand?" Trey asked, trying to remember whether he bought it or if it was a gift.

"Yeah, I'd say it's time for a little reality check," Joey said, downing his last sip of the pricey liquor. "Why'd you wuss out at the TV station?"

"I just want a break, not napalm my career."

Joey got up and helped himself to another glass of bourbon. He studied the calendar on the fridge. "So, what's your plan?"

"I asked Biv to look at my contracts," Trey said.

"Ha. You're his gravy train, man. He's not going to kill his golden goose," Joey said, gesturing to the jam-packed schedule. "We need to get a look at those contracts ourselves. Any way you can get copies? Don't you have a lawyer or something?"

"I have no idea. Biv set everything up. There's no way I can ask without him getting suspicious."

It took hearing those words come out of his mouth for Trey to realize he had become the celebrity he always said he wouldn't. He was insulated from reality. When did he start drinking bourbon that cost more than some cars? When did he get so famous he couldn't walk down the street? That reminded Trey of his failed attempt to get dinner.

"I'm starving. Hope those gyros get here soon," he said, his stomach rumbling loud enough for Joey to hear it.

The younger brother was lost in thought though. He had no idea how to get his hands on Trey's contracts, but he knew someone who just might.

***

Jackson Chapman woke up alone, the same way his wife had gone to bed. After finishing dinner at The Portobello Grille, he came home with every intention to make amends but found Audrey fast asleep. Not wanting to disturb her any more than the evening already had, Jackson went into his office, closed the door, and wrote his review. Over the years, he had figured out the precise time that he could both upset Martin Easley with a late submission, yet still get it into the next day's paper.

If you are a resident of even modest tenure in the greater Chicago area, it's highly likely you have dined at or have an opinion of The Portobello Grille. Owner Dave Talmidge's new menu is an invitation to update your attendance and enjoy refreshed ideas on his decades-old concept.

The roasted beet salad with goat cheese is a bridge to patrons new and old. The crimson tubers and cloud-like curds have not changed, but the drizzle of tarragon vinaigrette is a much better accompaniment than the previous citrus-based dressing. Many long-standing dishes are thankfully absent; such as the faded red tomato dip which assaulted the palate like sweet grout. Salbitxada takes its place, a Catalan classic that leans heavily on imported bixto peppers and raw garlic. Tomatoes, almonds and sherry vinegar round out the sauce. It is tradition-ally served in Spain with grilled spring onions. Talmidge puts his midwestern spin on the offering with fried Vidalia onion strips.

There is French influence as well, using lake trout in place of sole or flounder for a hyper local take on meuniere. The fish is lightly breaded, pan-fried and finished with brown butter and lemon. If this had been on the previous menu, I have no doubt the garnish would've been curly parsley. Here, they have shown growth by choosing to finely chop the flat leaf variety.

As for the signature grilled portobello cap filled with mashed potatoes and awash in short rib gravy, it too has evolved. A cauliflower and parmesan puree attempts to lighten the dish, but it is still a beef eater's offering, now topped with slices of herb-encrusted flank steak. This updating of the dish The Portobello Grille was built around speaks to the humility of the rebranding- one Dave Talmidge hopes he won't have to do again.

Four stars.

Jackson entered the kitchen and was immediately concerned. Audrey was an early riser, so breakfast without his wife wasn't abnormal. But she always put a single place setting at the counter stool, some sort of sustenance, and the morning paper folded neatly nearby. The blank space felt ominous. Jackson opened the fridge and pulled out a new bottle of orange juice. He removed the small foil tab and pulled out the garbage drawer. As he flicked it into the trash, he almost missed what was beneath the remnants of Audrey's breakfast. There, covered in coffee grounds and orange rind, was his review.

***

"I just make pork chops, man. I don't know anything about any fly cheese."

Supervisory Special Agent Ken Nakara had the wrong chef, but he already knew that. His investigation into the casu marzu viral image was not going as planned. After hearing a sense of urgency and importance in his boss's voice, Nakara had visions of a joint task force with half a dozen agents holed up in a large conference room with notes and pictures covering rows of dry erase boards. But it turned out that while Immigration and Customs Enforcement was happy to be part of the joint initiative on paper, they had no interest in providing any manpower or resources. Ken Nakara was very much on his own, which is why he was working on the weekend.

His first order of business was responding to a request for comment from Channel 2. He provided a basic statement saying they were aware of the viral image and looking into its origin. Next, he contacted the Chicago Department of Public Health which provided him with a list of all the people in the city who had registered for a Food Handler Certification. Crossing off anyone who worked at a brick-and-mortar restaurant or sold at Farmers Markets still left hundreds of names. Since the photo was viral, Nakara started looking into which of the remaining chefs had large social media followings. Enter Isaiah Williams.

The wafer-thin man standing behind an enormous barrel smoker did not look like the average pit master. But Williams was bona fide. He learned whole hog barbecue from his father whenever the family had the rare combination of money and occasion. The son brought that little piece of Estill, South Carolina with him, but once on his own, found that as the cities grew bigger, his kitchen grew smaller. So, Williams focused on his favorite cut- the pork chop.

"See how thick these are?" he said, proudly pointing to the enormous pieces of pig on the grates. "I was doing triple-cut before anyone was doing double-cut."

"How does someone just grilling pork chops get 145,000 followers on social media?" Supervisory Special Agent Nakara asked.

"First off, these aren't grilled. They're smoked. And these aren't just pork chops. See that bulge," the chef said, pointing to what appeared to be a baseball hiding inside each chop. "Some people just cut a little slit and put like a tablespoon of something in there and call them stuffed. Nah ah. I carve the center out and grind it with fat to make my own sausage. There's apples, pecans, sage and breadcrumbs. Folks call it 'Thanksgiving on a fork.' I can fit 85 on here, and I'll sell 'em out in less than an hour."

"And you just do this on the weekends?"

"Yep. I'm a copy editor at the Trib by day."

"What about anyone else doing this type of cooking?" Nakara asked.

"I'm a solo artist, baby. I tweet out my spot, get in and get out."

"Well, if you hear of anything that might help," he said, handing him a card, "please give me a call."

Williams nodded. It was clear he had nothing to do with the illegal cheese. As Nakara walked back to his car, he wondered how long it would take for one of his leads to pan out. The next name on his list would have to wait though. The hickory smoke clinging to his clothes was making him hungry. A second breakfast was in order.

***

The hired black sedan was supposed to be on its way to a photo shoot but was still parked outside the high-rise condo due to a disagreement between the driver and passenger.

"Fine! I'll call him," Trey shouted through the partition.

"Put it on speaker," the driver insisted.

"Trey?" Biv answered.

"I need to go to Chapman's, but this maniac you hired won't move."

"You've got a photoshoot."

"My dad called in a panic. And he never panics. So, whatever this photoshoot is for, it's going to have to wait," Trey implored.

"We need a new marketing shot for the knives," Biv said.

"You said you'd look at the contract!"

"I did. Look, I can buy you an hour or so, but you have to get there by eleven."

Trey wanted to lay into Biv, but his concern for his father took precedent at the moment.

The call earlier that morning was so cryptic it was unsettling. For the first time in his life, it sounded like the great James Chapman Jr. needed help.

Trey hung up the phone.

"You heard him," he said to the driver. "Chapman's Steakhouse. Go!"

Trey wasn't sure what to expect, but as they pulled into the restaurant parking lot, he saw something that had never hung on the front door of his family's restaurant. The red and white sign read, "Public Health Inspection Notice:

"Closed." Trey jumped out of the sedan and examined the sign for a moment before walking in.

"Dad?"

The restaurant was completely empty. Trey kept calling as he walked through the bar and finally into the kitchen. There he found James Jr., a ring of sweat around the neck of his shirt, frantically throwing boxes toward the back door.

"Dad, what's going on?"

James couldn't look his son in the eye. He motioned to the health inspection report on the counter. Trey skimmed it.

"Storing expired food?" he said, feeling less alarmed. "We can fix that. I can probably pull some strings and get someone from the Health Department back over here today."

"It's all expired," James said.

"All of it!? How is that possible?" Trey asked, looking around at the stacks of boxes.

It didn't make sense because Trey still pictured Chapman's the way it used to be, filled with loyal regulars, tourists and anyone with a reason to celebrate. There was a musicality to the laughter and clinking glasses. Knives conquering enormous steaks with a loud tap on the plate made their own percussion.

"I just thought if I could keep things going," James said, trailing off.

Trey wasn't there when the energy began to fade and the crowd dwindled. He had no idea that the few guests that came now were greeted by an intern. Trey Chapman didn't have time for his own restaurant much less his father's.

"How much trouble are you in, Dad?"

The length of the pause before he answered said it all. James Jr.'s eyes welled up. And Trey realized the last time he had seen his father cry was in that very kitchen seven years ago.

"I'm broke."

"What are you talking about?" Trey asked.

"People...they just stopped coming. I paid out of my own pocket for two years before I had to get the bank involved."

"How much do you owe?"

"A hundred and ninety," James said, his voice filled with shame.

All Trey had was questions. How could his father let this happen? But he knew a lecture wouldn't help.

"Maybe it's time," Trey suggested.

"The restaurant is all I've got," James said, not with pity, but with vigor.

"Dad, look around..."

"I don't even know why I called you!" James said, cutting him off. "You haven't even set foot in here since your mother died."

That was true. It had been seven years since the family gathered at the restaurant for the memorial of Josephine Chapman. It was supposed to be a celebration of her life, but all Trey remembered was finding his father sobbing in the kitchen.

"What do you want me to say? That I hate coming here because it just makes me think of her. You want me to apologize for having a life of my own?"

Josephine Chapman had died unexpectedly at the age of 63. The cause of death was a pulmonary embolism that doctors said was likely related to an estrogen therapy she was undergoing. The loss of their matriarch brought the family together both geographically and emotionally. Jackson was always around, having not lived more than seventeen minutes from his parents his entire life. But the eldest and youngest were far afield when they got the news. Joey, named after his mother because she had no intention of trying again for a girl and potentially ending up with a fourth boy, returned from a stint in Portugal. Trey was on the west coast promoting the latest of his fast casual outposts.

At the memorial, the brothers vowed to spend more time together. And for several months they did just that, creating an unofficial rotation to check on their dad. But it wasn't long before Joey left again. Trey would soon follow, his celebrity status surging to an all-time high.

James Jr. began spending every waking moment at the restaurant, the one he had always hoped his first born would take over. Instead, his son had rejected the family business, just as he had his own name.

"Your cookbooks keep the bed warm at night, *Trey*?" James said.

It was clear James wanted a fight, but his son wasn't going to give it to him.

"Good luck with all this," he said, and walked out of the kitchen.

He didn't stop until he reached the door of the hired black sedan waiting out front. Trey Chapman wanted to get away. Instead, he was going to a photoshoot.

***

Audrey was not a confrontational person by nature but had evolved to fill the need in her marriage. Jackson was a perennial people pleaser, a trait she mostly loved. He would much prefer to run a marathon than cause a stir. So, on the rare occasion that the couple was overcharged or somehow otherwise publicly wronged, Audrey became the squeaky wheel, and she was damn good at it.

She ascended the heavy staircase, resolved that this confrontation with her husband would be different. It had to be different. Her morning was spent on a park bench rehearsing what it was important for her to say and her husband to hear. Audrey simultaneously knocked on the office door and pushed it open.

"Yes, my love?" Jackson said.

"I have decided I won't let you put me in the situation you did last night ever again."

"The whole thing just makes me feel awful," he said.

"Then promise me that's the last favor you do," Audrey said, not asking.

"The new menu was actually delightful."

"I read your review. Dave Talmidge put lipstick on a pig and you sold it as the second coming of The French Laundry."

"You didn't even eat anything," Jackson replied.

"I saw enough," Audrey said, her arms folded tightly, "including the cockroach underneath the window."

Jackson had seen it too.

"It's Chicago, there are bugs everywhere," he dismissed.

"If you want to keep writing this fiction for your father's friends, you can do it without me."

"That's not fair, Audrey," he said, unsure of exactly what she was threatening.

"They don't deserve it! They don't deserve *you*!"

That was what Audrey had realized on the park bench earlier that morning. She hated how her husband allowed himself to be used and manipulated. But what bothered her the most was Jackson's talent being wasted. He should be introducing the city to new chefs and flavors through the lens of his vast knowledge and experience, not shilling for the old guard who don't care enough to even put up new drapes.

"Where have you been dying to go?" Jackson asked. "I'll let you pick the next restaurant."

"I don't want to pick the restaurants," Audrey said, exhausted. "I want you to pick them. That's the point."

"I do pick them," he said, motioning to the stacks of research and menus littered around the room.

As much as Audrey had hoped he would, Jackson simply didn't get it. He didn't see the trench his work was creating between them and was treating this conversation the same as all the others. Audrey was prepared for it though. Much of her time in the park was spent thinking about what was next. Her mind kept going to an invitation from another man, one she had been declining for half a decade. Despite her vow, she knew there was no other choice now but to accept.

"You think you owe him," she said, stepping outside the doorway, "but you don't. You owe everybody else."

Audrey left her husband to ponder those last words, and to make a phone call she promised she never would.

5

Joey was getting impatient standing outside the door to the nameless bar. He didn't like waiting, but his nostrils were being assaulted by the contents of the bag in his left hand. Finally, he heard the buzzer and click of the lock opening.

"I was beginning to think you weren't going to let me in," Joey said, walking up to the bar and placing the bag on the counter. Crete was immediately hit by the odor.

"There's a dumpster outside, you know?"

"I believe 'daring' and 'unique' were your exact words," Joey said, starting to open the bag.

Crete quickly stopped him.

"There better not be any maggots in there."

Joey didn't laugh.

"I trust you saw the news. I'm done for a while after this," he said.

Crete nodded in agreement.

"You sure these people are cool?" Joey asked.

"Yeah, it's just some yuppie. Apparently dating this foodie chick and wants to impress her. What do you got?"

"Unpasteurized cheese," Joey said, starting to open the bag again.

"No thanks," she said, firmly placing her giant hand on it. "What do I tell him makes this so special?"

"It has to age for a couple months before it can be sold. Let's just say your yuppie is getting an early release," he said, sliding the bag across the countertop.

"French?"

"It's from next door," Joey said, referring to Wisconsin, "but you can tell him Normandy."

Crete pulled out a wad of cash and started to peel off some bills.

"How about a little barter instead?" he asked.

"What do you need?"

"Some paperwork."

"I might be able to help," she said, pocketing the money and stashing the offensive bag in a cabinet behind the bar. "Get me an address and shopping list."

"Thanks," Joey said.

Crete waved a bottle of brown liquor at him. "Want a drink?"

"Sure."

Joey had no plans for the rest of the day. Joey didn't have any plans period. The only person who knew he was back in town was Trey, and that was only because his latest bender had ended in close proximity to his older brother's condo, which he believed was empty. It's not that Joey didn't want to see the rest of his family, he just didn't have good answers to the inevitable questions about why he had returned and for how long. So, there was no rush to see Jackson. Or his father really. He was starting to get consumed with the idea of breaking Trey free from his celebrity chains. Everything else could wait.

***

"Ninety back!" the stage manager yelled.

"How many times are we going to do this cheese story?" Joan Jones asked from behind the Channel 2 anchor desk.

"It's getting ten times the views of anything else on our site," said a little voice inside Joan's earpiece. "You should read the comments."

"Honey, I learned not to read the comments years ago," she replied to her producer.

The hair and makeup pit crew made final adjustments to Joan's ever-expanding mane as she rehearsed the story on the teleprompter.

"We have a tip line set up for this?" she asked, getting no response.

"Thirty back!"

"Jail?" Joan questioned, looking up from the script. "Did this cheese kill a white girl or something?"

No one laughed at her poor attempt at a joke, so Joan just smiled at the camera and waited for the red light to come on. The stage manager counted the last few seconds back from the commercial break using only his fingers, then cued the host with a wave.

"Welcome back! More on yesterday's story about the viral image of illegal cheese smuggled into Chicago that is quickly spreading across social media. I will once again warn viewers of the graphic nature of what we're about to show. We have confirmed that this is indeed casu marzu, a cheese that is filled with fly larvae. Our requests for comment from several local agencies have yielded a joint statement from the FDA and Immigrations and Customs Enforcement. They say they are aware of the image and investigating its origin. We here at Channel 2 have set up a tip line through our website for anyone with information on this bizarre situation. For the person or persons responsible, this could mean anywhere from a hefty fine to up to 20 years in prison. We will be sure to keep you updated on this investigation."

"20 years?" the waitress said, looking up at Joan Jones on the television above the bar. She was speaking to no one in particular. Ken Nakara sat in a nearby booth of the throwback diner and fought the urge to respond. He knew that prison was a rare result from this type of investigation, but still took his job very seriously.

"You sure I can't get you a coffee or anything?" the waitress asked.

"No, thank you."

Nakara was on his lunch break, but after two breakfasts, had no room to consume anything else. The remainder of his morning had been spent interviewing three more chefs and resulted in three more dead ends. He was beginning to rethink his strategy, but had a feeling social media was going to help him crack the case somehow. Unfortunately for Supervisory Special Agent Ken Nakara, his last online presence was MySpace. He referred to a hashtag as the pound sign. And had no idea what his daughters meant when they told each other not to "at" them.

The printed-out list of names looked more daunting than ever. Nakara placed it in a folder, left three dollars on the table, and went out to his car. He hoped the thirty-minute drive back to Lisle would help settle his stomach and clear his head.

***

"Why now?" Martin Easley asked, leaning forward on the mesh iron table.

He had been trying to get Audrey Chapman's help with her husband since he took over as editor of The Tribune's Food & Dining section five years ago. He used every tactic imaginable with Jackson; from friend to enemy, from sugar to vinegar, from boycott to forced capitulation.

At 55, Easley considered himself too old for such foolishness. He didn't believe a man with his accomplishments should have to. He proudly hung his undergraduate diploma from Brown and master's degree from Penn in his office, a site Jackson Chapman had entered only once. The writer considered the display vulgar. The editor considered the writer unmanageable. Easley always believed Audrey was the key to a truce.

"I'm tired of being complicit," Audrey said.

"Well, I'm sure you heard the surprise in my voice. I thought you were calling about Chapman's Steakhouse."

"Why would I call about that?"

"The health inspector shut it down," Easley said.

"Shut it down?" Audrey questioned, a little too loudly, drawing the attention of the nearby tables outside the coffee shop where they sat.

"I assumed you knew."

"No, that can't be right. They wouldn't. James wouldn't let that happen."

"I'm afraid the Chapman name just doesn't mean what it used to," Easley said.

Audrey knew exactly what he meant. She had warned her husband about riding his father's coattails. Now it appeared they were threadbare.

"Is Jackson's job in trouble?" Audrey asked, getting right to the point.

"That's entirely up to him, Mrs. Chapman."

Audrey finished the last sip of her latte and leaned back in the uncomfortable chair. Not only had she failed to make any progress on the problem with her husband's work, but she also knew whatever was happening at Chapman's Steakhouse would take all of his focus. It would put their marriage on the back burner. Audrey would be left to simmer.

"Thank you for meeting me, Mr. Easley," she said, standing abruptly. "I'm glad we talked."

She put her sunglasses on and weaved through the tables back out to the street. What Audrey needed was a long walk with no destination.

***

The only good thing about the photo shoot was Erica Tomlin. Trey never understood all the hours of makeup and outfit changes for someone to push a button on a camera a few times. And after the fan encounter near the park, the shutter click was giving him PTSD. The scene at Chapman's Steakhouse was all he could think about before his assistant arrived. Biv was smart enough to know he and Trey needed some time apart while his client went through this mid-celebrity crisis, so he sent Erica in his stead.

"I'm going to change lenses," the photographer said.

Trey used that as an excuse to walk over to his assistant, who was busy highlighting passages in a large book.

"School, huh?"

Erica didn't respond until she reached a stopping point. "You're the only person I've ever met who can make going to college sound weird."

"Maybe it's because I didn't go."

"Oh, so that's your problem. You've got an inferiority complex. And a stupid one, at that."

"Stupid?" Trey sounded more angry than confused.

"You studied around the world," she said. "Those Michelin kitchens were your classroom, and that's an education few people get. I'd say it's worth more than any university, and we can both agree things turned out okay for you without that little piece of paper."

Trey had never thought about it that way. "Yeah, but there's still a lot of stuff I don't know. I never even learned how to balance a checkbook."

"A checkbook? Be older. Look, I can't clarify veal stock and you can't add," she teased, closing the book and patting the chair next to her. "Everyone's got their thing."

"But I feel like everyone else has more," Trey said as he sat down.

"Mister-my-name-is-on-pots-and-pans-and-every-household-in-America-has-one-of-my- cookbooks-in-it thinks everyone else has more? That's about as rich as you are."

"You know what I mean. That's all I've got. I don't have hobbies. I don't have friends. I never see my family. I'm always on the road."

"Those are all choices," Erica said. "My family gets together every Sunday night for dinner. Every Sunday."

"That's really nice."

"Yeah, it is. But sometimes it's also inconvenient. My older sister and her husband have to drive in from Lemont with their 2-year-old. And I love my niece, but she can throw a fit about nothing. And being home Sunday means I can't make plans with friends or go to a concert or whatever."

"Wait, you still live with your parents?" Trey said, with a little laugh.

"Oh, don't worry, my father makes me pay rent. But that's not the point. We all have to give up something to get something. And when he and my mother are in the kitchen, cooking and clowning each other- those are my favorite memories."

"Who's the better chef?"

"Oh, she is, and she lets him know it."

Trey thought of his mother in the kitchen of their home growing up. She always wore this tattered white apron. And she commanded the space with a large metal spoon.

"My mom was too. Dad would probably never admit it. He had the restaurant, after all. And maybe he was better with steaks and a few other things. But my mom cooked almost every night. Sometimes he'd sneak a taste and suggest more salt or some fresh herb, and my mom would take her spoon and whack him. I mean really whack him."

"My mother loves to sprinkle flour in my father's hair when he's not paying attention," Erica said laughing. "Then at the end of the night he'll look in the mirror and say something like 'When did Don King get here!?'"

Trey grabbed her arm to keep from falling off the chair as he doubled over in laughter. He could've stayed there talking to Erica for hours but was snapped back to reality by the voice of the photographer.

"I'm ready, Mr. Chapman."

Trey tried to picture Erica's family at their Sunday dinner as he rode back to his high-rise condo after the shoot. He wondered if guests were invited. He had always dreamed of just showing up at someone's house randomly and taking over their kitchen. Trey had let that thought consume him all the way back to his couch, but then a loud knock on his door snapped him out of it.

"Morals clause," Joey said as Trey opened the door. He walked past his older brother and slapped a big stack of papers on the kitchen counter.

"What are these?"

"Your contracts," Joey said.

"How did you get my contracts?" Trey asked accusingly.

"Not important. What is important is that they all have a morals clause, which is your way out."

Trey picked up the stack and leafed through it. Joey was not getting the response he hoped for. He grabbed the top few pages out of his brother's hands and pulled out a page covered in highlighter.

"The morality clause gives the company the ability to suspend or terminate this agreement," Joey read, "in the event Mr. Chapman commits an act that falls within the purview of this clause, including behavior that is criminal, scandalous, or otherwise publicly reprehensible."

"So, I need some big scandal?"

"Something like that. And that starts," Joey said, turning to the calendar on Trey's fridge, "tomorrow at the Halting Hunger Charity Auction."

"You're sure that's the only way? What about a buyout?"

"We're talking millions. And it says you could still be sued for future profits. You gotta get *them* to dump *you*."

"I have no idea how to even begin that, and we've got another problem. Chapman's Steakhouse was shut down by the health inspector."

"What?"

"I went over there. It's bad, Joey. Dad's two hundred grand in the hole and he's been serving expired food."

"Shit," Joey said, opening cabinets. "You got any more of that Hirsch?"

"This is serious," Trey said, shutting the cabinet his brother was starting to open.

"Why do you think I'm looking for a drink?"

From an early age, Joey Chapman aligned with all the characteristics modern psychology had placed upon the youngest child in a family. He was highly social, confident and creative.

There was just one problem he couldn't solve, and that was how to keep his father's attention. Joey did a little of everything around the steakhouse because he was trying to find his niche, just as Trey had done from the moment he picked up a knife, and Jackson had done with his thirst for culinary knowledge. But James Jr. only saw a boy who couldn't focus. So, he often made up the errands he sent Joey on just to get him out from under foot.

Josephine Chapman had endless love and energy for all her boys, but she took extra care of her baby. Where James Jr. saw a lack of direction in Joey, she encouraged exploration. He went beyond the boundaries of his backyard as a child, investigated every nook and cranny of the city as a teen, and when he finished high school, decided to make the world his university. Joey's favorite part about returning from near or far was thrilling his mother with the story. But he never stopped seeking his father's attention.

The first time he truly remembered getting it was the day Trey announced he was setting out on his own. Joey heard yelling in the kitchen. He could only make out words here and there. *Ungrateful. Selfish. Abandoned.* He stood outside of the door and was terrified when his father came bursting out. But James Jr. looked down at his youngest as if he was meeting him for the first time. Joey happily accepted the affection that was meant for Trey because he knew it wouldn't last long.

Seven years ago, Joey found himself in the same position, absorbing the love and affection James Jr. wished he could still give to Josephine. Grief proved to be a powerful bond, but just wasn't strong enough to hold the Chapman family together.

"What are you going to do?" Joey asked, with no drink in his hand.

"Don't you mean *we?*" Trey shot back.

"What can I do? Seems to me you either bail him out with a check or the restaurant closes."

"It's not that simple, Joey."

"Never is," he said.

Joey was right and Trey knew it. He had searched for other options during the entire car ride to the photo shoot and every second after until Erica snapped him out of it. Still, he was no closer to figuring out what to do.

***

"Stop it, Ava!" Lily yelled at her little sister.

"You airdropped it to me first."

"No phones at the dinner table, girls," Ken Nakara said.

"She keeps sending me this gross picture," Lily said, holding up her phone.

Nakara instantly recognized it as the focus of his current investigation.

"Where'd you get that?" he asked.

"It's everywhere, Dad," Ava said.

"Listen to your father. Put that away," Angela Nakara said. "We're trying to eat."

"What is airdropping anyway?"

"You can just, like, send a picture right to someone's phone," Lily said.

"Oh, like a text message," he said.

"It's different," Ava said, rolling her eyes.

"So did someone just airdrop that photo to you, Lily?"

"No, I just grabbed it off IG."

"That's Instagram, Honey," Angela said, smiling.

"I thought it was posted on Twitter or X or whatever it's called?"

"You would, Dad" Ava said, which started both sisters laughing uncontrollably.

Supervisory Special Agent Ken Nakara was being schooled by his teenage girls. If social media was going to help him find the person responsible for smuggling casu marzu into Chicago, he needed help. Asking for it was another issue though. As he waited for the laughter to subside, he began to mentally psyche himself for the conversation he needed to have with his boss.

***

Jackson lifted the corner of the cardboard box and snuck a piece of sausage nestled next to the buttery crust. He appreciated the meaty disc that covered the bottom of a classic Chicago deep dish giving each bite some sweet, porcine goodness. But with the sauce being on top, the traditional version of the pizza did not lend itself to snacking. So, Jackson began ordering his with extra crumbled sausage. It came in handy on the drive home or the rare occasion when he had to wait for his wife.

With Audrey noticeably absent as the sun began to set, Jackson had taken the liberty of ordering dinner, still under the false impression that all was well in his house. It wasn't until he plucked the last visible fennel seed-filled bite from the sauce that he realized it was now cold. Jackson put the pizza in the oven and poured himself another glass of primitivo. He picked his keys up to move them off the counter and a small plastic soybean popped out of the pod on the keychain. The night he introduced Audrey to sushi, he watched as she tried to chew an entire edamame. They laughed hysterically as she spit the stringy pod into a napkin. Audrey came across the keychain a few years back and surprised him with it. It was silly, but a favorite sercy from his wife.

Jackson's day had been filled with the usual rigmarole- responding to emails, ignoring his editor, and researching where to dine next. Having just completed the review of The Portobello Grille, he was in no rush and on no particular deadline, so he allowed himself to be distracted by a magazine essay on Gullah cuisine. The remainder of his afternoon had been eaten up by a nap.

The smell wafting through the house was unmistakable to Audrey. As she turned the corner into the kitchen, she saw her husband holding her favorite bottle of red.

"A peace offering?" she guessed, incorrectly.

"A pizza offering," Jackson said, still unaware of how fractured their relationship was. He opened the oven and pulled out the box. Audrey poured herself a glass.

"How is your dad taking everything?"

"Taking what?" Jackson asked, sliding a piece onto a plate.

"The restaurant. Don't you know?"

"I really don't."

"The health inspector shut it down," Audrey said.

"What? Where'd you hear that?"

Audrey had every intention of telling her husband about the meeting with Martin Easley. After all, it was no adulterous rendezvous. She hoped the alliance with his "enemy" would send a message about her seriousness. But one piece of bad news was all Audrey cared to deliver at a time.

"My friend Robin tried to go," she said. "Apparently, there is a sign on the door."

Jackson pulled the phone out of his pocket and dialed his father. "This must be some kind of mistake."

Audrey sipped her wine as the phone went to voicemail.

"I should've known something like this was going to happen," Jackson said, exhaling deeply up towards the ceiling.

"How could you have known?" Audrey asked.

"The place was always empty. And the college kid at the front door. Maybe if I had just done the review..."

"This is not your fault, Jackson."

"He asked for my help, Audrey."

"Well, he shouldn't have!"

"I'm not going to abandon him. That's not what we do in this family!"

Jackson didn't mean it. At least not like that. But there was only one way for Audrey to take it, and she ran out of the kitchen filled with a shame that she hadn't felt in years.

Stanton Darlington was a businessman, golfer, drinker and husband- in that order. A perfect day would include buying a distressed company and selling it off in pieces while still leaving time for 9 holes before cocktail hour. It would not include his wife, Georgina, who was accustomed to seeing her husband almost exclusively in public. As the couple spent more and more evenings at soirees and galas among the social elite, the less the arrangement bothered her. Mrs. Darlington was happy to be part of the upper class even if it meant having a low-class marriage.

Georgina's pregnancy was not planned. She spent weeks thinking about how a baby would change her life before telling her husband. Stanton thought about it for less time than it took to get his checkbook and walk out of their lives forever.

The months before the birth were telling. Georgina's group of friends withered. The in-crowd apparently only liked to go out. The solitude gave her time to work through her anger towards Stanton and decide how she wanted to raise the baby. It would be hard enough even with money. Georgina decided she would not make it harder on her child by bad mouthing the father. Her daughter would be filled with noble strength. That's the exact meaning of the name Audrey.

Jackson knew all of this. That's what made what he had said so much worse.

***

Halting Hunger was started long before Trey Chapman picked up a pan, but he had become the face of its biggest charity event. The black-tie silent auction and reception were responsible for 75 percent of the annual donations, and the evening now filled the Grand Ballroom at The Drake Hotel to capacity. To be included among the 400 invitees was an honor. To be invited back was a matter of how wide one would open their wallet.

The exclusivity was a draw, as was the constant current of exquisite small bites and not so small glasses of champagne circulating throughout the room. But it was the unique items up for bid that made the night so anticipated. Table after table was filled with donations from the Chicago elite. One name famous. Oprah. Obama. Jordan. There were items you could wear and items you could hang. Items that you experienced garnered the most though. One of those was provided by Trey- a private dinner for eight cooked by the celebrity chef himself.

As was often the case, Biv Trammel was his plus one for the event. There was no need for a long pregame in the back of a hired black sedan because the duo had done this ten times before. Trey knew the routine. He shook a lot of hands, posed for photos, and said a few words at the end of the night. The business manager's main role was gracefully prying Phyllis Lipscomb off his client. The Halting Hunger CEO always latched on and liked to walk Trey around the party like a prized French Mastiff.

"Excuse me, Phyllis," Biv interrupted, "but I need to tear Trey away for a minute."

"One minute, promise?" she said.

Biv just smiled and motioned for his client to go first.

"What took you so long?" Trey asked, grabbing a glass of champagne from a passing tray and downing it.

"It's the same eighteen minutes we give her every year," Biv said. "And pace yourself."

"Did you bid on anything?"

"Original Indiana Jones movie poster signed by Harrison Ford. He's from Chicago, you know?"

"Okay, I'll tell you if you win," Trey said nervously. He pulled at the bowtie which felt like it was strangling him.

"You trying to rush me out of here?"

"No, it's just you never stay. Are you staying?"

"I'm going," Biv said, "but do me a favor. Go sit down and drink some water. And if you can, mention the cookbook in your speech."

Trey nodded and watched his business manager exit. As soon as Biv was out of view, Trey plucked another glass of bubbly going by and made quick work of it, trying to follow his younger brother's advice from earlier that afternoon.

"Get drunk?" Trey had asked.

"No, get really, really drunk," the younger brother had said. "Like that time in high school when you were at that house party in Buffalo Grove. What was it, Bacardi Limon? You drank the whole bottle, and they had to put you in a wheelbarrow to get you to the back seat of the car."

"That was bad," Trey recalled. "But Dr. Nevins said that I need to cut back on alcohol."

"We could come up with some elaborate plan, but look at what happened at the cooking demo at the TV station. You chickened out. The beauty of this plan is that there is no plan."

Phyllis Lipscomb waved at Trey from across the ballroom. He pretended not to notice and got lost in the crowd along the auction tables where he hid for nearly an hour. The champagne was starting to take effect, and the number of flutes he had consumed was now unclear. Trey was happy drunk. He picked up a pen and decided to do some bidding.

"$3,000 for a hat!?" he said to no one in particular. "Must be a good hat."

Trey crossed out the last bid on the sheet for a Lake Michigan fishing trip and wrote 69 which caused him to almost fall over laughing. He was so pleased with himself, he repeated it on the next several sheets without even looking at the items.

"Oh, no you don't," a woman said, taking the pen out of his hand.

Trey recognized the high-pitched voice and southern drawl before he even looked up.

"You can't bid on your own dinner," the man standing next to her chimed in.

"Madelyn and Shaun," Trey slurred.

"It's Scott," the husband said.

The Parkers had the annoying habit of placing the highest bid for Trey's personal dinner each year. Scott used it as an anniversary present for his belle who he had proposed to at *Trey*. Madelyn used the party as an annual reminder to their friends of how much money they had.

Trey found the whole thing unbearable but put up with it because of the large amount it brought to Halting Hunger.

"You're coming to our house again this year," Madelyn said, "even if we have to stand next to this sheet all night."

"What time should I *swing* by?" Trey winked at the wife and snatched the glass of champagne out of the husband's hands.

"Mr. Chapman," Scott protested.

"Come on. Forget dinner. Let's talk about what you guys really want to do."

Trey had reached the next level of inebriation. He had crossed from happy to lewd.

"You're disgusting," Madelyn said, storming off with her husband in tow.

Phyllis Lipscomb pushed through the crowd to find the cause of the commotion. Trey was teetering inside a ring of party goers who had all turned their backs on him. All except one. A young woman, dressed in a pantsuit, feverishly typed into her phone.

"Phyllis!" Trey shouted as soon as he saw her. "Philly. Philly cheesesteak."

The charming celebrity the CEO had escorted around just an hour ago was now unrecognizable. Trey's shirt was soaked with sweat, his bowtie undone, and his cheeks had turned blotchy and red. He fell towards Phyllis, almost knocking her over.

"Good Lord, Trey," Phyllis said. "You need to leave."

She forcefully guided him towards the nearest exit. Both were unaware that the young woman with the cell phone was trailing them.

"What about my speech!?" Trey yelled. "I've got to mention my knives. No, wait. Not the fucking knives. The book. What's that salad again?"

Phyllis shoved Trey towards a security guard.

"Please put him in a cab. Now."

She smoothed the front of her dress, took a deep breath and turned back to the room with a smile. The party was still in full swing. The disruption hardly noticed. Or so she thought.

***

Supervisory Special Agent Ken Nakara stood at a dry erase board looking out at the ragtag task force he had been given. Immigration and Customs Enforcement had sent over two rookies.

Two of the other three people seated in front of him were OCI agents. The third looked barely old enough to drive. The call Nakara had dreaded placing to his Deputy Director turned out to be incoming. The viral image of maggot-filled cheese was now national news. So, manpower, if you could call it that, was on its way. And before he even had time to microwave the community kitchen sponge, his conference room had filled up.

Nakara had decided to abandon his theory on chefs with large social media followings. The only thing he'd learned was how hard it is to remove the smell of hickory smoke from a shirt. In the length of time it took to drink his morning tea, he came up with a divide and conquer approach for his new team.

"ICE, I need you guys to look through historical cases of food smuggled into the city," Nakara said, making notes on the board. "Let's talk to who's done it in the past and see what we can learn. OCI, one of the local news channels set up a tip line. Let's get that information from them and start going through it looking for anything credible."

Nakara looked down at his notes. "Wallin, is it?"

"Yes, sir," said the youngest person in the room.

"Your background is tech?"

"Yes, sir. I can code in Python, Java and C++, and I'm trained in superencryption and cyphers."

"Cyphers?" Nakara said. "You know social media?"

"Social media, sir?" Wallin asked.

"Yeah. Facebook, X, IG? The original casu marzu image was shared on social media. I want you to try and figure out who originally posted it."

"Yes, sir."

"Yes, sir," mocked the older of the two ICE agents.

"Look, I'm sure you'd rather be spoiling plots to smuggle nuclear weapons into the country, but today your card came up 'cheese' so that's what you're going to do," Nakara said. "And Wallin could probably freeze your bank accounts or something, so I'd leave him alone."

Wallin flashed a mischievous smile.

Nakara dismissed everyone and got ready to drive back into the city.

***

Jackson pulled open the heavy door to Chapman's Steakhouse and was immediately hit by the smell of rotting food. All the lights were off, but he could make out a single figure sitting at the bar. He walked over, pulled out a stool and sat down next to his father. James held tightly to an old-fashioned glass. The bottle of scotch in front of him was empty and had been for a while. Jackson reached over the counter and grabbed another. He poured a drink for himself and offered a refill. James titled his glass towards his son. The harsh alcohol vapors were an upgrade over the decomposition wafting from the kitchen.

"This is where you ate your first steak," James said. "You were only one, maybe fifteen months."

Jackson had heard this story a thousand times, but still let his dad tell it.

"Your mother went away for the weekend and left me in charge of you and Trey. I didn't know what I was doing. All you did was cry. Around six o'clock, your brother started asking for food. I was here every night, so I had no idea what you were supposed to eat. So, I cooked up a couple filets. Figured they were the softest steaks we had. Your eyes lit up on that first bite like you'd seen God. I couldn't feed it to you fast enough."

James allowed himself to smile for the first time in two days.

"I wish I was old enough to remember," Jackson said.

"That's probably the only meal you don't."

"Mom used to always say my brain was in my taste buds. I couldn't remember Joey's birthday, but I could tell you what we ate at every one of his parties."

"I can say I taught Trey to cook, but you?" James said, taking another sip. "You've just got this gift. No idea where it came from."

"Here," Jackson said, looking around. "My playground was a steakhouse kitchen."

"You used to hide in the walk-in and eat until you were sick."

"What's going to happen to this place, Dad?"

"After you boys grew up, I had two things- your mother and this restaurant. I don't know what to do without them."

"I'm sorry I didn't write a review." Jackson couldn't help but apologize.

"Eh," James dismissed. "Why were you so hard on Dave? The decor thing. And you didn't have to bash the old dishes."

He couldn't help but make his son feel bad. James Chapman Jr. did not give out A's. He taught his sons from an early age that there was always room for improvement. They wished their father used the same advice when it came to showing affection.

With empty glasses in front of them, the smell of rot had crept back in.

"Let me help you clean this place up," Jackson said. But as his father tried to stand, it was clear that would have to wait. "Never mind, Dad. Let's get you home."

Jackson looked at the red and white health inspection sign as he helped his father to the door. He realized that the end of Chapman's Steakhouse wouldn't mean the end of the patronage he felt. The asks would still come. The obligation would still loom. Jackson was still walking on a tightrope held on one side by his father and the other by his wife.

***

The vomit-covered tuxedo on the floor was a bad sign. Trey fought through his headache trying to remember the previous night. He had flashes of Phyllis. And champagne. That explained the severity of his hangover. But he didn't remember leaving the Halting Hunger Charity Auction or emptying the contents of his stomach by the bed. He looked at the clock. It was almost lunchtime in the high-rise condo, not that there was any lunch to be found. Trey grabbed his phone off the nightstand. Dead. He plugged it in, gathered his soiled clothes, and tossed them in the tub. He turned the shower on and walked to the sink. As Trey began to splash water on his face, his phone erupted in buzzes and dings, startling the hungover celebrity chef.

Trey walked over to silence the noise. It was Biv. He could delay the inevitable dreadful conversation with his business manager for only so long. Curious as to what happened the night before, Trey decided to answer instead.

"Hey, Biv."

"What the fuck did you do, Trey!!!???" The voice boomed through the phone like it was on speaker, but it wasn't.

"I was hoping you could tell me."

"You think this is funny? You got so drunk you got kicked out of a charity event raising money to end hunger!"

"I'm not trying to be funny, Biv."

"Just go online. It's everywhere. Including the threesome you tried to arrange."

Trey opened his phone and saw 117 new text messages. He clicked on the first and read the headline above the link: "Trey-some? Celebrity chef makes drunken pass at couple during charity event."

"Jesus. What did I do?"

"I'll tell you what you did," Biv said, having clearly rehearsed this part, "is you cost yourself, and me, a lot of damn money. The knife deal is through. They pulled it this morning. You're lucky they've got some New York chef's face they can slap on the box otherwise they'd be suing us to infinity."

Trey perked up, forgetting for a moment about the throbbing in his head. The plan, or lack thereof, had actually worked.

"Anyone else?" he asked, trying not to sound happy.

"I've been doing damage control all morning. Feel free to open your email and familiarize yourself with your apology."

"My apology?" Trey went to his inbox and found the statement from Biv. He got angrier with every line he read. "You do not issue statements for me! You're a business manager, not my PR."

"If I didn't do your PR there would be no business to manage."

Both sides of the line went silent.

Biv had taken Trey from local talent to national celebrity. He was used to pushing when he needed to push and pulling when he needed to pull. The drama that came with his client's fame was an unfortunate package deal. But Biv Trammel weathered all the slings and arrows because he knew Trey Chapman would've never reached this pinnacle without him.

Unfortunately for the business manager, Trey was starting to realize that too.

6

T he drive from Lisle to the Department of Public Health on South State Street took a lot longer than it should have. It gave Ken Nakara enough time to go from being excited about leading his own task force to feeling the pressure to deliver on an increasingly high-profile case. His last request for a mile long printout of everyone in the city with a food handler certification was met with extreme pushback, so Supervisory Special Agent Nakara was not surprised that he was plopped in front of a computer terminal on this visit and sarcastically wished "good luck."

While the ICE agents were looking to track down past smugglers, Nakara was hoping to find instances of food-borne illness. Any such incidents treated by a medical professional would be recorded and kept on file at the Department of Public Health. There were just two hurdles to this line of inquiry. It's estimated that one in six Americans get some type of food poisoning each year, and with 2.7 million people in Chicago, that's a lot of cases to sort through. The second and even larger problem was narrowing those down to illness caused by illegal foods. Most headline-grabbing outbreaks of salmonella, E. coli, and listeria are traced back to garden-variety foods. Romaine lettuce has gotten such a scarlet letter from contamination that some salad mixes now say "Does Not Include Romaine" on the package.

Nakara decided to begin his search with the low-hanging fruit, dairy actually, and typed in "cheese." He read through case after case, but they all seemed linked to queso fresco or a similar homemade Mexican cheese. No evidence of a rogue smuggler. No results for casu marzu.

He tried seafood next and found two records involving Japanese Puffer Fish. Fugu, as it's known, is not necessarily illegal in the United States, but few chefs have the proper training to prepare it. A wrong slice can release a tetrodotoxin which when ingested can cause paralysis and asphyxiation. But farm raised fugu is growing in popularity and believed to not contain the toxin, so fatalities from the delicacy have been extremely rare worldwide.

While entertaining, the process of going through the records had become increasingly frustrating for Nakara. Looking at his watch, he realized he hadn't moved in nearly two hours. He got up to stretch his legs and beg for help.

Nakara stopped the first person who walked by. "Are you familiar with the records system?"

"Sorry, I'm a nutrition educator," the man said.

"Okay. Thanks."

As he paced the hallway, Nakara knew that he was looking for a needle in a haystack, and that the needle may not even exist. He needed an expert. He needed Wallin.

***

Crete stared at the security camera feed on the little television. The figure standing outside the nameless bar had a hoodie pulled up tight. Since he was not gaining entry, he took off his sunglasses and looked straight into the camera.

"Is that Trey Chapman?" she said, squinting at the image.

Joey overheard from a few seats down the bar. "That's my brother."

"Trey Chapman is your brother?" Crete was baffled.

"Yeah, I told him to meet me here. Hope that's cool."

Crete pushed the button to open the door, and Joey waved Trey over to the bar.

"Hoo hoo, sounds like you had one hell of a night. Looks like it too."

Trey tightly closed his eyes and motioned for his brother to quiet down.

"Drink?" Crete offered.

Trey declined and the bartender walked away.

"Did you really try to have a threesome at the party?"

"Everything's a blur."

"I bet Biv is pissed," Joey said, grinning.

"Out of his mind. The knife company dropped me."

"Holt shit. It worked. The no plan plan actually worked."

"Yeah, but I can't do this anymore," Trey said. "I got like a million calls and texts. Jackson. My assistant. Everyone's either pissed off or disappointed."

"You've got an assistant?"

Trey glared at his little brother. "If losing all these appearances and endorsements means losing the people I care about, it's not worth it."

"No one's saying you can't tell them. You just can't tell them right now. This is like *Brewster's Millions*."

Trey clearly didn't get the reference.

"You've never seen *Brewster's Millions*? Richard Pryor?" Joey whipped around in his stool. "This guy inherits 300 million bucks, but he only gets it if he can spend thirty mil in thirty days without telling anyone why. Everyone thinks he's insane, until it's all over and he explains it."

Trey nodded as the plot slowly made its way through the haze of his hangover.

Crete motioned for Joey. He left his brother to think and walked down to the other end of the bar.

"I've got another job for you," she said.

"I told you I can't right now."

"Easy money."

"For what?" Joey asked, still set on turning it down.

"Whatever. It's the same yuppie as last time." Crete leaned in and whispered. "And he's willing to pay a grand now."

"What did he pay you last time?"

"Five hundred."

"Five hundred for that little bit of cheese?!" Joey asked, a little too loudly.

Trey looked over and wondered what his brother was getting into.

"I told you he's just some rich idiot trying to impress his chick."

"Give me his info and we'll see," Joey said, and walked back to the other end of the bar.

"What was that all about?" Trey asked.

"Oh, just some temp work."

"What is it you do, Joey?"

"Various and sundry things."

Trey laughed. Joey's life beyond high school was a mystery to the Chapman family. They rarely knew where he was, and the topic of his employment made for a fun party game. Jackson liked to think he was some sort of modern-day pirate. Trey had almost convinced everyone that Joey was a spy.

"You'd tell me if you were in trouble, right?" the older brother asked.

"You're in it worse than me. What's next on your calendar?"

"I'm not even sure."

"Well, one down, Mr. Brewster," Joey said. "One down."

***

Estcourt Station is a tiny village at the top of Maine. If you want to get there via paved roads, you have to drive down from Canada. According to the latest census, there are no year-round residents. But as the northernmost point in New England, Estcourt Station is the logical starting point for an adventure Jackson had daydreamed about for the last five years.

The Chapman family did not take vacations growing up. That was entirely due to James' inability to be away from the steakhouse. He believed it would crumble without him or catch on fire or some other calamity only his presence could prevent. The closest they had come was a day trip to Muskegon. Little Jackson didn't get to experience the world, but he learned early on that he could send his taste buds around the globe. The desire to get his other senses involved had increased exponentially when Martin Easley entered his life.

Jackson had always planned to document his epicurean road trip of the east coast. Estcourt Station played no role in the culinary portion of the journey but served as a grand jumping off place. From there, he wanted to see and taste how communities from Maine to Florida took the same ingredients- seafood, corn, potatoes, rice and fresh vegetables- and created wildly different dishes. Half of the clutter in Jackson's office had nothing to do with Chicago. It was research trying to tie specific towns on the eastern seaboard to the countries and even cities of their original ancestors. Jackson wanted to compare the cuisines of each place. How much had the recipes changed? How much had stood the test of time? It was much more than just a trip down the Atlantic. That's when Jackson realized it was a book.

The idea was daunting though. Writing a review took a couple of hours. A book would take months. Years? Then there was Audrey. If she knew about the idea, she wouldn't stop until it was in print. But even if he wanted to tell his wife, she was currently neither talking to him nor staying at the house.

Jackson looked across the table at the empty seat and took another bite of sweet potatoes. He had stopped the car the moment he saw the neon sign, always a sucker for a "meat and three." There was something about being able to see all the options before choosing; to be served by the same hands that labored over the cooking. No other type of restaurant offered the same feeling of homemade.

Jackson almost went with the fried chicken, but a good, smothered pork chop is hard to find. That made the sweet potatoes a no-brainer to help soak up the salty gravy. Green beans and creamed corn rounded out his three vegetables. The plate was a brumotactillophobic's nightmare. This type of southern dining was not for those who had a fear of their food touching. Jackson had no such phobia. He swirled his fork around the plate, each bite a new combination. It was delicious, but without Audrey, the comfort food just wasn't able to live up to its name.

A young woman, who didn't look out of high school, walked over to the table and set down an armload of plates.

"Uh, I didn't order any of this," Jackson said.

"It's on the house, sir."

There was the fried chicken he passed up, pot roast and country fried steak. Small bowls dotted the table filled with lima beans, mac 'n cheese and mashed potatoes.

"Save room for dessert, Mr. Chapman!" said an older woman headed his way in a flour-covered apron. "This here is my award-winning shoofly pie."

Jackson let out a deep sigh. "Well, this is all very nice, but…"

"I just can't believe you're finally here reviewing my restaurant," the woman said.

That was the problem with not being anonymous. People always assumed Jackson was there as a critic.

"I'm sorry, but I'm not," he told the owner.

"What do you mean?"

"I'm just trying to have a quiet dinner."

"I've been writing and calling the paper for years and you finally come out, but you're not doing a review?"

"I really am sorry for any misunderstanding."

"There's no misunderstanding, Mr. Chapman," she said as she started removing the plates from the table. "I've read every review you've ever written. I know we're not welcome."

"That's not true," he protested.

"I'd like you to leave," the owner said.

Jackson slid back in his chair and stood up. He thought about telling her how much he enjoyed the food, but knew she didn't want or need to hear it. He just nodded and left. As Jackson walked toward his car, all he could think about was escaping. About how no one would recognize him in Maine. Or Maryland. No one would know he was writing a book. For the first time, the idea sounded just a little less daunting.

***

Ken Nakara did not let the fact that he was leading his very first task force disrupt his normal morning routine. He helped get Lily and Ava off to school, kissed his wife and then drove into the z-shaped building visible from the interstate that housed the Food and Drug Administration Office of Criminal Investigations. He enjoyed his morning tea, responded to emails, then walked down the hall to start his briefing promptly at 10am.

"ICE?" he asked, standing at the front of the room.

"We are still going through the recent history of known smuggling operations," the younger of the two Immigration and Customs Enforcement rookies said.

"It's mainly narcotics and firearms," the other one said. "No cheese."

Nakara wasn't sure if they were actually working on the case or not, but he was stuck with them either way.

"OCI?"

"The Channel 2 tip line is a joke. Everyone who knows nothing thinks they know something," said the first agent.

"Oh yeah. One guy thought it was his grandma," the other said.

"I liked the guy from King Arthur. Who was it? Merlin?"

"No, no, no. My favorite was Steve Urkel. Got any cheeeese?"

"Who's that?" Wallin asked.

"He was on a show called Family Matters," the first agent said. "Before you were born."

"Alright. Alright." Nakara had had enough. "Wallin, how are you coming on the photo?"

102

"The image was originally posted from an account that has since been deleted. I'm still working on finding the owner. But the weird thing is how bad the resolution is on the picture."

"Why does that matter?" Nakara asked.

"Most phones have a 10 or 12 megapixel camera these days. If the person who took the picture was the one who posted it, it would be a lot clearer. It just doesn't make sense."

"Well, keep looking into it. Also, I'm going to need your help on another search later this week back in the city."

"Whatever you need, boss."

Supervisory Special Agent Ken Nakara's needs only seemed to be growing. He didn't have the cheese. He didn't have the person who had eaten it. He didn't have the person who served it. He sure as hell didn't have the person who smuggled it into the city. All he had was a photo, and an apparently poor quality one at that.

***

Grease was starting to soak through the white paper bag sitting on the front seat. Audrey had set out for a drive, not quite ready to return to her husband, and soon noticed she was headed toward the Chapman family home in Hinsdale. That gave her the excuse to check on James. The burgers and fries were just a bonus.

As she pulled into the driveway, Audrey barely recognized the place. The large brick house, which had once looked so stately, was now hidden by overgrowth. It screamed of years of neglect, even though she and Jackson had visited just a few months ago. The brick walkway to the front door seemed to crumble beneath her feet. Audrey knocked and knocked again. She was about to leave when the door finally opened.

James Chapman Jr. was almost unrecognizable, except for his voice.

"Audrey."

"I brought burgers," she said, holding up the bag.

"Little Joe's?"

"The one and only. Crinkle cut fries too."

James stepped aside so Audrey could enter. Everything he did seemed in slow motion.

Inside, the house was a time capsule. Nothing had changed since the boys left. Most of the rooms had remained untouched since Josephine's death. The walls and roof were simply a shelter for James when he was not at the restaurant. Neither place felt like home anymore.

James sat down at the kitchen table.

"Double cheeseburger, right?" she said. He nodded. Audrey handed him the white paper wrapper now completely soaked with grease. "Let me get some napkins."

James took a bite. It was small. Like when a child is asked to taste a new food. As Audrey sat down, she saw something in her father-in-law for the first time since she became a part of the family- weakness.

It was strength that had immediately formed a bond between Audrey and Josephine. The Chapman matriarch liked to say that she raised four men: three boys and a husband. She would never speak the words out loud, but always believed that if any of her sons could benefit from marriage, it was Jackson. He didn't have Trey's world-conquering aspirations or Joey's wanderlust. He was traditional in the most beautiful sense of the word. Josephine saw that in her daughter-in-law; someone who desperately wanted to send down roots so she could grow.

Audrey did not shy away from talking about her fatherless childhood. She, in fact, did not shy away from talking about anything. Josephine loved that. They shared an unapologetic disposition and were no match for the Chapman men once they got going.

"The first time I saw one of these burgers," Audrey said, adding another soiled napkin to a growing pile on the table, "was right after Jackson and I started dating. We had come over to pick up an old book or something in his room, and the same white, greasy bag was on the counter. Josephine picked up the burger and took an enormous bite. My jaw just dropped. I couldn't help but laugh as the prim and proper Mrs. Chapman had cheese and ketchup and grease rolling down her chin. Then she started laughing too."

James smiled. "That about sums her up."

"I miss her," Audrey said.

"I hope you didn't drive all this way just to tell me that."

Once she had a destination, Audrey thought of all kinds of things she wanted to say. She wanted to ask how he could let the restaurant fail. She wanted to tell James that his son had been an ass. That Jackson was still seeking the approval his father had never given him. That she needed her husband to be his own man. But she couldn't say any of those things to the slumped figure across the table, hunched forward, his face inches from a virtually untouched burger.

James Chapman Jr. was withering right in front of her. Audrey tried to cheer him up. She tried to get him to talk. She tried to get him to eat. When it was clear none of those would happen, she got up and put a hand on his shoulder.

"I'll put this in the fridge for you."

It was time to go home.

***

Joan Jones got the reaction she wanted. Glenn Bitman was completely caught off guard.

His office had prepared him to do a four-minute interview about the city's prosecution rate of gun crimes, of which he had just gotten a very high-profile conviction. Despite having a wiry mustache and rat-like nose, he knew nothing about cheese.

"You must be aware of the story, sir. We broke it right here at Channel 2 and quite frankly our viewers have shown concern about such an item being smuggled into our city. Can you assure us that the person responsible will be brought to justice?"

The fact that the casu marzu story was now national news had completely changed Joan Jones' opinion on it. She had gained over 10,000 followers on X in less than a week, and never missed an opportunity online or on-air to take credit. The Midwest anchor with the oversized hair considered herself the protector of her concerned public, and made sure the maggot-filled cheese was somehow included in every newscast. She had delighted herself in the makeup chair when she came up with the idea to spring the topic on an unwitting 30-year-old assistant district attorney.

"Yes, I, uh, am aware of the story," Bitman stammered.

"Is your office looking into it?" Jones pressed.

"I don't have the answer to that."

"Well, I shouldn't have to inform you that there is a joint task force investigating the crime as we speak."

"If a case is brought to our office, then we will look into whether or not it is worthy of prosecution."

"Mr. Bitman, are you saying smuggling cases are not worth prosecuting?" Joan Jones knew she was being completely unfair. There were hundreds of attorneys who worked for Cook County. The young man on the right side of the TV screen with sweat beading up on his forehead could no more speak about the illegal cheese case than he could about animals rumored to have been stolen from the Lincoln Park zoo.

"I really appreciate you having me on, Joan. We're very excited about our success with gun crimes. If we hear anything about the other case, you'll be the first to know."

"Thanks for joining us, Mr. Bitman. We'll be right back."

The red light above the camera turned off. "Clear!" the stage manager called.

"What was that, Joan!?" the producer screamed from the control room into her earpiece.

"It was gold."

"You know their office is going to call the station," he groaned. "And the show is two minutes heavy now."

Joan didn't care about either. That interview would be posted on the Channel 2 website in a matter of minutes. The social media team would share the link. Her spotlight was growing by the second, and she would do anything to keep the bulb burning bright.

***

The door to the high-rise condo was already unlocked. Trey slowly entered and scanned the room. It appeared empty, so he turned around to flip the lock.

"Hey stranger," Erica said, coming out of the bathroom.

"Jesus!" Trey jumped. "How many people have a key to this place!?"

Trey clutched his chest. Even the slightest excitement now made him feel like he was having a heart attack. His ailments had become as much mental as they were physical.

Erica pointed to the fridge. "New calendar."

Trey walked over to take a look. "Wasn't I supposed to go to Ohio?"

"Orlando. Biv said the *Trey Chic* guys are pissed after the charity debacle."

"Fine with me. They don't give a shit about the food anyway. Fast casual," Trey scoffed.

"Do you?"

"Do I what?" he asked.

"Do you care?"

"About the food? How could you even ask that?"

"Can you even tell me where all the locations of *Trey Chic* are?"

Trey thought for a second. Some of them? Sure. All of them? No. But the celebrity chef had grown an ego the size of his restaurant empire, with stubbornness to match.

"Can *you*?" Trey snipped.

"Houston, Indianapolis, Pittsburgh, St. Louis, Milwaukee, Tucson, Baltimore, Boston, San Diego, and Orlando, of course," she said with a giant grin.

It sounded right, but she could be making it up for all Trey knew.

"Bravo," he said sarcastically.

"There's food in the fridge."

Trey pulled out the familiar brown bag from his restaurant and emptied the takeout containers onto the counter. "Want some?"

"I have to go," Erica said.

"No pencil dress," he said, gesturing at her sweater and jeans. "Guessing we don't need a hostess tonight."

"I have class." Erica picked up her bag and headed toward the door. "You should really come in one night. Everyone knows you're back in town. Can't hide forever."

Erica left Trey with his mouth as full as his mind. He would love to come in and see his guys. To cook a dinner service alongside them. But the longer he was away from his namesake restaurant, the more awkward the idea of that reunion felt.

Trey shoved in another forkful of food from one of the containers and turned to the calendar on the fridge. With Orlando off his plate, his schedule certainly looked more manageable. But he knew that was just temporary. Next up was his annual lecture at the DePaul University Driehaus School of Business.

"Can't get drunk at that," he said to himself. Trey needed his little brother's help again.

***

"Did you or did you not take this photo?" Nakara said, holding up a copy of the viral image.

The chubby, long-haired high school kid being questioned quickly weighed his options.

There was no way he could get the skateboard out of his backpack in time to make a break for it. Running was out of the question. Then there was the issue of the gun.

"Are you a cop?" the kid asked.

"No." Supervisory Special Agent Ken Nakara was not going to waste time explaining where he worked, and honestly hated doing it.

"Look, we know it was your X account," Wallin said. "Just because you deleted it doesn't mean it can't be traced."

"You brought the IT guy?"

"I seriously doubt you're some international smuggler," Nakara said. "You're currently skipping remedial math to skate in a parking lot, kid."

"How do you know that?"

"We called your school," Nakara said.

"And you forgot to turn geotags off your new account," Wallin said. "Yeah, we know about that one too."

The kid took out a candy bar and unwrapped it. He looked at both men before taking a bite. They waited impatiently while he chewed.

"Seems like there should be a reward for information," the kid finally said.

Wallin knocked the candy bar to the ground.

"Dick!" the kid shouted.

"You want a reward?" Nakara asked. "I'll wait five minutes after we're done before I call your truant officer."

"Okay, I posted the picture, but it was off some guy's phone."

"What do you mean?" Nakara asked.

"This preppy loser sitting at the table next to me was telling his friend all about that maggot-filled cheese and showing him on his phone. I wanted to see it, so I used my phone to zoom in."

"Then you cropped that picture before you posted it. That explains why the image quality was so degraded," Wallin said to Nakara.

"You're degraded," the kid muttered.

"Where was this?" Nakara asked.

"Revival Food Hall. On Clark."

"What did he look like?"

"Like this guy," the kid said, pointing to Wallin. "But with like a Beatles haircut and sweater vest."

"Funny," Wallin said.

"Did he mention anything else about where he got the cheese or where he ate it?"

"No."

"Why'd you delete your account?" Wallin asked.

"I saw the picture on the news and something about an investigation. I don't need that."

Nakara got out his phone and began dialing.

"Yo, who are you calling?" the kid asked.

"Your truant officer."

"Damn, what about my five minutes!?"

Nakara was stone-faced. The kid pulled out his skateboard and took off on it.

"Want me to go after him?" Wallin asked.

"No," Nakara said.

"You really calling his truant officer?"

Nakara nodded and began walking back to the car as the phone rang. The viral image of casu marzu was the only reason anyone even knew about the illegal cheese. Without it, there would be no investigation, no task force. And now it was a dead end.

***

"How long have you been in town?" Jackson asked, handing his little brother a beer.

"Not long," Joey said. He took a sip and looked around the kitchen. "You still only got one bar stool?"

"Go to the study," he said, playfully pushing Joey out of the room.

"Seriously, that's weird, man."

Joey walked down the hallway and gestured with his bottle at a photo of Jackson and Audrey on the wall. "Where is the old ball?"

"Out," Jackson said.

They entered the study and Joey immediately flopped down on a baby-soft leather couch.

"Why do you have this and an office?" Joey asked.

"I haven't seen you in over two years and you want to talk about the layout of my house?"

"R.P.P., I guess," Joey said.

"Am I supposed to know what that stands for?"

"Rich people problems."

"We're not rich," Jackson said, seated in a large wingback chair framed by enormous shelves filled with old books.

"Okay," Joey said flippantly.

Joey and Jackson had never been close. Their last name was about all they had in common growing up. The middle brother was a homebody. The youngest would sneak onto the "L" and see how far he could get before having to get home for dinner. They differed on favorite foods, favorite movies, test scores, clothes, hairstyles and girls. Every penny Jackson earned from chores and summer jobs

111

went into the bank. Joey always had a plan for how to spend his next dollar. He had no interest in compound interest. This created a class-like divide under the Chapman roof that only seemed to widen between the brothers with age.

"What brings you back here?" Jackson asked.

"Just sort of felt like the right time." Joey finished his beer and started to set the empty bottle down on the marble coffee table. As soon as the youngest brother was happy with the amount of horror on his older brother's face, he slid it onto a nearby coaster. "Relax."

"If you want another, you can get it yourself," Jackson said.

"I'm good."

Joey leaned back and closed his eyes.

"Are we racist?" Jackson asked, completely out of nowhere.

"I'm not," Joey said, without missing a beat. "But I don't know about you."

"What do you mean you don't know about me? You're my brother. And I'm not racist!"

Joey motioned around the room with his head. "You do have a study."

"This is serious, Joey."

"I guess you're waiting for me to ask what this is all about, so go ahead."

"I was just trying to have a quiet dinner at this soul food restaurant, but the owner thought I was there to review it. When I told her I wasn't, she said it was because African Americans weren't welcome in my column."

Joey didn't respond, he just stared at his brother with a blank look.

"Well?" Jackson finally asked.

"Not exactly sure how the ball is in my court here, brother. They don't exactly sell The Tribune where I've been living. Is she right or not?"

"No. I've interviewed lots of African American chefs and restaurant owners."

"Lots?" Joey asked. "Let me ask you a question. You still writing reviews for all of dad's friends?"

"Sometimes. When it's warranted," Jackson said defensively. "But that has nothing to do with race."

"Maybe not to you. But how many old white guys has she had to read about over the years? You know what they say about perception and reality," Joey said standing up. "I'm gonna grab that other beer."

Joey walked to the kitchen leaving Jackson alone with his thoughts.

As the youngest brother rooted around in the fridge, he heard the front door open. Audrey came down the hall and set her purse on the counter.

The sight of Joey as he popped up caused her to scream.

"Ahhhh!!!!"

Jackson came running in.

"Dammit, Joey," Audrey said, trying to slow her racing heartbeat. "What are you doing here?"

"Nice to see you too," he said, twisting off the bottle top.

"Hi," Jackson said to his wife, using the word as a probe to see if they were alright.

She was still focused on the unexpected guest though. "How long are you in town?" she asked.

"I'm not sure, especially now with everything happening with Dad and the restaurant."

"Have you seen him yet?" Jackson asked.

"No. I'm still trying to figure that out," Joey said.

"I'm really worried about him. I've never seen your dad look frail," Audrey said.

"When did you see him?" her husband asked.

"This afternoon. I was just out for a drive and next thing you know I was on the front porch with a bag of Little Joe's."

"Now I want a burger," Joey said, drinking half of the beer in one gulp.

"He barely ate anything. The house is a mess. It's like the restaurant was the only thing keeping him..." Audrey stopped herself from saying the word.

James Chapman Jr. would outlive them all. That's what the brothers used to say. He was too stubborn for death. They never considered their father's mortality until they were faced with their mother's. But in seven years they'd never actually discussed it out loud.

"I'll check on him," the youngest brother said.

"That'd be good." Jackson was worried, but needed to settle things with his wife before he could focus on anything else.

Joey picked up on the discomfort in the room. "Thanks for the beer," he said as he polished it off and put the bottle in the sink. "Good to see you, Audrey."

He made no attempt to hug her on his way out of the kitchen and let himself out of the front door.

"Are we okay?" Jackson asked.

"I really want to be."

"So do I." Jackson wrapped his arms around Audrey. The slight hesitation from his wife spoke volumes. He wished he could tell her what she wanted to hear, but there was still so much guilt over the restaurant, and now his father's health.

There was, of course, one other way to make everything right. All Jackson had to do was tell Audrey about the book. But he couldn't.

7

Trey Chapman was in the best mood he could remember in weeks. He was unable to reach Joey during the short car ride to the 11-story building on the corner of Jackson and State, so he was free to be his normal self at his annual DePaul University lecture. Even more so without Biv in attendance. The event was open to any of the 3,500 undergrads enrolled in the Driehaus College of Business. Lately, crowds had started to panic the celebrity chef, but the familiar surroundings gave Trey a sense of calm despite the packed house.

"I know why culinary students want to listen to me," he said, slowly moving across the front of the room, "but I know about as much about business as I do about bitcoin." Trey whispered loudly to a girl in the front row, "Can you teach me about bitcoin?"

The audience erupted in laughter. He was in his element.

For the most part, his speech hadn't changed in years. Trey talked about learning his skills at an early age in the family's restaurant. He was more comfortable in a kitchen than a classroom, so his formal education ended in high school. His culinary school was a series of pressure-filled stops across three continents. After Chicago, Trey learned classical French cuisine in Rouen and Japanese fusion in the Minato ward of Tokyo. A stop in Chile was an introduction to indigenous ingredients rarely seen outside of Patagonia. Each experience made an impression on his palate and helped hone who he was as a chef.

"How many of you have ever eaten a cheeseburger?" he asked the crowd. Nearly every hand went up. "What words come to mind when you think about taking a bite of your favorite burger?"

"Greasy," one voice said.

"Melty," said another.

"Toasty."

"Beefy."

"What else?" Trey asked.

"High as shit," one kid yelled from the back.

When the laughter died down, Trey continued. "You don't need a cheeseburger in front of you to know how a cheeseburger tastes. A preconceived idea is locked in your brain. For the rest of your lives, your mind will pretty much be made up every time you sit down to one. Will it be better or worse than what you're used to? That's where your taste buds come in. But don't you think it's a little unfair that your taste buds get the last say when it comes to how something tastes?"

This was Trey's favorite part of his lecture. He waited an extra beat for it to really sink in.

"All I've ever wanted to do with my cooking was give your taste buds a fair shot."

There are probably very few chefs who can trace their culinary philosophy to a single experience, let alone a single ingredient. Trey Chapman still got goosebumps when he thought about his. It was during his three-month apprenticeship in Santiago. His duties extended beyond the kitchen to the garden and hills above the restaurant. One April morning, he was escorted to a wall of bushes bursting with a small, maroon fruit. Before he filled his basket, he had to try one. *It sort of looks like a cranberry. Is it tart? No, maybe more like a cherry.* Trey's mind could only guess. He plucked a murta, as it was called, off the nearest shrub and sank his teeth in. "*Strawberry!*" his tastes bud shouted. But not like the strawberries he was used to. There was a floral sweetness, and then acid. The experience existed entirely in his mouth, with his brain simply along for the ride.

Trey opened six months later with a 10-course tasting menu that was part omakase and part molecular gastronomy. Diners had no idea what they were getting. His mind-bending presentations deceived the eyes. The experience began where it should- taste. Every other sense was left playing catch up.

A young woman in the front of the room shot up her hand, but began talking before Trey had a chance to interject. "So, the Seared Beef Salad with Thai Dressing in your latest cookbook, the one you've been making on TV. How exactly does that fit in with your culinary philosophy?"

"You can't really trick the mind when you know the recipe," Trey said, thankfully getting enough laughter to lighten the room. "Cookbooks are for home cooks. For home cooking. What I like about that salad," he said, making it up as he went along, "is the way sweet, sour, salty, bitter and spicy play pinball on the tongue."

Trey poured his heart and soul into his first cookbook. He shuttered the restaurant for a month and holed himself up in the kitchen translating each of his dishes into something that could be made without the fuss, but with all of the flavor. It was an offering to those who couldn't get to or afford visiting *Trey*. It sold through the roof, spreading his name across the country, and paved the way for his restaurant expansion. But every cookbook after that couldn't possibly have the same care, the same time, the same attention. His most recent publication was sculpted more by deadline than desire.

"Your name is on restaurants, cookbooks, pots and pans," the young woman in the front continued, "but history has taught us that empires that spread too far will fall. How much farther do you want to, or can you, go?"

Trey's cheeks began to flush. The students usually asked about his favorite celebrity encounter or if there were any foods he didn't like.

"Whoa," Trey said, pulling at his collar. "I wasn't prepared for cross-examination. I believe the College of Law is next door, Miss."

Trey had one thing right. The young woman was not a business student.

"I guess now is as good a time as any to open the floor to questions," Trey said. "Softballs are encouraged."

The first question came from a baby-faced student with an adult mustache.

"What happened to your dad's restaurant?"

"Any questions about *my* restaurants?"

"Look, I'm just trying to get some answers."

"If you have questions for my father, then why don't you ask him," Trey said, looking visibly agitated. Trey noticed as someone in the first row pointed their cell phone at him. "Are you filming this?"

"That was my internship."

The kid asking questions was Benny Perez from the Hospitality Leadership program in the Driehaus College of Business.

"There are no interns at Chapman's Steakhouse."

"Shows what you know," Benny said.

"Stop filming," Trey said sternly to the kid in the front.

"Was it rats? People are saying it was like rats or something?"

"It wasn't rats!" Trey yelled.

It felt like the room was shrinking. His vision tunneled.

"Well, is it going to re-open or what?" Benny asked.

"How should I know!?" Trey took his anger out on the kid with the phone. "I told you to stop filming!"

He grabbed the cell phone and threw it against the wall.

"Okay, I think we're all out of time," said a professor who rushed to escort the unhinged celebrity chef out of the room.

Unfortunately for Trey, he had only destroyed one of the recordings. The inquisitive young woman who had grilled him earlier was filming from behind a stack of books. She checked to make sure she had gotten the outburst. The video would get way more clicks than her story from the Halting Hunger Charity Auction.

***

Joey Chapman sat on a bench across from Buckingham Fountain thoroughly enjoying both his coffee and watching the man he was supposed to meet pace back and forth. The yuppie in the ridiculously bright red jacket checked his watch again. There was no doubt in Joey's mind that Anderson Strout was a fake name. The hastily thrown together Facebook page may have been enough to fool Crete, but didn't come close to passing Merlin's test. And the meeting itself had been too easy to arrange. Using the number provided by the bartender, Joey gave a vague story about a unique food item he was about to get delivered. The fountain, the jacket and the quick meet-up were all Strout's idea.

The question Joey had been mulling all morning was "Why Crete?" Anyone looking to shut down the nameless bar had countless other avenues to do so, starting with the fact that it wasn't an actual bar. It was a modified stock room that had been sealed off from an abandoned department store decades ago. The owner of the boutique hotel that now occupied the rest of the building knew about it and knew enough to leave it alone. Crete had no business permit or liquor license, but as far as Joey could tell, she had no enemies either.

The only way he was going to learn the truth was by following Anderson Strout, but the fake yuppie didn't seem to be in any hurry. Joey finally checked his watch. It had been nearly forty minutes since the agreed upon meeting time. He didn't have any coffee left. He was running out of things to occupy his stakeout.

Strout finally made the move to leave the park, and Joey used his empty cup as an excuse to head towards a trash can and begin tailing him. The obnoxious red jacket was easy to see from a distance, so he hung back as the fraud headed west away from the lake. All of a sudden, Strout seemed to pick up the pace as he made a quick right on State Street. Joey had to break into a jog to catch up and was barely able to see the man slip into a building at the end of the block. The youngest Chapman had no idea that it was the same building his older brother had been escorted out of just hours before. DePaul University shared the space with several other tenants, but only one name jumped out at Joey as he scanned the directory- the Department of Public Health.

Anderson Strout was The Boogie Man.

***

The two men seated at the computer terminal on the second floor of the building were a much bigger problem for Joey Chapman, but only if they could catch him. Ken Nakara had brought his secret weapon and watched anxiously as Wallin typed search queries into the records system.

"Nothing for casu marzu," Wallin said.

"Yeah, I got that far."

The tech expert clicked away at the keyboard for another couple minutes before reading through a handful of results. "There are a few instances for cheese, mostly queso fresco, but nothing that indicates smuggling."

"How about if we search for cases involving other illegal foods?" Nakara suggested.

"Okay," Wallin said. He waited with his fingers lightly resting on the keyboard. "You're going to need to give me some examples."

"Sorry," Nakara said. "Let's try ortolan."

"Ortolan?"

"It's a small bird from France."

Wallin executed the search and looked up from the empty screen. "No ortolan."

"Try ackee," Nakara instructed.

"Another small bird?"

"No, it's a fruit from Jamaica."

"Why is it illegal?" Wallin asked.

"Technically, it's only illegal in its unripe state. It can contain high levels of a toxin that causes dehydration, vomiting, and in rare cases, death. But you can buy it canned or frozen."

"Is this what you do all day?" Wallin asked.

"Just do the search," Nakara ordered.

One result popped up. "I'll be damned," Wallin said, opening the case file.

Both men read through the text on the screen. Nakara got to the end and jumped out of his chair. "Print it out!"

"I don't get it. How does some guy getting sick on unripe fruit help?" Wallin asked.

Nakara pointed to the name on the screen. "Ackee is the national fruit of Jamaica. Does that look like a Jamaican name to you?"

Wallin shook his head.

"I think we need to talk to Dustin Miller."

***

Nothing good ever came over email. Jackson was fond of saying it and couldn't help but think it every time he turned his computer on. He preferred a tactile experience for all correspondence and enjoyed sitting down with a stack of letters each day after he heard the metal mailbox on the front door clang shut. Usually there was a gin and tonic involved. The ritual, however antiquated, felt civilized.

Jackson believed he was the last child in America taught on a typewriter. Even Joey learned on a bulky Macintosh. The middle Chapman had no say in making the switch and had once protested to his middle school teacher by describing the keyboard and mouse as alien. The antagonistic relationship only worsened when the computer became the preferred method of communication for Martin Easley.

An average day would bring anywhere from ten to twenty emails, with a quarter coming from his detested editor, who never seemed to run out of restaurants to push. But as Jackson opened his inbox, there were no questions from fans. Even more extraordinary, there was just a single email from Easley. Mubashir Mediterranean was a Lebanese restaurant he had recommended reviewing once before, but something about this seemed different.

Jackson turned off the monitor and walked out of his office. The air in the household was still filled with tension, but he needed a sounding board. He found Audrey folding laundry in the master bedroom.

"He only sent one email."

"Who?" she asked, plucking a shirt out of the basket.

"You know who." Jackson hated saying his name.

"Is that unusual?"

"Very," Jackson said, sitting down on the bed. "In fact, I can't remember another such instance."

Audrey continued to work her way through the pile.

"Well, where do you want to go for dinner tonight?" he asked, changing the subject.

"Is it for a review?"

"I know I'm not supposed to ask, but I'm asking."

"Will you match these?" Audrey said, tossing a handful of socks at her husband. "Why don't we go somewhere Martin suggests for once?"

The words pierced Jackson's ears. He would have been less hurt had his wife asked for a divorce.

"How could you side with him?" he said, whipping around.

"I'm not siding with him."

"That's exactly what you're doing."

"I'm not siding with him," she said, sitting down by her husband. "I just met with him."

Jackson jumped up as the words landed. "What!?"

"I didn't know what else to do. I thought he could help."

"How could he help?" Jackson fumed. "He's the problem!"

"He's not. Martin really cares. Christ, we wouldn't have known about your dad and the steakhouse being shut down if it weren't for him."

"But you said…" Jackson started.

"I know what I said. I didn't want to hurt you. I don't want to hurt you. This isn't about James or Martin. I'm trying to save your job."

"They can't fire me!"

"They can," Audrey said solemnly. "And Martin will."

The empty inbox finally made sense. That single email wasn't a suggestion. It was an edict. And for the first time in his career, Jackson Chapman had lost his appetite.

***

"The kid isn't the problem."

Biv let himself all the way in and shut the door. Trey went back to the well-worn track in his carpet that he'd been pacing ever since the hired black sedan dropped him off at the high-rise condo.

"Recognize her?" Biv asked, holding up a picture on his phone.

"Yeah, that's the girl at the lecture who was asking me all these crazy questions."

"Her name's Lindsay McKeil. Tabloid trash. And she's apparently decided to make you her meal ticket."

Trey stopped. "Why?"

"Because you keep giving her a story!" Biv ran his fingers through his hair. That's the problem with a crew cut. It grows out quickly. The business manager's bright white buzz had started to lay down. "First, it was the charity catastrophe. Now she's got a video of you losing your shit on a 20-year-old kid."

"He ambushed me."

123

"Nobody ambushed you. Look, I'm sorry about your dad's restaurant, but we have a lot more on the line."

It stood out the second Trey heard it. Biv never said "we." As much as Trey had tried to get him to share in the credit, his business manager had always preferred to stay out of the spotlight. He was a true silent partner. At least he always had been.

Biv Trammel was a decade into a modestly successful career when he heard about one of Chicago's native sons returning home to open a restaurant. Despite the ten-course meal at *Trey* being out of his price range, he made a reservation. After his first bite of the second course, he asked if the chef would come out. Trey was irritated when he arrived at the table and noticed how early into the meal the diner was. He stood there with his arms crossed. Biv did not waste his time or words. "The first course made me want to tell everyone I know. The second made me want to tell the world. Are you happy being a chef or would you like to be a global brand?"

It wasn't something Biv had ever delivered, but he was nothing if not confident. Trey was impressed enough to set up a meeting but underwhelmed at the suggestion of a cookbook. Biv went down a timeline of restaurant expansion and kitchen endorsements, which were music to the chef's ears. Getting the name Trey Chapman into as many homes as possible, though, was the first step. So, the deal they struck started with a cookbook. If Biv could line up a publisher, Trey would write it, and that's exactly what happened.

A second location for the namesake restaurant was the next order of business. Biv was stunned to learn that *Trey* was wholly owned by the chef. Most first-timers needed deep-pocketed backers. But it wasn't hard for Biv to connect the dots from the loan officer back to James Chapman Jr. He often wondered if his client had any idea of his father's involvement.

The financial setup at *Trey* created an opportunity for the business manager to become a business partner. The Chapman name didn't open doors in LA or New York, and Trey was still not a well-enough known commodity. Biv had a choice to make. He could happily live off a small percentage from cookbooks and endorsements or put his life savings on the line and co-sign on a seven-figure loan. The more he weighed the decision, the less it seemed like a risk. Biv had never believed in anyone the way he did Trey Chapman. With the stroke of a pen, Biv Trammel became a 50% partner in the New York location, and would go on to repeat the process four more times.

"What do *we* really have on the line, Biv?" Trey paused just long enough for effect, but not a response. "There was a $9,000 bottle of bourbon in my cabinet. I have no idea if I bought it or how it got there. I don't have a clue how much money I have. I haven't had a second to stop and count it, much less enjoy it."

Biv stared out the window, looking down on the lake. "You think you'd have this view if you were just a chef?"

"A lot of good it does me if I die from a heart attack," Trey shot back.

Biv turned and looked him right in the eyes. "You were the one who left the kitchen, who traded those rubber mats for red carpets."

"I'm serious, Biv! Dr. Nevins said all this stress could kill me."

The business manager knew after the visit to the doctor that Trey wasn't in the best health, but after this long together, he had developed a keen ear for embellishment.

"It's not just me, you know," Biv said. "A lot of people depend on you."

Trey hadn't thought about that. It was one thing to try and get out of endorsements from major companies, but what about the hundreds of people that worked at his restaurants. The ones who were paid by the hour. Trey sat down on the couch. All of the grand openings and popped champagne flashed through his mind. He could see all the smiles. He could see that the life he had taken decades to build was now inescapable.

***

Joey's life was the exact opposite. He was bound by nothing but gravity, and the occasional need to extend his visa abroad. The youngest Chapman had made Europe his playground, bouncing between countries on a whim. He loved nothing more than going to sleep on a train and waking up with all the possibilities of somewhere new.

The last time he relocated by rail was to the Italian town of Ravenna, just steps from the Adriatic Sea. Joey didn't speak a lick of the language. He just sort of got by, like he did with everything in life. It was supposed to be a quick stop on the way to Venice, one spurred by romantic stories of art and architecture recounted by a recent fling. But one day of wandering through the history and beautiful mosaics turned into two.

Before the week was up, Joey had secured a room above a restaurant with a pair of empty nesters. He occasionally helped the wife in their kitchen or the husband on his boat. He had no schedule, just an insatiable quest to find the best piadina in the city. The rustic flatbread filled with various meats and cheese and folded into a sandwich was his only meal each day. It was a simple, carefree existence. Or it had been.

The water he looked out on seven years ago had a different name, but there was a room, a nice couple and odd jobs. The news of his mother's death was so unexpected the phone call drained the color from his world. He had four thousand miles to think on the way home from Portugal. Overwhelming grief turned to guilt. There were promises made about his family, his future. There would be big changes. They would be short lived.

Joey returned to Europe because it felt more like home than Chicago ever did. But his travels did not have the same purpose, not without his mother to tell them about. So, he thought about his father. The longer Joey stayed, the more he worried about getting that call again. He was not bored in Prague or Munich or Ravenna. His departure always had to come before his father's.

Actually going to visit the great James Chapman Jr. was another matter altogether, which is why Joey had avoided it for more than a week. If it weren't for the restaurant closure and report from Audrey, he probably would have delayed it even more. But as he pulled up to the back of Chapman's Steakhouse, Joey immediately regretted waiting. The dumpster was overflowing, and he could hear the buzzing of flies even with the windows rolled up. The stench once he got out of the car was toxic, and the unseasonably cold September air seemed to trap it near the ground. Joey never used the front door to the restaurant, but for once wished he had.

The kitchen smelled of the same rot, just smothered in bleach. The main dining room didn't offer much relief. Joey found his father sitting in the corner, lit only by sunlight coming through a handful of open curtains.

"The rumor is true," James said.

"Very goth in here," Joey said, sitting down across from him. "Have you thought about renting it out for Halloween?"

"It'll be rubble before then."

Audrey's account was not exaggerated. James was so hunched over that Joey couldn't look him in the eye. "Doesn't have to be. What do you want to happen, Dad?"

"What I wanted didn't happen," James said.

"Yeah, I can see that. Or I could if the lights worked." Joey was desperately trying to see if there was any fight left. "I can get the trash picked up in an hour and a cleaning crew in the kitchen tomorrow. Trey can cut a check to the bank..."

"No." James cut him off. "I'm not asking Trey for money. I've wasted enough for this lifetime."

"It's a little late to be proud."

"You want to help?" There was finally a little strength in his voice. "Sell all the booze. That's how you can help. Can you manage that?"

Suddenly, Joey was fourteen again, being given a task just to keep him occupied. He didn't need to be around to watch the restaurant, or his father, implode though. The visit was over, and the answer was the airport.

"Bye, Dad."

As Joey stood up from the table, he felt his phone buzz. It was a text from Trey. His father may not need him, but his brother did.

***

There were thirty seconds left on the microwave when one of the rookie ICE agents walked into the community kitchen at the Food and Drug Administration.

"What's for breakfast?" he said.

A safe distance away, Ken Nakara waited patiently with his mug in his hand. "It's a sponge."

"High fiber, huh?" the ICE agent said, retrieving creamer from the fridge.

"I'm sanitizing it."

"Germaphobe. Figures." The rookie stuck his nose inside the carton and took a whiff.

"E. coli sickens over 250,000 people worldwide each year," Nakara said.

"You must be a hit at parties."

The ICE agent splashed some creamer into his coffee and left just as the microwave mercifully beeped.

Ken Nakara was still coming to terms with the lie he told his Deputy Director as he sipped his morning tea. Technically, not telling her that the viral image was a dead end was a lie of omission, but it counted the same in his book.

Nakara gingerly handled the hot sponge and doused it with soap. As soon as he had any good news, he planned to come clean. He was hoping someone in the conference room down the hall had some. After copious scrubbing, Nakara placed the sponge back in the sink and gave his mug one last rinse.

Standing in front of his task force, Nakara felt more like a substitute teacher than the leader.

"For those of you that don't know, we were able to determine who took the viral image, but unfortunately that individual was not involved with the

128

smuggling, serving or consuming of the illegal cheese," he said. "Wallin, where are we on locating Dustin Miller?"

"Should have that information by this afternoon."

"Good." He turned to the ICE agents. "Safe to say you guys still have nothing?"

"Yep," one rookie said.

"OCI, anything promising from the tip line?"

"No, but the station has requested that you come on for an interview," the older agent said.

"Absolutely not."

"Joan Jones is all in on this," said the younger one. "This could get you, like, promoted."

"Why would I go on TV?" Nakara asked. "We have nothing."

He wasn't happy with the source of their motivation, but if it materialized anything then he could use it to clear his conscience with the Deputy Director first.

"You want me to talk to Joan Jones, then get me something to talk about."

8

The ride out to "Little Palestine" was quiet and uncomfortable. Audrey's attempts at conversation didn't get far. Jackson was still hurt, and the forced trip to Bridgeview by his editor only made it worse. They drove down South Harlem Avenue, past dozens of Middle Eastern restaurants and grocery stores, before pulling into the parking lot of Mubashir Mediterranean. Ornate script on the front window advertised "Authentic Lebanese Cuisine."

Audrey was barely inside the front door when she was overwhelmed by the smell of toast and char.

"Oh my god, the bread," she said, pointing to a basket of pita on a nearby table.

All Jackson could see was vinyl-padded banquet chairs and clear plastic table-cloths. A young man approached carrying a stack of menus.

"Two, please," Jackson said.

"Right this way."

They were led past three small open booths and even an empty four-top before being seated at an enormous table with two place settings. The critic was not anonymous, but he didn't like giving restaurants advanced warning, which Martin Easley clearly had.

"Here are some menus," the young man said, "but you won't be needing them. I'll be right back."

Audrey smiled as the young man disappeared. "I don't think we've had Lebanese in ages."

Jackson, distracted by his anger, didn't hear her.

"Are you going to be like this all night?" she asked.

He finally looked up. "I can't do this."

"What? Eat?"

"I won't be forced to review what *he* wants me to."

"Then don't write it. Let's just enjoy the meal." She waved her hands over the large open space between them. "This apparently very large meal."

Jackson leaned in and whispered loudly, "Then what? Get fired?"

"I don't know, but..." she was interrupted by a trio of servers who filled every inch of the table with small plates and baskets.

The young man began pointing at all the dishes. "This is pita. Hummus. Tabbouleh. Baba Ghanouj. You know, with eggplant. Falafel. Ful. It's fava beans. Manakish. And Kibbeh, our national dish, made with lamb. Enjoy!"

After a few awkward seconds of silence from Jackson, Audrey looked up and said, "This looks wonderful. Thank you very much."

The young man and servers each nodded at the couple and stepped away.

"You can be upset with me, and mad at Martin, but I will not tolerate you being rude," Audrey said.

Jackson said nothing. He aggressively ripped off a piece of pita and slammed it into the creamy chickpea dip. Paprika stained olive oil ran down his fingers as he shoved the bite into his mouth. Audrey just sat and watched as the caveman-like sampling continued. It took several minutes for Jackson to realize she hadn't touched the food.

"Aren't you going to eat?" he asked with his mouth full.

Audrey had two choices. She could dress him down, and rightfully so, since the man sitting across from her didn't resemble who she married. It would cause a scene, an embarrassment for both them and the restaurant. The food would go to waste. Their night would be ruined, and the implications on her husband's career would still be unknown. Or she could take him back to a time they were unimaginably happy. When he was still unconvinced he had won her heart. A time when every thought and every gesture had that one singular goal.

"Make me a bite," she instructed.

"What?"

"Make me a bite."

"Audrey..."

"I know you remember. Was it Al Madi?"

Jackson wiped his mouth with his napkin. "Al Wadi."

"Our table looked a lot like this. I'm pretty sure you ordered one of everything." Audrey could see her husband go back in his mind. "It was a pretty grand gesture. I wasn't quite sure if you just wanted to put on a big show or what. And I had no idea what any of it was."

"Except maybe hummus," Jackson said with the smallest hint of a smile.

"That's right. But the rest of it? I must've had a terrified look on my face because you looked me right in the eye and said..."

"Let me make you a bite."

"I don't think I picked up my fork the entire night." Audrey reached a hand across the table and gently placed it on top of his. "I just watched as you made each mouthful the perfect combination. I know you explained what everything was, but I'll never remember."

Jackson gave her hand a squeeze and then picked up a crispy brown fritter off one of the plates. "Do you remember kibbeh?"

Audrey shook her head.

"It's like a meaty hush puppy with minced lamb, onion and bulgur wheat." Jackson carefully split it and wrapped half in a shred of pita. He added a dollop of thick white sauce, then a drizzle of something green. "The garlic yogurt dip is classic. And this is a hot sauce made from fresh jalapenos called shatta."

Jackson held a napkin underneath the oversized morsel as he went to hand it to Audrey, but she leaned forward instead. *Feed me*. Her husband obliged.

For the rest of the night, there was no talk of a review or Martin Easley, and nowhere else either Chapman would rather be.

***

Trey walked past his name on the window and causally opened the door to his restaurant. The hostess's eyes lit up, but he put a finger to his lips and pointed at the man standing next to her who was staring down at a computer screen.

The chef made his voice comically deep. "Table for one." He waited for a second before trying again a bit louder. "Table for one!"

The man finally looked up and just shook his head. "Two weeks. You've been back in town two weeks, and you just now come by?"

"It's not like you've been calling me day and night either, Edward."

Trey walked around the hostess stand to give the restaurant manager a hug.

"Hey, I saw what happens when someone pulls out a phone near you."

The hug turned into a playful headlock before the chef let go. Edward fixed his ruffled suit.

"You picked a good night. We're booked up."

"Always love to hear that," Trey said.

"And you know what really gets them in the mood to spend money?" Edward asked.

"Oh, don't do it, Eddie."

But there was no stopping him. The restaurant manager turned and yelled, "Ladies and Gentleman, the great Trey Chapman!"

The room came to a halt, and the diners started clapping and cheering. Some stood up, others craned their necks just to get a view of the celebrity chef. Trey mock covered his face in embarrassment, but this was better than any drug. He took his time, weaving through tables, shaking hands and smiling for pictures, eventually reaching the back hallway that led to his office.

Trey was more than surprised to find the space occupied by Erica Tomlin.

"What are you doing in here?"

"I could ask you the same thing," she said, making no attempt to get up from the desk.

"This is my office."

Erica laughed.

Trey noticed the spreadsheets scattered in front of her, covered with various shades of highlighter.

"Homework?"

"Cost review in Miami. The break-even is the highest of all your restaurants. Biv asked me to give it a fresh set of eyes."

"I thought you just printed new calendars and stuff," Trey said, a bit sheepishly.

"You *really* don't know anything about me," she said.

"I know. You keep saying that."

Erica was just one of the people that Trey had been thinking about over and over since his conversation with Biv. He had no idea how many hundreds of people were employed directly or indirectly by his celebrity. The sole purpose of coming to the restaurant was to look through the records for each of his namesake locations. He was hoping there was something in there that would help him unwind everything. But to do that, he needed the computer, the one that his assistant was firmly planted in front of.

"Maurice know you're here yet?" she asked.

"No." .

"He'll be *relieved*." Erica put an odd emphasis on the last word, and it took Trey a minute before it clicked.

"Sammy's out again?" Trey rolled his eyes. "Don't wait up."

Despite being barely five feet tall, Maurice Ochoa stood in complete control at the end of the kitchen. He wiped the edge of a plate clean and pushed it down the metal table to a server waiting to run it out. As he mopped the sweat off his forehead, the machine in front of him spit out another ticket. He clipped it to the rail above him and called out.

"Ordering! Two gem and one soup."

"Heard!" everyone called out in unison.

Trey originally hired Maurice as a prep cook before the restaurant opened. It was just the two of them testing recipes at all hours of the day and night. The short Ecuadorian was game for anything. He understood the vision and proved it to the point he was named sous chef when *Trey* launched. He stood by his boss's side when Trey closed the restaurant to write the first cookbook. And he was rewarded when Trey's career took off and took him out of the kitchen. That's what Maurice liked the most about working there. The boss was rarely around.

Trey burst through the swinging doors, and was welcomed with hollering and the clanging of pans from everyone except the head chef who didn't stop to look up.

"MoCho!" Trey had coined the nickname the first day they worked together and refused to call his friend anything else.

"Sammy's a no-show," Maurice said.

"Heard," Trey responded, grabbing an apron.

"Hop on the grill and relieve Julian."

Trey walked over to the station and took the tongs from a skinny kid swimming in a filthy apron. "Last time I was here you couldn't wash lettuce right. Now you're on the grill?"

The executive chef happily slid in and lightly prodded a large piece of beef. As chef de tournant, Trey would spend the night going from station to station, giving breaks as needed.

Having worked his way up the ladder, Trey was well aware of the hierarchy in professional kitchens. This step down was unheard of. But the boss was out of practice. He knew to leave his ego at the door and let Maurice do the frantic ballet at the end of the long metal table just as he did night in and night out.

Edward popped his head through the swinging doors. "You're about to get a push!"

The machine sprung to life and printed out four tickets in rapid succession. Maurice flew into action calling out orders, and the kitchen filled with frenzied energy. Trey just stared at the grill. There was a secret happiness to not being in charge. These nights were now the only time the great Trey Chapman got to cook. Not drizzle a sauce from a squeeze bottle. Or use surgical tweezers to place microgreens. Or simply wipe the edge of a plate before it went out the door. To cook. Actually cook.

***

Dustin Miller was definitely not Jamaican. Ken Nakara was sure of that much. The red hair, freckles and translucent skin of the man approaching his car alluded to a lineage from a much different island.

"Welcome to Mister Suds. Early bird special ended two minutes ago, but you can still have it if you want."

The Supervisory Special Agent was so eager to follow up on his ackee hunch that he broke from his morning routine. He was out the door before his daughters left for school, and didn't stop at the office for his ritual cup of tea or emails. The car wash provided both an opportunity to question Miller and clean some of the miles off the seven-year-old Toyota Camry that he'd been racking up going back and forth between Lisle and the city.

"Sure, I'll take the special," he said, rolling up his window and getting out.

Miller handed him a slip of paper. "Pay at the register inside."

"Actually, I was wondering if I could ask you a few questions."

"You a cop?" Miller asked, taking a step back as if preparing to run.

Nakara was aware of the car wash attendant's rap sheet and left his gun at the office so as not to spook him. The skittish man had a history of fleeing the scene of his various offenses.

136

"No. I just want to know about the ackee fruit that made you sick."

"Seriously?"

"Seriously."

Miller grabbed the long hose off the hook and began vacuuming the agent's floor mats. "It was disgusting," he yelled over the loud humming sound. "I threw up for a couple days. Had to get an IV and everything. You know how much that cost without insurance?"

"Could you please turn that off?" Nakara shouted.

Miller pointed to a car that had just pulled up behind them. "I got people waiting." He went back to the floor mats.

"How did you get it?!"

"This guy I used to work with. Real rasta dude. We were smoking one day and this car pulls up. My man comes back with a couple bags. I was like, 'what is that?' He says 'ackee.' I just thought it was some slang for a new drug or something. He gave me a bag and when I got home and opened it, it was just some fruit."

Miller walked around to the other side of the car.

"And you just ate it?" Nakara asked.

"I told you. I was high."

"I'm trying to find the person who sold your friend that fruit. Can you tell me anything about him, what he looked like, the car?"

"You know how many years ago that was?" Miller asked.

"Yes," Nakara said.

The car wash attendant popped up. "He did have a strange name though. It was like a magician or something. I laughed for like twenty minutes when my guy told me. Marlin. No, that's not right. Merlin."

Nakara froze. He had heard that name before.

"I need to get in touch with your friend," he said with a sense of urgency.

"Oh, I haven't seen that dude in years. If you find him, tell him I said what's up."

Nakara remembered. Someone had mentioned Merlin on the Channel 2 tip line. The Supervisory Special Agent finally had a lead, but before he could follow it up, he had to wait for his car to be washed first.

***

The latest edition of The Tribune landed on Jackson Chapman's face with a "thwack." He thrashed in the bed before blinking his eyes open.

Audrey hovered over him, looking very agitated. "What is wrong with you?"

"What's wrong with me?" he said, still trying to make sense of the rude awakening. "Did you just hit me with the paper?"

"You think you're hurting Martin, but you're not. You're hurting the restaurant, the owner, the chef, and all the people who work there."

"What are you talking about?" Jackson asked, knowing full well what she was talking about.

Audrey snatched a section of the paper from near his head and began reading. "The Middle Eastern tradition of flavorful dips stops with Mubashir Mediterranean. The ful medames was a watery mess lacking both the punch of fresh garlic and much-needed acidity of lemon. The baba ghanouj was barely recognizable as eggplant underneath a blanket of careless acrid char. High hopes for the Lebanese national dish of kibbeh were dashed by an exterior fried to an impenetrable crisp."

She threw the paper at him a second time.

"Did you think that I wasn't going to read it?"

Jackson sat up. "Are you questioning my taste?"

"I'm questioning a lot of things."

"Audrey, I've eaten those dishes dozens of times, I know exactly how they're supposed..."

"Don't you dare!" She sharply cut him off. "Don't try to paint me as the girl who doesn't know better. This isn't about me. I've eaten thousands of meals with you. I can tell what you think the moment something hits your tongue, and we both know that food was incredible."

Jackson would never admit the truth. When they got home from dinner, he said goodnight to his wife, went to his office and allowed his mind to go down a dangerous rabbit hole.

Why had his editor suggested just a single restaurant? Why Mediterranean? Audrey's request to make her a bite started to seem rehearsed. The memory felt convenient. *Had she and Martin planned the entire thing?* Jackson tortured himself. The only outlet was the blank screen in front of him.

"You can't write a bad review because you're mad at me or mad at him," Audrey said. Jackson still hadn't responded to the accusation and seemed set on not doing so. "Make it right, or I will," his wife threatened, then stormed out of the room.

"What does that mean?" he called after her.

Jackson sat in bed wondering if his wife was headed to make some apology to the restaurant, or even worse, another meeting with his editor.

***

Joey stood in front of the nameless bar holding a bottle in each hand. He looked up at the security camera until he heard the familiar buzz. As he had hoped, the space inside was empty, which wasn't always a guarantee, even at such an early hour of the day.

"I don't remember ordering anything," Crete said as he walked up.

Joey set the bottles on the counter. "Just a sample. I've got a whole trunk full, and then some."

She leaned in to take a closer look at the labels. "Lagavulin 16-year. Nice. Flor De Cana 25. Even better. How hot is it?"

"It's not. I need to offload the entire bar from Chapman's Steakhouse."

"Chapman?"

"My dad."

"Some family you come from," Crete said. "Is it all this good?"

"Most of it."

"Okay, whatever I don't want, I can find a buyer for. Get you cash by next week."

"Thanks." Joey took a seat at the bar. "Hey, how'd you get in touch with Anderson Strout again?"

"He called me up out of the blue. Said a mutual friend gave him the number."

"Who was the friend?"

"Wouldn't say. Wanted to respect his friend's privacy. But I told you, I looked him up."

"The Facebook page?" Joey asked.

"Yeah."

"Fake. Anderson Strout is The Boogie Man."

Crete looked confused. "This guy hid in your closet as a child?"

"No, he's a health inspector. How do you own a bar and not know that?"

"You think this place has ever been inspected?" she said, motioning around the room with her head. "It'd take a warrant to get me to open that door."

"I just can't figure out why he's coming after you," Joey said.

"We can just be done with the sexist bastard if you want."

"How do you know he's sexist?"

"First time he called he was surprised a woman answered."

Joey got a terrible feeling. Anderson Strout wasn't going after Crete. He was coming after him. "Did you know there's a whole task force trying to find me?"

"Yeah, your cheese has taken on a life of its own."

"I need to find out if Strout's a part of it," Joey said.

Crete raised her eyebrows and gave a little nod. "Want me to send someone to find out?"

"Like with a baseball bat? No, thanks. For now, just don't talk to him. If he leaves you a message or anything, let me know."

"Okay. Option's on the table though."

Joey stood up. "You got a dolly I can use?"

"Get you one out of the back," she said and disappeared.

Joey stared at the TV behind the bar with the security feed. If Anderson Strout had stood in front of that door, he was already way too close.

***

The sound of Tibetan singing bowls playing through the speaker hidden behind a large white orchid had lulled Jackson into a trance. He stared blankly at a charcoal drawing of a lotus flower hanging on the wall and hadn't noticed that the fluffy robe he was wearing had started to slip open below his waist. After the unpleasant morning with his wife, Jackson needed to clear his head and decided to move up his monthly appointment at the Lake Day Spa. Twenty minutes in the sauna lined with Himalayan salt had started his meditation, and now the addition of the music in the back waiting room was causing his eyes to grow heavy.

Trey walked through the door wearing the same robe. "Jackson?"

"Trey?" the younger brother said, squinting through the dimly lit room.

"I can see your nuts," Trey said, pointing at his brother's now bare lower body.

Jackson fumbled to close the robe. "What are you doing here?"

"Guessing the same as you. Biv thought I needed to relax."

"Didn't take you for a day spa kind of guy."

"I'm not," Trey said. "But you seem pretty comfortable."

Trey walked over to a crystal water cooler with slices of citrus fruit. He filled a glass, and finished it in one gulp, then sat down in the chair across from his brother.

"How you been?"

"I've been better," Jackson said.

"Me too."

"You know you could tell me if this is part of some court-ordered rehab or anger management program."

"And there are other ways to tell the world that you're a pretentious, middle-aged white guy," Trey said. "Buy a sports car or something."

They both smiled. Unlike most brothers, their relationship had never been competitive. Jackson's days wearing an apron next to Trey were short lived. One of the cooks at Chapman's Steakhouse nearly sliced his index finger off in front of them. The younger brother was scarred for life. The older brother thought all the blood was "cool." Their shared love of food split in two directions after that, but actually brought them closer together. Trey was always trying to invent something new and Jackson was his happy guinea pig. Their relationship was symbiotic, and the foundation for both of their current success.

"Were you planning on calling?" Jackson asked.

"Yeah, you know my crazy schedule."

Jackson didn't. "How long you in town for?"

"I'm not sure."

"We should probably talk about dad and the restaurant."

"Yeah," Trey said.

A man walked in and motioned for Jackson to come down the hall. Trey gave his brother a funny look.

"It's deep tissue," Jackson whispered, shaking his head.

"I bet it is." Trey got up and walked back over to the water cooler. "Hey, what are you and Audrey doing tomorrow night?"

"Audrey and I are..." Jackson paused.

Trey sensed the awkwardness. "Even better. I've got this nonprofit thing. It'll give you and I more time to catch up. The food is always amazing."

"Okay."

"Great, I'll have Biv send you all the details." Trey turned to the man waiting in the doorway. "Watch out, this guy's a little loose with his robe etiquette, if you know what I mean."

Jackson just shook his head at his brother on his way by. "I'll see you tomorrow."

***

With a clean car, Ken Nakara hightailed it back to the FDA Headquarters in Lisle, which for him was two miles an hour over the speed limit. His last-minute attempt to assemble the task force for an urgent briefing had hit a roadblock with the rookie ICE agents, who texted that they were on a stakeout that would apparently last several days. From a procedural standpoint, Nakara had a good mind to call up their superiors and either confirm the assignment or prove it to be bogus. But he didn't have the time and was happy to have them out of his hair. So Supervisory Special Agent Nakara stood in front of three fifths of his crack squad in the conference room.

"We have our first break. Several years ago, a guy smuggled an illegal fruit into the city going by the name Merlin."

"Somebody mentioned that on the tip line," said the older OCI agent.

"Exactly," Nakara said. "What other information did they provide?"

The two OCI agents looked at each other sheepishly.

"Well," the younger one started, "we got so many joke ones."

"That is to say that if we believed something to not be credible..." the other one trailed off.

"Spit it out," Nakara ordered.

"We didn't read it," the younger one finally admitted.

"Really, any of them."

"Well, where is it?"

The two agents pointed to three legal boxes filled to the brim on a table in the back of the room. Nakara closed his eyes and pinched the bridge of his nose.

"Find it," he said, but neither man seemed to move. "Now!"

The OCI agents shot out of their chairs and started digging through the mounds of paper.

"Wallin, I need you to work your magic on every database you can get your hands on. Arrests. Department of Public Health. Whatever. Get me any result in the city having to do with a Merlin, even if it's about a kid in a Halloween costume."

"Yes, sir."

Nakara called to the guys in the back. "And call Channel 2. I'm ready to go on with Joan Jones."

***

Audrey finished the last sip of her latte and checked the time on her phone. As she was about to leave, Martin Easley weaved through the iron tables outside the coffee shop where they had met once before and plopped down in a chair across from her.

"Meetings," he said, a little out of breath. "They always take longer you think."

"It's okay."

"Well, I'm all ears," he said, unwrapping a scarf from his neck. He placed his bag on the table and pulled out a water bottle.

"I told Jackson about our meeting, and he was furious. Then, when he got your email suggesting Mubashir, he felt like he had no choice. So, he took his anger at us out on the restaurant."

Martin took a long sip. "I thought as much. I've eaten there twice and found the food to be remarkable."

"Well, I feel terrible for them," Audrey said, leaning in. "What can we do?"

"The paper could suspend him. But that, of course, would only worsen the situation. And frankly it would open us up to a lawsuit since his reviews are a matter of his own personal taste and opinion."

"What if I wrote something?"

"Like an op-ed?" Martin asked. "It would be like the paper taking a side in your marital feud. We couldn't publish that."

"Well, what can I do?"

"I don't know, Audrey. Tell all your friends to go. Give Mubashir some publicity on social media."

"No. I want people to read it." She looked right at Martin. "I want *him* to read it."

He shrugged. "My hands are tied."

"What are you going to do about his reviews going forward?" she asked.

"Your husband is acting like a cornered stray. I'm going to see what he does with a little space."

Audrey tilted her head back and looked up at the platinum gray sky. An act of contrition wasn't likely coming from her husband. She really thought that the editor could help make things right. Instead, she had doubled the number of unhelpful men in her life.

***

Joey sat in his car and watched the door of the sandwich shop on Halsted Avenue. He had tailed Anderson Strout there from the Department of Public Health building downtown. Whatever he was doing inside, he was taking his time. Ghosting the fake yuppie at their Buckingham Fountain meetup seemed to only have increased his interest. Anderson, or whatever his name was, had left three voicemails on the burner phone. Joey had to find out more and following him was the extent of his current plan.

It was more than an hour before Anderson emerged from the restaurant. Joey watched him drive out of the parking lot, then headed in. The space was narrow, with tables on one side and a long counter on the other, and noticeably void of any other people. Joey pulled out a stool and was just about to sit down when a guy who looked no more than twenty emerged from the kitchen wearing a dirty apron.

"Hey, we're closed."

"Health inspector?" Joey asked.

"How'd you know?"

"I think that guy wrote up a place I worked at once. Improper food temperature or temperature control. Some bullshit. Anderson I think his name was."

"Yeah, Andy." The young guy picked up a stack of papers off the counter and read the full name. "Andy Truman. He found like nine violations and kept asking where my manager was. I was like, 'I don't know. Dude won't answer his phone.'"

"That's rough," Joey said. "They closed you?"

"Yeah. I swear this guy had it in for us. He spent like twice as long as any other inspector."

"Guess I gotta find another place for lunch."

Joey turned and walked back out to his car. Not only did he have Anderson Strout's real name, but he was sure Andy Truman wasn't a part of the task force charged with finding the casu marzu smuggler. There's no way he would still be doing hour-long health inspections if that were the case, but it didn't explain why he was moonlighting as a sort of vigilante food cop. Joey's morning had produced two answers and a much more troubling question.

***

"You nervous?" Joan Jones asked.

Ken Nakara had never been on television before, and the studio was a little bit overwhelming with all of the cables, cameras and lights. He couldn't help but touch the powdery makeup on his face. Nerves were not an issue though. The Supervisory Special Agent had spent the better part of the last twenty four hours preparing, which included a video Wallin had put together of Joan's interviews regarding the case. Nakara would not let himself be ambushed like Glenn Bitman, the young assistant district attorney.

"One minute back!" the stage manager yelled.

"Just excited to be here," he said.

"I'm sure the producer went over everything," she said, waving a notecard, "but I'm going to start with some questions to help the audience sort of understand what it is you do."

"Fine by me."

Understanding what he did was one of the reasons Nakara's boss approved the TV appearance so quickly. All the worry he had about the call with his Deputy Director was immediately put to rest. Since this type of high-profile case was rare for them, she saw it as an opportunity to make the public aware of the agency. Nakara's motivation for the interview was twofold. He hoped to strike a chord with someone watching who had actual information and could help with the case. And he wanted to scare the smuggler into making a mistake.

"Fifteen seconds!" the stage manager called out.

Joan Jones looked at the return monitor off to the side of the set and gave her oversized hairdo one final pat. Nakara just sat and smiled. The stage manager counted the final seconds back from commercial with his hand and pointed right at the anchor as the red light on the camera went on.

"Welcome back to Channel 2 News at Noon. I'm Joan Jones, and we have a very special guest with us. This is Ken Nakara. I want to make sure I get this right. You're an agent with the Food and Drug Administration Office of Criminal Investigations?"

Nakara nodded. "Supervisory Special Agent. That's correct."

"Say that five times fast," Jones said, mugging for the camera. "Now when I think of the FDA, I think of people approving new prescription drugs and making sure our beef is safe to eat. Can you tell the folks at home what it is you do?"

"Sure. We're in charge of investigating any theft, fraud or counterfeiting of drugs, beef and everything else the FDA regulates."

"And you are the head of a task force that is trying to catch the person responsible for smuggling the casu marzu, that maggot filled cheese, into our city?"

"Yes."

Jones leaned in close. "Do you have any idea who it is?"

"We have identified a possible serial smuggler who we believe has been bringing illegal food items into the area for several years, if not longer."

"Years?!" Joan's eyes went wide, and she put her hand on her chest. "Well, I pressed the assistant district attorney and he assured our viewers that he would prosecute this case, so the big question is, are you going to bring him a suspect?"

"That's our goal. We have identified the street name this individual went by, and I would encourage anyone watching who has solid information to please use the tip line to help bring him to justice."

"Well, you have to tell us that name."

Nakara knew at some point Joan Jones would go off script and try to keep herself at the center of the hype machine.

"Revealing that information would not only compromise the investigation but make our job a lot more difficult."

Joan Jones was out of questions on the card from her producer, but desperately wanted to keep the interview going. "Does the district attorney's office have the name?"

"You can rest easy knowing that everyone who needs it, has it."

Jones could hear a voice from the control room in her ear telling her to go to commercial.

She stared at her guest. He wasn't going to be rattled. The next best thing was a juicy hook for her viewers.

"Well, when that information is made public, do you promise to come back and give us all the details?"

Supervisory Special Agent Ken Nakara knew better than to agree, but he did anyway. "For you, Joan? Sure."

She wrapped the interview, gave the information for the Channel 2 tip line, and tossed to a commercial break. As soon as the red light above the camera turned off, she sprung out of her chair. "I'm going to hold you to that now."

A producer motioned for Nakara to get up, but he just sat there for a moment. There was something about Joan and that studio that gave him goosebumps. For the first time, he felt like they were actually going to catch Merlin.

9

Trey twisted the top off a tiny plastic bottle and sniffed the bright green liquid inside.

"It's a wheatgrass shot," Biv said. "Supposed to be good for you."

"This one smells like the inside of a lawn mower."

He put the lid on and tossed it into the seat back pocket of the hired black sedan.

"You can't say I'm not concerned about your health," the business manager said.

It had been a week since the celebrity chef thought he was being kidnapped and eventually dropped at the doorstep of Dr. Richard Nevins. In that time, Trey hadn't followed a single one of his recommendations. The most exercise he'd gotten was the panic attack-induced run from the tour group near the lake. And his drinking had only increased. So, it was no surprise that his arm pain and chest tightness hadn't gone away. But he could live without the vial of foul green juice.

"We picking Jackson up?" Trey asked.

"No, meeting us there. I wanted to run through a few things with you."

"I got it. There's no speech. I just sit at the head table with the other celebs that the nonprofit wants to show off. Even I can't screw this up."

That's what Biv thought about the lecture at DePaul University and the Halting Hunger Charity Auction. He was going to be glued to his client's side for the time being.

"No, the Orlando trip is back on. I finally got Donnie and them calmed down, but they want to see you in person. I told them it still counts as one of your *Trey Chic* appearances."

Trey groaned. "How many of those do I have left?"

"This year? Ten. And since we're already down that way, we're doing a night in Miami. The numbers aren't good. I'm hoping a public appearance will get some buzz and boost things."

Trey was silent, something that Biv had grown increasingly used to over the years. As they continued down the road in the hired black sedan, all the chef could think about was cooking at his restaurant. Being with MoCho and the guys in that kitchen the other night was the most fun he'd had in months. One second they were all cracking jokes on each other, the next they were scrambling to help when the sauce station fell behind. They were a team in sweat-soaked uniforms. Orders came in. They knocked them out. Trey had disappeared as MoCho sent out the final dishes of the night. He reappeared with an armful of beers for everyone. That feeling at the end of a service was better than any red carpet or throng of screaming fans.

The car came to a stop outside a nondescript white building and Trey's door opened.

"Welcome, Chef Chapman," said a woman holding a clipboard. "Your guest is already inside."

"Thank you."

Trey and Biv walked up the steps and into the nonprofit headquarters. The event was always held in the main lobby, which was the largest space in the building. Modern art that looked like it was painted by a child adorned the walls all the way up to the vaulted ceiling.

Circular tables were spread throughout the floor, not for seating, but for tiered cascades of some of the best food in the city. Each was sponsored by a top restaurant, including *Trey.*

Jackson had filled a small plate beyond capacity and was waiting by the door when his brother arrived.

"I'm going to shake some hands," Biv said. He turned to Jackson. "Don't let him out of your sight."

The brothers laughed as the business manager stepped away, but he was not entirely joking.

"I see you've helped yourself," Trey said. "Anything good?"

"I've already had three of these," Jackson said, pointing to a one-inch square sandwich drenched in a dark brown sauce. "It's a take on torta ahogada, but with mole. Like Guadalajara and Oaxaca had a baby."

"I hope there's some left."

"What do you do here?"

"Hide mostly." Trey realized his joke hadn't landed because he only had half of his brother's attention due to the food. "Nothing. I'm an honorary board member. At the end of the night, I sit up there with a couple other celebs while some big wigs talk."

"Anyone cool?"

"Some old rocker I've never heard of and a former mayor."

"What's this nonprofit for?" Jackson asked as he picked up the last bite off his plate.

"I honestly don't know."

Trey was absolutely obsessed in the kitchen. He once counted individual salt grains for a recipe. But outside of the restaurant, he was not a details kind of guy. When things took off, he had deferred to Biv, and that's how his calendar quickly filled with so many events like this one.

"I think I saw xiaolongbao over there," Jackson said, pointing with his empty plate.

"I love those little juicy pork dumplings." Trey motioned for his brother to lead the way. "Hey, what's going on with you and Audrey?"

"We're fighting about my work."

"Wasn't that always your thing though?" Trey had to raise his voice a little as they weaved through the crowd. Jackson paused briefly to give his brother a look. "Hey, don't act like we don't know. She hated all the reviews you did as favors for Dad."

"It's different this time. She's really upset, Trey. I'm honestly afraid of what she might do."

"Like divorce you?"

Jackson paused to get his food bearings. "I don't think she'd let me off that easily." He spotted the dumpling table to their left. "Aha."

The brothers each picked up a flat-bottomed spoon holding one of the fragile steamed packages. Underneath was finely shredded ginger and a dark liquid. They recognized the aroma before it had even reached their noses.

"Black vinegar," they said simultaneously. Trey slid the entire bite into his mouth.

"That's not how you're supposed to do it," Jackson said.

"Don't tell me how to eat." Trey picked up another spoon and scarfed it down.

The younger brother liked to both honor the tradition and drive his brother nuts. He took a small bite out of the side of the dumpling and let the fatty juice inside pour out onto the spoon. He let it mix with the vinegar and ginger, then slurped it down. The pork-filled wrapper was saved for a bite all on its own.

"I could eat a hundred of these," Jackson said.

"I bet you could." Trey gave his brother's stomach a pat. "What next?"

The Chapman brothers weaved around the room, attempting to sample one of everything over the next hour. They talked about the food, the unseasonably cold weather Chicago was having for September, pretty much anything to avoid the one thing they needed to discuss.

"Should we talk about Dad?" Jackson asked.

"I meant foodwise, but yeah, I guess we should. Have you seen him?"

"Yeah, you?"

Trey nodded. "It was bad. Losing the restaurant is one thing, but I think he might have put the house up as collateral. He's so sad and angry that he'd rather pick a fight than actually let me help him. And he was so drunk."

"So drunk," Jackson echoed. "You could bail him out, right?"

"Yeah, but no one has been coming for years. Did you know he had an intern working there?"

"I think everyone knows after you assaulted him on video."

"I didn't assault him. And it was some other kid's phone." Trey saw Biv heading towards them. "Never mind. Hey, you know Joey's in town?"

"Yeah, he surprised me."

"Trey, they need you up front in about two minutes," Biv said.

"I've got a trip coming up soon," Trey said to Jackson. "We should all get together before that. Joey knows this place. We can come up with a real plan for Dad and the restaurant."

"Great."

"Really good to see you." Trey squeezed his brother's shoulder.

"Stay as long as you like," Biv said, motioning for his client to go first. "Make sure you get some of those little Middle Eastern meatballs at the table near the bar."

And just like that, Jackson was back to thinking about his wife.

***

James Chapman Jr. looked into the mirror behind the bar and rubbed the snow-white stubble on his face. It wasn't so much that he hadn't shaved in days, it was how easily he'd fallen out of his routine. He was a double-edge safety razor man. The kind that butterflied open in the middle to pop a new blade in. Each day started with coffee and a clean shave. When that stopped, so did everything else.

James the restaurant owner always wore a suit. James the restaurant failure wore a windbreaker. And dress pants. He did not own jeans. No matter how much he tugged at his collar, there was no making his outfit look respectable. He started to regret not fixing himself up for the meeting.

The air was noticeably less toxic though, and a quick walk through the kitchen confirmed that the youngest Chapman had ignored his bitter old man and helped anyway. Even the dumpster outside had been emptied. James made his way back to the main dining room and did a slow loop. He ran his finger along the ornate plate rail on the wall. He tapped the brass foot rail of the bar with his shoe. His attempt to soak in all the details that made the restaurant so special was interrupted by the sound of the heavy front door opening, and a young man in an expensive suit walking in.

"You from the bank?"

"Yes."

"Where's Alan?"

"He couldn't make it. My name is Sable."

"Sable? Like the fur?" James shook his head. "Jesus."

"As Alan explained on the phone, I'm here to go through the next steps." He pulled out an envelope and handed it over. "I'm sure you still have the originals of the loan agreement, but I brought a copy just in case."

James tossed it onto a nearby table without even so much as a glance. "I know what it says."

"Great. Then we'll start by sending someone over to inventory the place." Sable pulled out a chair and gave it a quick examination. "If there's anything of value, we'll arrange a sale to help recoup the bank's loss. Of course, you'll need to remove any personal effects."

Sable motioned with his head at a picture of Josephine Chapman on the wall.

"Now wait," James said, starting to lose his temper. "I still have 21 days."

"Technically, that's true."

"Alan and I were going to talk about my options."

"What's there to talk about?" Sable asked, putting his hands in his pockets. "You either become current on what you owe or you don't."

"You can't just waltz in here and talk to me like that. I've been a customer of that bank longer than you've been alive!"

"Let's say you do find the almost $200,000 you owe in time. Then what? How are you going to keep paying with no restaurant?"

"So, you're just going to tear it down?" James couldn't take it anymore. "This is a piece of the city's history!"

Sable glanced around. "I'm sure it was."

"Get out," James said, walking over to the table with the envelope. "Take your papers and get out."

Sable turned and headed for the door instead. "Three weeks."

"And tell Alan we're not done here."

James watched out the window as the young man got into his car and drove off. He walked over to the chair Sable had pulled out and carefully slid it back under the table making sure it was perfectly aligned with the others. The absolute stillness in the room made it look more like a museum than a restaurant. James just stood there, struck by the silence, unable to think of a single thing he would've done differently.

***

Jackson was busy researching the book he had not committed to writing in an effort to take his mind off the troubles that seemed never ending at both work and home. Among the stacks of papers and other periodicals that littered his office, was a clipping on the Feast of the Blessed Sacrament. He had become fascinated by the more than 100-year-old tradition, which is recognized as the largest festival of Portuguese culture in the world. Attending the 4-day event in New Bedford, Massachusetts was not only on his bucket list, but an important stop if he ever made his much-romanticized journey down the East Coast. But his eyes kept darting from the newsprint in his hands to his computer screen.

Martin Easley hadn't sent a single email in two days. The empty inbox was a far worse mental torture than his usual smattering of suggestions. Jackson could only guess as to the meaning. Was his editor mad about Mubashir? Was he actually free to choose whatever restaurant he wanted to review next? Was he about to be fired? Jackson needed to get away from the computer. He also needed a snack. Reading about the feast had made him hungry, but he knew there was no chance of a Portuguese roll filled with marinated tuna, onion and parsley waiting downstairs. Instead, Jackson was surprised to find his wife standing at the counter as he rounded into the kitchen.

"Audrey. I didn't know you were home."

"Well, I am," she said, flipping through a stack of mail.

Jackson attempted to find a safe subject. "I saw Trey last night."

"About time he called. Hasn't he been back in town for weeks?"

"He didn't call. It's a funny story actually." Jackson opened the pantry and began to survey its contents. "I ran into him at the Lake Day Spa. Then he invited me to this nonprofit thing so we could catch up. The food was incredible."

"The only reason you saw your brother was because you randomly bumped into him?" Audrey threw a handful of junk mail into the garbage. "Even Joey had the decency to come by."

Jackson thought she was missing the point but knew better than to mention it. He pulled down a box of olive oil crackers and tore it open. "Well, it was good to see him. I think all three of us are going to get together soon and talk about Dad."

He took a bite and chewed as he waited for a response from his wife, but none came. Jackson opened his mouth again but opted to put a second cracker in over letting more words out. The blank computer screen upstairs was better than this tension. He tucked the box under his arm and started walking out of the kitchen, but Audrey had no intention of letting him retreat.

"Are you going to apologize to Mubashir?"

Jackson only turned back halfway. "I thought we had moved past this."

"Why on earth would you think that?"

"I told you, there's nothing to apologize for, Dear." He walked back and set the box on the counter. "I'm glad you enjoyed the food. It was a wonderful evening. But my review is my review."

Audrey was not surprised or saddened. She wasn't hurt. Their marriage was strong enough to survive this. She just hoped it was strong enough for what she was planning to do. There was only one conclusion in her mind, only one place to make things right. She didn't need Martin Easley's help. But she would need her husband's forgiveness.

"I'm sorry," she whispered. "I'm sorry you feel that way."

As Audrey brushed past him, Jackson had no idea that those were two completely different sentiments.

***

The stakeout that was keeping the Immigration and Customs Enforcement agents busy, which may or may not actually exist, was only one of the reasons that there was no morning briefing for the casu marzu task force. The original Channel 2 tip line message mentioning Merlin had been located, but the name was apparently only overheard at an unidentified underground bar. Ken Nakara had sent one of the OCI agents on a wild goose chase to try and locate it. The other was busy sorting through the thousands of new tips that resulted from Nakara's appearance with Joan Jones, none of which had mentioned the smuggler's correct street name so far. The two remaining members of the task force were having an early lunch together.

Besides a functioning microwave, the community kitchen at the FDA office in Lisle, Illinois also had several small, round tables with wooden chairs that seemed designed to encourage going back to work. Supervisory Special Agent Nakara sat perfectly upright as he removed his sandwich from a zip top bag.

"Didn't you have that yesterday?" Wallin asked.

"I have it every day."

"A chicken sandwich?"

"Yes, a barbecued chicken sandwich," Nakara said, waiting for the inquiry to end to take a bite.

"Why?"

"I like barbecued chicken." Cooked to a minimum 165 degrees Fahrenheit, but he didn't say that part.

Wallin eyed his boss's Tupperware container of broccoli. "No chips or even pretzels?"

"Broccoli has vitamins A, C, K and calcium." Nakara looked at Wallin's microwave burrito. "You should take a multivitamin."

Wallin shrugged and took a bite. Nakara, satisfied that the conversation was over, also began to eat. Lunch was normally a solo endeavor. The contents of his reusable bag never changed, but since breakfast and dinner were always at the dining room table with his wife and daughters, Nakara enjoyed varying the location he took his mid-day meal. Halfway through his sandwich, he was beginning to regret accepting the invitation to join the young, tech expert in the community kitchen until a strange beep emitted from Wallin's phone. He put his burrito down and checked it.

After a few quick taps, Wallin's eyes lit up. "Whoa. It worked!"

"What?" Nakara asked begrudgingly.

Wallin held up his phone, showing a map of Chicago covered in small red dots. "I decided to look into some of the metadata around the original viral image. These dots represent anyone in the city that interacted with that post within 24 hours."

Nakara realized this was not going to be brief and put the other half of his sandwich back in the plastic bag. "Interacted?"

"Yeah, retweet, quote tweet, like, share, etcetera."

"Okay. How does that help us?"

"The only reason I could map them is that these people have geotags on, basically telling the whole world where they're posting from." Wallin could tell that he didn't have the right audience to appreciate his work, so he pulled back on the geeking out. "Never mind, just watch this."

He hit a button, and all the red dots started moving around the map.

"I wrote a program that tracked all those people's posts. This animation is them going backwards in time from when they interacted with that cheese picture." The dots froze and Wallin zoomed in on a large concentration of them in one location.

"What are they all doing together there?" Nakara asked.

"My guess is eating maggot-filled cheese."

Nakara didn't really get it, but he got it enough. "You think you found the exact location the casu marzu was served?"

"I think so. I just need to go back and look at those accounts and see if I can figure out what happened at that address."

"Impressive, Wallin."

"Thank you, sir." He scarfed the rest of his burrito and picked up his phone. "I'll let you know when I have something."

Ken Nakara once again had good news and the rest of his lunch to himself.

***

"Your other brother is Jackson Chapman, the restaurant critic?" Crete stared at the table in the corner where Joey's two brothers sat.

"We all have the same last name. How are you just now piecing that together?"

"Well, you all certainly have your own claim to fame, huh, Merlin?" She leaned down and lowered her voice. "Any more information on the yuppie?"

Joey looked around, but there were only two other people in the nameless bar, and they only seemed interested in quickly raising their blood alcohol levels.

"His real name is Andy Truman. I don't think he's on the task force. Has he called anymore?"

"Nope. You?"

"Yeah, left a bunch of messages. Does he know about this place?"

"Sort of." Crete motioned to the door with her head. "I made the cheese exchange out in the parking lot."

"Damn. Okay."

"What are you guys having?"

"Entree." Joey looked over at his brothers. "Probably easier to just give us a bottle."

She obliged, along with three glasses.

Joey carried everything back to the table, still unsure if he was going to tell them about the trouble coming his way. He had been going back and forth for days. An escape plan had been put in place the moment the maggot-filled cheese showed up on the news. Joey stashed a bag in an airport locker and was prepared to take the first flight available out of the country. Leaving unexpectedly wasn't out of the ordinary, but he knew it meant staying away from Chicago, and maybe even the States, for a while.

He sat down and poured three drinks. Did he owe his family an explanation? Or was it better to just keep them out of it entirely? Joey raised his glass, hoping the answer was inside. His brothers followed.

"Been a while since we were all together," Jackson said.

"Yeah," Trey agreed.

"Should we just get it out of the way?" Jackson asked.

Joey sat back. "Oh, are you going to tell Trey you're a racist?"

"What?" Trey looked from Jackson to Joey.

"Oh, he didn't tell you?"

"I'm not a racist!" Jackson said a little too loudly, drawing the attention of the other two patrons and the bartender. "I was talking about Dad."

"Do I even want to know?" Trey asked.

Joey leaned toward his oldest brother and whispered, "It's a whole white privilege guilt thing. I'll tell you later."

Jackson was not amused. He downed his drink, grabbed the bottle and poured himself another.

"Well, I don't want him losing the house," Trey said.

"Agreed," said Jackson. "I'll pitch in." He looked at his little brother.

"I'm happy to offer support of the moral variety."

"I'll cover it," Trey said, "but I don't see the point in saving the restaurant. I know it means a lot to him, but if it's just been bleeding for two years..."

The other Chapmans nodded.

"It's a shame though. Pretty incredible space," Jackson said.

"Iconic." Trey refilled his glass and held up the almost empty bottle. "Going fast."

Joey motioned for a refill of his own.

"Should we all go see him together?" Jackson asked.

"I'm on a plane tomorrow," Trey said.

"Convenient. Joey?"

"Pass." He stood up and swiped the bottle off the table.

"You just said you'd offer moral support," Jackson said.

"That's true, but I'm still not going." He turned and headed toward the bar.

"Once again, everything falls on me. Just like when Mom died. You were off being the celebrity chef and Joey was God knows where. I was left with Dad and trying to plan a funeral and pick up the pieces. Why would I expect this to be any different?"

Jackson got up.

"Where are you going?" Trey asked.

"Restroom. That okay with you?"

Joey saw the sour look on Jackson's face as they passed each other. He sat down and refilled all three glasses. "What's that all about?"

"A lot of things, I'm guessing."

An hour later, the brothers were well into a third bottle of brown liquor. Joey had decided that he would keep his current problem to himself. The family had enough to deal with. Trey, too, was fighting with the idea of telling Jackson about his desire to exit the spotlight. But he was so confused about how he planned to do so that it only made sense to keep it a secret.

"You guys want to crash at my place?" Trey asked.

"I was planning on it," Joey said.

"Probably a good idea. I honestly don't know if Audrey and I are still in a fight or not."

"From one to ten, how scared are you of your wife?" Joey asked.

"Three. No, five and a half." Jackson raised his glass, but somehow missed his mouth, soaking his shirt in booze.

"You're cut off." Trey went to snatch his brother's glass but knocked it to the floor where it disintegrated.

"Jesus, you guys still can't hold your liquor," Joey said. "Trey, you might want to put your clothes hamper away."

"That was high school!" Jackson slurred.

"Joey, I still can't believe Mom and Dad let you stay at my apartment. You were like twelve."

"They didn't. I told them I was at Anthony Stropetti's."

"Was that the kid with the unicycle?" Jackson asked.

"No, I made him up."

Trey swigged directly from the bottle. "What!?"

"How do you not know about this? He was my excuse for everything." Joey said. "I hopped the bus to your shitty apartment in West Town and watched you guys get drunk on like two beers. Then I wake up in the middle of the night to Jackson pissing into your laundry."

It was a good thing the rest of the patrons of the nameless bar had cleared out because the brothers laughed hysterically for several minutes. Crete walked over and took what was left of the third bottle and the two glasses that were still intact. The night was over.

Jackson stood up first. "That was probably the last time we all stayed under the same roof."

"I should just make you sleep on the bathroom floor," Trey said.

Joey nodded across the bar at Crete, then led his brothers out. "Let's get some tacos first."

10

The hired black sedan pulled up outside the high-rise condo just five hours after Trey's head hit the pillow. He basically lived out of a suitcase at this point, so all he had to do was zip it before heading downstairs. The 35-minute ride to PWK, a small executive airport just north of the city, gave him a few more minutes of sleep. But he was rudely awakened for the second time that morning as his business manager flung the car door open.

The smell hit him first, then one look at his disheveled client told him everything he needed to know. "I thought you hated flying hungover."

"I hate flying, period," Trey said, shielding his eyes as he stumbled out onto the tarmac.

"Well, you've got two and half hours to sleep it off."

"You know I can't sleep on planes." Trey covered his ears to muffle the noise of the jet engines starting up.

Biv tossed their bags at the foot of the steps. "Hope it was worth it."

Trey followed his business manager onto the plane and didn't have to think long about the answer. It was. And that familiar feeling after getting together with his brothers had returned. He wished they were closer, in every meaning of the word. But as the plane started taxiing, Trey knew that would never be the case unless something changed. And in the throes of his worst hangover since the Halting Hunger Charity Auction, the celebrity chef was in no position to brainstorm. He collapsed into a seat and pulled the window shade down.

"When we get there," Biv started, but Trey put his hand up.

"Not yet. Please."

"Fine." Biv pulled out a bottle of ibuprofen and tossed it his way.

Trey looked over at him as he opened the bottle and popped a couple of the small, white pills. As a business manager, Biv Trammel was the best. But as a life companion, he was not.

And that's what he had become over the years. They shared everything; every trip, every success, every failure- not that there were many of those. They had no one else to share them with. And as the wheels lifted off the ground, Trey and Biv started another adventure together.

Trey's anxiety rose as the ground disappeared beneath them. He never had a fear of flying when he traveled the world to learn in restaurants. It was these tiny planes. No one ever talked about the turbulence. It was so much worse than commercial flights. Or how the slightest storm could cause long delays or even postpone a trip. He concluded that anyone jealous of these private charters had never actually been on one. The novelty had worn off long ago and now all Trey could do was close his eyes and pray for his headache to go away.

The Colonial Plaza location of Barnes & Noble was a 3-iron from the Orlando Executive Airport, but that's where the good news ended. Although the car ride was short, the line outside the bookstore went down the block. Trey and Biv were led through the back entrance, and the celebrity slipped into a new chef's coat. The cheers that rang out from the crowd as Trey took his seat were no longer energizing.

"No demo at the news hit, right?" Trey asked, opening the first box of black markers.

"Yeah, you're making the same Thai salad," Biv replied.

"I won't be able to grip a pan, much less chop after this. Can we cancel?"

"They've been promoting the appearance all day. I'll tell them no demo. We'll turn it into an interview."

It was a small victory, but Trey still felt defeated. He gave Biv the nod he was ready for the onslaught, and the velvet rope was opened. First to the table was a blonde-haired woman with a deep tan, white mini-skirt and matching visor.

"What's your name?" Trey asked.

"Mary!" She excitedly handed over her copy of the book. "I'm your biggest fan! We've been to the restaurant in Miami and are so excited you opened one up right here in Orlando."

Trey wanted to correct her. The new restaurant couldn't be more different from the ones he had poured his sweat and inspiration into. He was quite frankly sick of *Chic*. But these events were about efficiency and repetition. Ask the name, sign the book, and don't forget to smile. No one got more than forty-five seconds. There wasn't time for pleasantries, much less unpleasantries.

He finished his scrawl on the title page and handed it back. "Thanks for coming, Mary."

The visor colors changed, but everything else stayed the same for the next ninety minutes including the throbbing in his head. Every person was his biggest fan. They all had every cookbook. Some even showed up wearing his line of aprons. Maybe it was the hangover, but Trey couldn't remember feeling this spent at a signing. His fingers cramped so badly that he signed the last five books with his left hand. No one ever knew the difference though. As the velvet rope closed after the last fan he could've cried, but he felt so dehydrated he doubted anything would come out. The clock on the wall showing 11am was the most painful sight of all. The day had only just begun.

A triple espresso and the car ride across town didn't offer much relief. The celebrity frenzy started again the moment Trey entered News 6, including a dozen photo requests between the front door and the makeup chair. The normal coating of anti-shine didn't cover the lack of sleep on his face, so Biv pressed the makeup artist to cover the bags under his client's eyes. Fully spackled, Trey was led on stage.

A man in his late thirties with jet black hair gelled into place bounded over and stuck out his hand. "I'm Alex."

"Trey." He winced under the grip of his handshake, which seemed aggressive for a local news anchor.

"You okay?"

"You ever signed 200 cookbooks?"

"Sorry to hear we're not doing the demo anymore," Alex said, taking a seat. "Hey, my mother said if you ever need any Cuban recipes, she's happy to teach you."

"I'll keep that in mind."

"One minute, Alex!" a voice yelled from somewhere in the background. The anchor flashed a notecard at his guest. "Don't worry. No curveballs."

Trey faked a smile. The same six questions were handed to every host, anchor and interviewer at each stop. He and Biv used the first couple TV appearances to fine tune his answers. After that, Trey was on autopilot. This would be no different. The chef delivered his well-rehearsed and brief explanation about the cookbook and his favorite recipes in an almost trance-like state.

"Well, Trey Chapman, thanks so much for joining us," Alex said when it was all done.

"Thanks for having me."

"The new cookbook is in stores everywhere," the host said, holding a copy up to the camera. "Before we let you go, what's next, Chef?"

Trey just stared straight ahead. He hadn't heard the question because the interview was over in his mind. But he knew from Biv's frantic gestures behind the camera something wasn't right. He turned to the host.

"What's next?" Alex asked again.

"Uh, I think we're headed over to the new location of *Trey Chic* but that's not 'til later."

"I meant for you and your empire?"

Trey blanked. He didn't have an answer, prepared or otherwise. If his head wasn't so clouded, maybe he could have used the opportunity to end it all. He could say something that would implode the business. Outrage his sponsors. Something that would spread on the internet even before the private jet touched back down in Chicago.

"You're just going to have to wait and find out." The sentence came out as a tease to the viewers, but really Trey was talking to himself just as much.

Biv didn't even wait until they were fully inside the hired black sedan before he started in.

"What was that!? Have you lost your hearing now too?"

Trey flopped into the car and fumbled with the ibuprofen lid. He took two more and chased them down with an entire bottle of water from the pocket on the car door.

"Take it easy," he said, catching his breath. "It's Orlando. This whole place is basically a swamp."

"A swamp with the internet. How long do you think it'll take your tabloid friend, Lindsay McKeil, to find that interview? You think she won't chop that up and turn it into her next hit piece?"

"I need some food." Trey was done with the riot act.

Biv wasn't. "You think all the people who depend on you care if you're hungover? Do you think they have the luxury of getting so drunk they can't do their job properly the next day? So why do you get to?"

That's the part that had the celebrity chef the most confused. He honestly didn't even know how many people depended on him. And he didn't want to imagine what it would mean for their lives if he walked away. Or ran. Or whatever it was going to take to just be James Chapman III again.

"Eat. Shower. Sleep. I don't care," Biv said, no longer looking at his client. "You've got three hours. Get your head on straight."

Trey could feel the water slosh in his otherwise empty stomach, but he could barely keep his eyes open. Food would have to wait.

The nap passed in what felt like five minutes, but the square alarm clock on the postmodern bedside table said otherwise. All Trey wanted to do was stay in the cloud-like bed, but he only had a half hour before yet another hired black sedan would be waiting for him. It was barely enough time for a meal or shower, and he was in desperate need of both. The sweat and booze that had been seeping out of his pores all day clung to the chef coat he was still wearing. It needed to be dry cleaned. Or burned.

Trey sat up and wrestled the offensive piece of clothing off. The sleep had helped, but his hangover was most certainly still there. He walked out of the bedroom and got his bearings in the suite for the first time. The main living area had a small dry bar with a stone high top, two stools and a minifridge. Over by the window was a C-shaped couch with a circular ottoman inside that reminded him of Pacman. Trey found what he was looking for on top of the desk near the entryway. He picked up the room service menu and dialed the phone.

"Yes, I'd like a cheeseburger. Rare. Nothing on it. Just mayo on the side please. And an order of fries. No ketchup or anything, just another side of mayo. Thanks."

He put the phone down and went back through the bedroom to turn on the shower. Steam started to coat the mirror as he finished undressing. Trey liked the water so hot you could almost poach an egg in it. He liked to plug his ears and pretend he was standing underneath a roaring waterfall. It had been over three decades since he shared a tiny bathroom with his two brothers in the Chapman family home, but he was still making up for it. Still making up for the days when all he got was a lukewarm stream. Still trying to forget when it was an ice-cold trickle. If it wasn't for his hunger, Trey would've spent every extra second he had pressed against the warm marble tiles. Instead, he turned off the water and put on the fluffy hotel robe, still dripping wet. He never saw the point of drying off first. As he tore open the plastic on the hotel slippers, there was a knock at the door.

"Room service!"

Trey slid his feet into the plush softness, then walked through the suite and opened the door. The sight of the white linen-covered cart made him salivate. As soon as the waiter left, Trey lifted the steam lid and pushed his finger lightly into the top of the burger. After a smear of mayonnaise on the bun, he took a bite and admired the pink hue inside. Perfectly medium-rare. He had long ago discovered that the elevator ride always brought the patty up a few more degrees and adjusted his order accordingly. The mayo part was something he picked up in France, for both the burger and fries. But he was still a mustard traditionalist when it came to his Chicago hotdogs. Trey didn't even bother wheeling the cart over to the couch, he just sat right in the entryway. Each bite made him feel a little more like himself. There was nothing more familiar than eating a cheeseburger in a hotel suite. And that realization made Trey instantly feel worse.

***

Even through the dark tinted windows of the hired black sedan, the flood lights that illuminated the front of the restaurant seemed harsh. Trey had to squint as he stepped out and onto the red carpet. Then came the familiar clicks from the platoon of photographers and the screams from the army of fans behind them. He looked down, trying to buy his retinas an extra minute to adjust, but the sensory assault continued, this time in the form of a thick Boston accent.

"City of Light!"

Trey looked up and saw the conspicuously large necklace of St. Michael. He didn't need to see the man's face to know it was Donnie Byrnes.

"Orlando. It's called the City of Light," Donnie said, gesturing to the wall of giant bulbs he'd brought in for the event. He stuck his hand out. The last thing Trey wanted to do was shake it, and his hand still aching from the cookbook signing was just one reason why. But in front of all the cameras he had no choice.

"Very literal," Trey said to Donnie. He looked over at the two guys standing next to him. "Fellas."

Trey had never committed their names to memory. The shorter one always wore a V-neck that showed off the top of his chest, revealing more of a dislike for cardio than an affinity for weights. The other one had a strong chin that looked like it had been featured in frequent fights as a kid.

"You're up," Donnie said, motioning for Trey to pose for the photographers.

He walked over to the background with the *Trey Chic* logo plastered on it and forced a smile. Biv replaced him next to the Southie trio. It was his idea to partner up, and sold Trey on how much more quickly they could grow his brand. The namesake restaurants in Chicago, New York and elsewhere took up to eighteen months to open. Donnie and company promised to cut that by two thirds, which was fitting because it seemed like their formal education had ended with fractions. It didn't take Trey very long in the first meeting to figure out that the capital they were venturing came from their parents. But Biv pointed to their successful burger chain across the northeast as proof of their fast casual concept and eventually convinced his client.

"Let's do a few together," Donnie said, and they all entered the frame and put their arms around their celebrity chef.

Trey found out too late that the hangers on didn't want a partner, they just wanted his name. Promises of control came down to contractual fine print. The Boston contingent paid some kid at M.I.T to write a program analyzing the cost of every dish in Trey's cookbooks. They set the menu entirely based on profit margins, at least the required 60% of it that needed to have its namesake's DNA. The rest of it seemed to share its genetic code with Applebee's.

"You're not going to freak out and punch a camera guy, are you?" the one with the V-neck joked while nudging Trey in the ribs.

He had wanted to punch his business manager. The first *Trey Chic* opening was the cause of the biggest fight in their entire relationship. The menu was a bizarre mishmash that Trey was afraid would sink him. But the local critic didn't want to make an enemy of the celebrity and was convinced behind the scenes to paint it as an "eclectic slice of Trey Chapman's evolution as a chef." The bigger problem was that it was packed every night. There was no arguing with the revenue, and he had to accept that the expansion of his empire was nothing more than a cash grab.

"Take Trey inside," Donnie said to his guys. "There are some VIPs in there waiting to meet you."

The one with the chin led the way. Donnie held Biv back though.

"We want to go international. Thinking Toronto first."

"Now's not the best time," the business manager said.

"It's a quick flight from Chicago."

"Is it?" Biv asked, sarcastically.

"You know we can pull out any minute. Especially the way Trey's been acting lately."

"Sounds like the opposite of going international."

"He shows up in Toronto, we cancel two of his other appearances," Donnie said.

"Three." Biv was always negotiating.

"We'll send you a proposal. Let's get you some ribs."

They were, of course, not a Trey Chapman recipe, something the chef couldn't get past the moment he spotted them inside the restaurant. It seemed every VIP eager to meet him wasn't even eating his food. He couldn't take any more undeserved compliments. His bones couldn't take any more handshakes. According to the back of the bottle, Trey wasn't allowed to take any more ibuprofen. All he could do was think of the hotel bed and wait for the day to end.

***

Miami was just a fifty-minute flight from Orlando. There was no bookstore appearance or local news interview. The only thing on the agenda was a stop at the Coconut Grove location of *Trey*. But that didn't mean there was nothing to complain about.

"Planes have schedules," Biv explained. "This isn't an Uber."

"I'm just saying, if we're the ones paying for it, 8am seems a little aggressive. I could've used a couple more hours of sleep."

"Then go to bed earlier."

Trey looked out the window. Just a few minutes outside the city, the landscape turned green. Hundreds of small lakes and ponds added dots of blue. The view was almost peaceful. Almost. Every little bump and drop made Trey's heart skip. He was not a "think happy thoughts" kind of guy, but anything that could help the anxiety was worth a try.

"So 55 soon?"

Biv looked up from his phone. "Yep."

"Hard to top your 50th though."

"I certainly haven't eaten any caviar since."

"You were using it like cocktail sauce- on the shrimp, on the stone crabs." Trey stretched his hands from the floor to near the top of the cabin. "That was like the Eiffel Tower of seafood."

"That was when we decided we needed a restaurant in Miami."

"*Needed*." Trey emphasized the word.

"Well, when you've had that much champagne."

Biv's phone dinged, and he opened the message. He read silently, but Trey could sense it wasn't good. The business manager handed the phone across the aisle. "Lindsay McKeil."

"Diva Chef Ditches Demo" Trey said, reading the headline out loud. There was a screenshot of his mouth agape staring at the camera at the end of the News 6 appearance. He raced through the story, getting more upset with each line. "Trey Chapman pulled his celebrity card and refused to do a cooking demo on-air that was agreed to well in advance. A source at the station said hundreds of dollars of food went to waste. The chef was distant and aloof throughout the interview leaving many to question if he was on drugs at the time. That's bullshit! How can she write that!?"

There was enough truth though, that's why Biv chose not to respond. He just looked out his window. Trey didn't need any help misplacing his anger, and eventually realized he didn't have an audience. The business manager didn't speak again until they were walking down the small set of stairs from the plane to the tarmac.

"I'll see you at the restaurant at five," he said to his client, then picked up his bag and walked away from the hired black sedan.

"Where are you going?"

Biv didn't have an answer, he just knew he needed a break. He had the rest of the day to figure out if that was enough.

***

One hour. That's all it had taken for Trey to get bored. After being dropped off at the hotel, exploring his latest suite including a long shower, and having breakfast, he found himself wandering aimlessly down South Bayshore Drive. Most people would love to have a free day in Miami. But he had no interest in sand, and even less interest in visiting South Beach. So, for the first time since he thought he was being kidnapped, Trey Chapman took Dr. Nevin's advice and went for a walk. He figured it would kill some of the remaining hours before the trip once again turned to business, and the sunshine and fresh air would certainly do him good. At least it would have, had Trey not caught a glimpse of a familiar condo building down a side street.

"How'd you get in?" The woman who answered the door didn't seem surprised nor upset.

The way she let her robe hang spoke volumes about how she knew the man standing in front of her.

"I'm a celebrity."

"How'd you know I'd be here?"

"A guess?" Trey said, sounding somewhere in between sheepish and suave.

"A guess?"

"Well, you usually close down the kitchen around 10. Outta there by 11. Late night dinner followed by drinks, of course. And because you're now a responsible adult, asleep by 2. So, I thought you might be just rolling out of bed. And I wondered if you wanted to roll back in," Trey paused ever so slightly, "Su."

That wasn't her name. And it would be easy to mistake it as some reference to the second in command in a kitchen. But Teresa Ramos was a pastry chef, and one of the best in the city.

She turned and headed toward the bedroom. Trey followed, still mesmerized by the loose curls that swayed as she walked. He hadn't seen her in almost two years, but her hair looked the same as when they had met decades before. There was black and cocoa and brown sugar and tan- all the colors of tiramisu. Trey fell into the covers and was about to say something, but she stopped him.

"We both know you're going to ruin it. Just not yet."

For the next hour or so, he obliged.

Their New York romance had started as a matter of convenience. Proximity and opportunity were two parts of an equation that played out often in restaurants. Trey and Teresa didn't know anyone in the city and worked the same late hours that excluded them from the normal dating scene. The two attractive twenty-somethings could only bump into each other in the kitchen of that Italian fine dining restaurant so many times before nature took its course.

It was a fling. That's what they told each other. Manhattan was merely a shared stop on their culinary paths. But before one of them could leave, it got serious. And almost as soon as it got serious, Trey was packing for France. After the heartbreak, they tried to stay in touch. But time and distance are undefeated.

It took years for him to go days without thinking about her. Eventually his only reminder was the sight of the Italian layered dessert with all the tones of Teresa's hair. Then there was Biv's 50th birthday party and the Noah's Ark of all thing's shellfish. They had no room, but the business manager had a sweet tooth. He just wanted to take a peek at the dessert menu. There, at the bottom, was her name. And the second he read it, Trey Chapman knew he *needed* a restaurant in Miami.

It was an expensive excuse to reconnect, one that Biv never knew about. The trade winds quickly blew the old flame back to life. Trey spent more time leading up to the opening than he had at any of his other namesake restaurants outside of Chicago. But Teresa hadn't forgotten the first go-round. As good as it felt, it was temporary. The celebrity chef's time in Miami had an expiration date. The fling didn't even make it that far though. Trey asked her to be his executive pastry chef. He thought it was a grand gesture. Teresa saw it as going from equal to employee.

She didn't need a job nor a daily reminder of life without him. There was no agonizing when she told Trey she didn't want to see him again. At least not on her part. He made attempts. They were ignored. And for two years he had stopped trying, until an hour before when he knocked on her door.

"I forgot how much I missed cafecito."

"Aren't there Cubans in Chicago?" Teresa asked, leaning against the metal counter.

Trey gestured at the palm trees and blue sky with his tiny cup. "Yeah, but we don't have this."

She took another sip of the frothy, brown liquid. "How long are you here?"

"Just tonight."

"A save-the-restaurant trip?"

Trey set his cup down and stared at her. "What's that supposed to mean?"

"Cooks talk."

"How bad is it?" he asked.

"I don't know exactly, but one of your guys works in my kitchen now. Said they had gone from doing 300 covers a night to 80. He was afraid of the place going under, so he jumped ship."

Trey knew when Biv added Miami to the itinerary that it was serious, but he never imagined that the restaurant could actually be failing.

"Come with me tonight," he said.

"I have to work."

"Right." Trey didn't want whatever this was to end. "Come back to my hotel. I could use another shower."

Teresa finished the last sip of her coffee and stood up straight. "Another time maybe."

He felt stupid. Not because of the rejection, but because he hadn't figured it out sooner.

They could've had coffee at her place. She had led him out into the open. A public place where there would be no scene.

"It really was nice to see you, Trey."

A place where he would have to watch her walk away.

***

The afternoon was a caffeine and emotion-induced blur. Trey had managed to carry himself back to the hotel, but every step was consumed by replaying the events with Teresa. The carousel in his head continued as he laid on top of the sheets. Not even the rush of scalding water during his second shower of the day could get him to think about anything else. It was only when he stood in the mirror putting on his clothes that he finally saw something that bothered him more than the morning. Trey was tired of putting on a chef's coat and not being a chef.

Biv was waiting at the curb as the hired black sedan pulled up. The scene couldn't have been more different from Orlando. There was no red carpet. No flood lights. The two guys with cameras standing near the entrance could easily be mistaken for tourists.

Trey got out of the car and looked a little confused. "I thought this was going to be a thing."

"It's not." Biv waived at the photographers who turned their lenses on Trey. "This is more about what's going on inside, but your face in the papers won't hurt."

The business manager opened the door and they both entered the restaurant. It was one hour until service, but there was no music and no energy, just a waitstaff that seemed to shuffle about. A man with a gray ponytail spotted the duo from far across the restaurant and waved frantically as he walked over.

"Who is that?" Trey whispered.

"Andres. New GM."

"What happened to Marco?"

"He quit."

"What a surprise!" Andres yelled, now halfway to the door.

"You didn't tell them?" Trey said, still in a whisper, but with a hint of anger.

Biv stuck out his hand to hopefully cut off the embrace he knew was coming, but Andres still managed to land a half hug.

The new general manager opened his arms wide again. "Trey! So wonderful to meet you."

It wasn't the hug that bothered the celebrity chef so much as it was the gentleness, like he was being consoled at a funeral.

"What brings you in?" Andres asked, finally uncoiling.

"It's been a while since we've seen the place in action. How many reservations are there tonight?"

"Twenty three."

"That's it!?" Trey exclaimed.

"We get our fair share of walk-ins too."

"Well don't mind us," Biv said.

"Let me know what I can do!"

Trey nodded and they quickly moved away from the eager man. "How long has it been this slow?"

"Too long." Biv pointed to the kitchen. "You want to go see Oscar while I check on the bar?"

"Sure."

Trey went through the swinging door, and it was hard to tell who was more surprised- the guy whose name was on the restaurant or the kitchen full of people who had never met him.

"Is Oscar here?"

"Someone asking for me?" boomed a voice from around the corner, which didn't seem like it could have come from the scrawny man who popped out. His bright red and slightly flaky face caused Trey to pull back in horror.

"You gotta stop getting your chemical peels in the back of a windowless van."

"It's a sunburn."

"You told me Belizeans don't get sunburns."

Oscar laughed and gave his boss a classic bro hug. "What's with the surprise inspection?"

Trey had never seen a kitchen like this, much less one of his. An hour before service should be frenetic. Each station buzzing with activity, playing a game of chicken between being ready and that first ticket printing. But no one moved with any pace or sense of purpose. It told him everything he needed to know about the restaurant. These people had never been slammed, never been in the weeds, and would have no idea what to do if it ever happened.

"Apparently, we're not keeping you guys busy enough back here." Trey leaned in. "Who are all these people?"

Oscar motioned for them to head down the hallway and waited a bit before he started speaking. "I know, it's a lot of new faces."

"*All* new faces. Where are the people I spent weeks training?"

"Most were short timers, just here to get a little experience and get your name on their resumes. But don't worry. These are good guys. You'll see tonight."

Two hours into service, Trey had seen enough. His recipes had been put through a game of telephone. At each station, he witnessed a new affront to his dishes, and it was too much for the perfectionist to handle. He began to wonder if no one came because the food was bad and went on a rampage tasting everything in the kitchen. Trey flung a spoon into the sink and the metal clang startled everyone, including himself. Without saying anything, he turned and pushed his way through the swinging doors, nearly knocking Biv down on the other side.

"You're supposed to look through the little window before you come flying out. That's what it's there for."

"We need to shut it down!" Trey's outburst would've startled diners had there been any.

"Whoa, whoa. What happened?" Biv asked.

"The food isn't right. It's no wonder this place is crumbling," The fire was gone, and his words came out as breathless exhaustion. "I taught every person in that kitchen. Entire days were spent on getting a single component right. I literally put my hands on their hands. I thought I was helping train the next great line of chefs. But these guys... it's just a job. They're barely cooks."

Biv could see it in his client's eyes. Trey had walked into that kitchen already near his breaking point.

"Let's go home."

"I thought it wasn't like an Uber,"

"I called the pilot this morning," the business manager said. "I had a feeling."

"What did we have tomorrow?"

"Doesn't matter." Biv steered them out a side exit. The last thing they both needed was another encounter with Andres. "How long do you need to pack?"

The bumps were the same flying at night, but the worry about the restaurant, the tabloid reporter and the morning with Teresa didn't leave any spare room for that particular anxiety. Trey stared into the darkness outside the window. His retreat to Chicago came with one crumb of clarity. There was no one reliant upon him in Miami.

11

In a relatively short amount of time, Patrick Schuler had carved out quite the life for himself thanks to his gamble on underground dinners. The tangible changes included upgrading from a less than safe apartment on the South Side to a penthouse loft in the swanky River North section of the city. He loved being able to walk everywhere. He loved the view of the Chicago River. He loved the high ceilings, exposed brick walls, and the Carrara marble countertop in the kitchen. What he didn't love was the man standing next to it wearing a gun.

"So you have heard about the illegal casu marzu cheese?" Supervisory Special Agent Ken Nakara asked.

"Yeah. It's all over the news."

The frequency with which the story had been appearing was making Schuler increasingly nervous, and rightfully so.

"And what's your occupation?"

"I'm a chef."

The notepad Nakara was holding did have information in it, but he knew it by heart. Flipping the pages was more for effect.

"I couldn't find a current employer. Are you working now?"

"Yes." Schuler was smart enough to know he was the mouse in this game, but that didn't mean he had to give himself up to the cat.

"Where?" Nakara clicked his pen like he was going to write down the answer.

"Here and there."

Once Wallin's computer program had delivered an address and date, it didn't take long to find the owner of the building. And once they had the name of the renter, it was even easier to piece together that he was an underground chef who liked to serve the macabre. Nakara didn't need to see the look on Schuler's face when he opened the door to know he had the right person, but apparently, he needed to make that clear.

"What'd people like better at your last dinner- the rattlesnake or the antelope?"

Schuler smiled. "You forgot about the snails."

"No, I didn't. No one really likes snails."

"You'd be surprised what people like."

Nakara closed his notepad. "Then why don't you tell me about it."

"Oh, the FDA doesn't want to hear about my cooking," Schuler said, all of the sudden feeling a little more comfortable.

"The Office of Criminal Investigations does."

The two men stared at each other, Schuler pleased with the stalemate and Nakara trying to break it.

"Whoever happened to serve the cheese isn't looking at jail time. I'm guessing the D.A. will go for a fine and be done with it, assuming there's some cooperation involved. We just want the guy who sold it to you."

Schuler had been set on stonewalling the gun-toting man no matter what it took. He had focused so much on trying to not get caught up in the case that he had never considered the alternative. A financial slap on the wrist was nothing compared to the publicity. Of course, if he led anyone back to Merlin the only big break in his life would be his femur.

"I only met the guy once. He was taller than me. Maybe fifty. Wavy, blonde hair."

Nakara started taking notes. "Where'd you meet?"

"Parking lot in Greektown." Schuler didn't hesitate. He had thought about this interrogation a lot.

"What kind of car was he driving?"

"Didn't see. He just sort of appeared from behind a dumpster."

"How'd you contact him?"

"Cell number. It's not working anymore, but I can get it for you."

"What's his name?"

"I don't know his real name. Just goes by Merlin."

Nakara stopped writing and looked at Schuler.

"I know. Silly nickname, right?" the chef asked.

The Supervisory Special Agent had lots more questions, but all that mattered was that one answer. He was on the right track and closer than ever to catching the smuggler. Patrick Schuler planned to do everything he could to keep that from happening and started thinking about an empire of his own.

***

Jackson Chapman had looked at dozens of pictures of *kratai kood maprao*, but for the life of him couldn't see a rabbit. The traditional Thai coconut shredder consisted of a wooden seat with a metal blade at the end tilted upwards that supposedly looked like the furry woodland creature or *kratai*. The tool was the inspiration for the name and cuisine of a restaurant on Kedzie Avenue that Jackson had wanted to try for some time. The idea was shelved, however, as soon as Martin Easley had suggested Rabbit Thai in one of his many emails.

Due to the current precarious relationship with his editor, Jackson felt it best to comb through those old recommendations for his next review. And with colder weather setting in, there was nothing he liked more than a bowl of khao soi. The coconut curry noodle soup from Northern Thailand was the signature dish of the restaurant, and the focus of his critique.

Audrey was not anywhere to be found in the house as Jackson lumbered down the steps to find breakfast and see his work in print. The kitchen was as empty as he had left it the night before, so he walked to the front door to get the paper off the mat. He returned and tossed it on the counter, then started a pot of coffee. Jackson fumbled through the fridge while it brewed but found nothing of interest. He turned his attention to the Tribune and flipped directly to his column. But before he could even enjoy the headline, the critic was infuriated by the half page ad directly underneath.

This is an advertisement encouraging all readers to try Mubashir Mediterranean restaurant for themselves. Anyone familiar with hummus, baba ghanouj and pita, in my opinion, will not be disappointed. Bridgeview is the closest I've ever been to Lebanon, so I won't pretend to know how authentic the kibbeh are, but my mortal taste buds enjoyed every bite. I hope that you'll make the trip to South Harlem Avenue and make up your own mind.
-The Critic's Wife

Jackson threw the paper down in disgust and grabbed his phone. He dialed his wife, but it went to voicemail.

"Hi, you've reached Audrey Jackson..."

For a moment, he considered leaving a message, but that would let her off too easily. He ended the call and paced around the kitchen. There had to be someone he could take his anger out on. Only one name came to mind, and he couldn't press the buttons quick enough.

"This is certainly a surprise," Martin Easley said.

"I know you were involved! You and my wife have been conspiring against me!"

"Jackson, I have no idea what you're talking about and if you don't cease yelling, I'm going to hang up."

Jackson lowered his voice the slightest amount possible. "The ad?! Underneath my review!"

The line went silent for a minute, then there was the rustling of paper as Martin investigated the source of the outrage.

"This is incredibly inappropriate," he said after digesting the copy.

Jackson wanted to continue shouting, but now it seemed his editor was on his side. "So, it wasn't you?"

"No. In fact, she did approach me about writing an op-ed, but I told her I wouldn't have anything to do with it. She clearly found a way to circumvent that."

"Well, the paper needs to run an apology. This is an embarrassment!"

"I certainly agree with you on the latter, Mr. Chapman," Martin said, "but this has to be the end of your marital feud playing out in the paper. In fact, I think it would be best if we held your reviews for the time being."

"You're suspending me!?"

"Call it whatever you want to call it."

Jackson screamed into the phone. "But she did this! She put the ad in the paper..."

Martin fulfilled his promise and hung up, but the loud tirade continued for nearly a full minute before the critic realized it. He tried Audrey's phone again, but still there was no answer. Jackson couldn't just sit and wait for his wife to return home. He stormed up the stairs trying to figure out where to channel his rage in the meantime.

***

Standing outside the Department of Public Health gave Joey mixed feelings. If the casu marzu task force really was onto him, then it was a pretty dumb move. But Andy Truman had continued his relentless quest to meet up, which only increased Joey's desire to find out why. The number of voicemails on the burner phone now numbered in the double digits. So, the stalking was not only necessary, but he was starting to enjoy it.

187

Joey checked the time as Andy left the building, knowing that the thorough health inspector would be gone for a minimum of one hour. Now all he needed was to find his office and an excuse to get in, which he was hoping the contents of his inside jacket pocket would provide. First, he had to make a call.

"Chicago department of public health," said the voice on the other end of the phone.

"Is this Larry?"

"No, Arthur."

"Sorry, wrong number."

Joey made his way to Room 200 and opened the brown-framed double doors with glass panes that led to the main reception area. He walked up to the window and tossed a plastic bag of sweaty lunch meat onto the counter.

"Can I help you?" said the large man behind the glass.

Joey put on his thickest Chicago accent. "Yeah, I was told I needed to get this checked for listerine."

The man stepped back. "Do you mean listeria? I don't think we do that here."

Joey pressed his phone to the thick glass for a moment, praying the receptionist wouldn't look too closely.

"Look, all I know is that I'm supposed to go to the lab." He started to push the bag underneath the window. "Or you can take it."

"No. No. No." The man reeled back even farther.

"I was here a couple months ago. They wanted to check my lettuce for salmon. It's Arthur, right?"

"Yeah, and I think you mean salmonella." The receptionist looked back and forth between the man in front of him and the greasy plastic bag. "You know where you're going?"

"Yep," Joey said, swiping the lunch meat and heading down the hall.

Arthur immediately pulled out a disinfectant wipe and scrubbed the whole area.

Joey did not know where he was going, but that had never stopped him before. Once past the gatekeeper, he proceeded slowly, but confidently through the building. In less than five minutes, he found himself staring at the nameplate outside Andy Truman's office. Joey slipped in and closed the door behind him.

The windowless room was dark and tiny. A cheap-looking desk took up almost half the space, and the roller chair behind it looked like it should've been replaced years ago. The only other piece of furniture was an ancient metal bookshelf and file cabinet combo- the type hipsters would pay big bucks for. Joey rummaged through the paperwork inside, but it was just old inspection reports. He turned to the side wall. The series of neatly framed pictures and newspapers were basically an autobiography. The first paper was a story about tracking down the cause of an outbreak of food borne illness that had sickened thirty-five people across Cook County. Although the ink had faded a little with time, it was clearly Andy Truman pictured among the heroes.

The next clipping was about uncovering a Chinese restaurant full of illegal snakehead fish. While not a major health concern, the invasive species could devastate native populations if released into rivers or other waterways, so Truman was awarded a medal by the mayor. He also posed next to several fish and game wardens, known in Illinois as Conservation Police Officers. Once again, the picture was of a much younger Andy Truman.

Joey got the feeling that this was the story of a career that started with big possibilities. One that had since stalled out. He sat down at the desk and picked up the one personal item in the entire office. It was a photo of Andy and a boy who looked to be about twelve. The other person had been cut out, only a few strands of long hair remained. Joey gently set the silver frame back down. It was hard not to feel sorry. But he couldn't let Truman use him to try and resurrect his career or salvage his marriage or impress his son or whatever it was he was doing.

Thanks to a previous less-than-legal situation, Joey knew that all employees of the city of Chicago had to change their passwords every ninety days. His assumption that Truman was like most people and had to write the ever-rotating combination down was correct, and he found it on a sticky note underneath the desk calendar. Joey logged on and opened the inbox. It wasn't hard to figure out which emails were from the health inspector's boss. And he had a feeling Patrice LuFont would like to know what her employee was doing while on the clock.

***

Having not been able to sleep on the plane, Trey was completely drained by the time he got back to his Gold Coast high-rise condo on the wrong side of midnight. And with nothing better to do, he had slept through most of the following day. He was happy to be home, even if the word didn't have the same meaning as it did for most. Trey had missed his brothers more in two days than he had in the months-long stretches they often went without seeing each other.

Unfortunately, he couldn't get either to answer his texts, so he reached out to the one person who always responded, and secretly hoped it wasn't simply because she was paid to do so.

Trey was looking out the peephole and opened the door before Erica Tomlin even knocked.

"That was a little creepy."

"Want me to close the door and start over?"

She shook her head as she let herself in. "How was Miami?"

"Which part? The restaurant caving in on itself or my ex publicly embarrassing me?"

"I thought you were going to say News 6, but I want to hear more about this ex."

Trey flopped down on a counter stool. "The whole trip was terrible, okay?"

"New calendar," Erica said, waving a piece of paper.

"Do I even want to look?"

"Guess the bright side is you don't have a lot of time to go to the restaurant. Maurice said you were in the weeds the other night every time you took over the grill."

"MoCho," Trey said, "is a known liar. Did you bring me any food?"

"Nope." Erica put the new calendar on the fridge. "You can't get your own dinner?"

Trey's mind flashed to the crowd of tourists with cameras that had him surrounded by the lake. "It didn't go well the last time."

She pulled out her phone and tapped away for a minute. "Pizza will be here in an hour."

"You should have some."

"Can't. I have class."

"What subject?"

"Oh, now you're interested?"

Trey had spent the entire day isolated from the world and needed more human contact. The fact that he actually liked being around his assistant was a bonus, and the flight home had given him time to realize he needed to make better connections with the people in his life. He pulled out the other counter stool and patted it with his hand.

"If you must know," Erica said, pushing the seat back in, "it's mathematical foundations for business. I have two courses left before I get my MBA."

"That's fantastic. What do you want to do?"

"I want my own restaurant empire."

Trey ran his fingers through his hair. "They're not all they're cracked up to be."

"I don't want *your* type of empire. I'm developing a model based on a completely different business that I think could be applied to restaurants."

"Well, if I can help in any way…"

"Oh, don't worry, I'll cut you and Biv in." Erica looked at her phone. "I have to go. Don't forget, pizza is on its way."

"Thank you."

As soon as she left, Trey checked his phone, but there were still no messages. He got up and examined the new calendar on his fridge. Not that he ever truly unpacked, but there was no sense in it based on the latest schedule. The cookbook tour, chock full of interviews and signings, was about to start back up in four days. Trey walked over to the window and looked down at Lake Michigan. Boats sped across the water and people bundled in jackets and scarves walked along the shoreline. There was even a couple picnicking on the sand. Trey had left so many times before, but he realized what starting that cycle again would mean. There would be no more late nights with his brothers. He wouldn't be around when the bank came for Chapman's Steakhouse and his dad. And as conflicted as all those relationships had been, he knew being away meant widening the divide to a point he could never get back across. Trey walked into his bedroom and defiantly emptied his suitcase onto the floor next to his bed. He texted Joey again, determined to not only get the trip canceled, but to finally craft a plan to turn off his celebrity spotlight for good.

***

Despite having twenty-four hours to rein in his emotions, Jackson had failed. His attempt to wait up for his wife succeeded only in the sense that his night had been sleepless. Audrey still hadn't come home, nor returned his numerous calls. The only remaining distraction in his life was the pending exchange with his father, which he had been putting off. However, it seemed like a slightly better option than waiting by the front door all day.

The drive out to the family home in Hinsdale was a mental game of ping pong between the conversation he was about to have and the one he'd been trying to. Jackson was not prepared for either, and the sight as he pulled into the driveway further confirmed it. The garage door was open and littered with half-filled boxes and packing material. He got out of the car and hoped that there was some other explanation besides the obvious.

Jackson pulled out a hastily wrapped picture frame. It was the family portrait that had hung above the fireplace as long as he could remember. The three Chapman boys were all dressed in white against a white background. Their heads, arms and feet seemed to float. It was the source of endless jokes, but it made their mom happy, which was all that mattered.

"It would be more helpful if you put things *in* the boxes," James said, walking out with another armload.

"Dad, what's going on here?"

"I always considered you the smart one."

There was renewed strength in his voice, underneath the sarcasm. The hunched man who had withered for a week was unrecognizable. He was even clean shaven. All that was missing was a suit and matching hat.

"You're not moving. We talked it over and Trey's going to pay off the debt."

"I told you I'm not taking his money," James said, continuing to pack. "I don't need the house. And I'm not losing the restaurant."

"You can't sell the house."

"Why? Because of the memories? It's just a bunch of walls, windows and doors, son."

"Yes, because of the memories. Our entire childhood happened in there. And mom..."

Jackson didn't know how to finish the sentence.

James did. "Your mother isn't the house. And every second inside is a re-minder that she's gone. The only place I've been happy in the past seven years is my restaurant. So, I'd rather live there if I have to."

"You're going to live at the restaurant?"

"I don't know yet."

Jackson kicked one of the few boxes that was already taped closed. "What about all your stuff?"

"I've got a storage unit off Ogden."

"Dad, this is crazy!"

James stopped packing. "Maybe you should get your own house in order before telling me about mine."

Jackson was caught off guard. His father had seen the ad. Of course he had, he read every review. If he wasn't ready for the conversation with his wife, Jackson certainly wasn't ready for a confrontation with his dad. He put his hands up and started walking backward out of the garage.

"The restaurant is gone. It's only a matter of time before they take the building. Where are you going to live then?"

He turned and got in his car but hesitated before driving off. That couldn't be his last memory of the house. Jackson blocked out the garage and focused on the front door. He could still hear exactly how it sounded when he and his brothers would run through and slam it shut. The brass knocker always landed with a thump a half second later. He could hear his mother's voice, her constant plea to close it quietly for once.

As Jackson drove away, he finally understood why his father had to sell the place.

***

Trey stood in front of the 5-story row house in the West Loop and was sure he was in the wrong place. The ornate stonework and carvings on the historic building were way out of his brother's league. He checked the address on his phone one more time before ringing the bell. He was relieved when Joey answered the door.

"This is where you've been staying?"

"Pretty nice, huh?" Joey waved him in, but Trey hesitated. "I'm watching it for a friend."

"Do they know?"

Joey rolled his eyes and turned to walk down the hall. Trey gingerly stepped into the tiled entryway. He pushed the door shut behind him with his foot, and kept his hands jammed into his pockets.

"Are you serious?" Joey asked.

"I'm not leaving any fingerprints."

"The guy's name is Herman. He's a YouTube star and fitness influencer. Whatever the hell that is. We met in Barcelona, and he mentioned this place and that he was never here. Said I could stay anytime I'm back in the city. Really nice guy." Joey opened the fridge. "I'd offer you a beer, but I'm all out. Water?"

"Sure." Trey sat down at the marble kitchen table which looked like it weighed two tons. Joey tossed him a bottle. "What's up?"

"I'm ready to get my life back. There's no one relying on me in Miami, or anywhere else. My conscience is clear. I just need you to help me figure out how. And don't say get drunk."

"You could fake your own death."

Trey shook his head at his brother.

"What?" Joey asked. "Then you take your millions and go live on an island somewhere."

"Death is the opposite of getting my life back. The whole point is to be able to do this more. I want to hang out with you and Jackson. I want to be able to help Dad."

"I don't know how much longer I'm going to be around."

"Why do you have to leave?"

Joey looked down at the ground. "I just do."

Before Trey could argue, Joey popped off the counter. "You gotta get arrested!"

"What?"

"That morality clause thing," Joey said, starting to get excited and pace around the kitchen. "They all mentioned committing a felony. You get led away in cuffs. The picture's all over the papers and internet. No one wants to be partnered with a criminal."

"Wait, I don't want to go to prison."

Joey stopped for a second. "Neither do I."

There was something in the way he said it that made Trey take notice.

"Look, you're a celebrity," Joey said, sitting down next to his brother. "Celebrities don't do time. You'll get a fine or something."

"That's crazy, Joey."

"Is it any crazier than flying around the country signing cookbooks and making the same salad on local news for the rest of your life?"

The description was reductive, but not wrong. His days were spent making money he didn't need and making other people happy. The last thing Trey truly did for himself was the very first restaurant. It was those ten dishes. The career climb after that was certainly his idea, one he thought about a lot. But he couldn't have known that he didn't want the fame until he had it.

Joey could see how distraught his brother looked. "We've kicked this around a lot. Everything else is just a stop gap."

"No, I'm just going to tell Biv and we'll do whatever we need to do to get out of the contracts and close the restaurants."

"I read the contracts. You gotta pay through the nose and you know they'll still sue you. You'll spend years in court fighting lawsuits. And I'm not a lawyer, but you could probably still end up in jail. At least this way it's over quick and you keep all that money you've been killing yourself for. Literally. Isn't that what the doc said?"

Trey stood up and started pulling at his hair. "This is nuts! How is it that me being a criminal is starting to make sense!?"

"You know what you need? You gotta clear your head. When was the last time you went for a run?"

"Planned?" Trey asked, still traumatized by the tourist incident near the lake. "A long time ago."

"You run until your brain turns off. Then when it turns back on, whatever pops in first is what you should do."

"I don't even have any workout clothes."

Joey pointed at the ceiling. "Herman's got a million. His whole closet is full. Brand new with tags and everything."

"I'm not stealing some stranger's clothes."

"He gets 'em for free. I told you he's some fitness guru. Didn't that doctor tell you to start working out more?"

Joey was right. Even if Trey didn't come up with an answer to his life's biggest question, he could at least get a good sweat in. He went upstairs and a few minutes later reappeared in a blue zip-up sweatshirt and bright orange compression pants.

"A little tight," Joey laughed.

"You think?"

"Your legs look like bratwursts."

"Enough," Trey said, tugging at the material. "I'm going to run back to my place. Can you bring my clothes over there later?"

"Yeah, I'll pick up lunch. All of a sudden, I'm craving sausage."

Trey flicked his brother off and left. He only had a few days before his next business trip, which one way or another, he wasn't going on. The odds of the run providing the clarity he needed were slimmer than his pants, but with the clock ticking, anything was worth a try.

***

Jackson hadn't given up on trying to distract himself and, with no restaurant review to plan for, hoped that a culinary mystery would keep the ad and his wife out of his head for at least a few minutes. The bottom shelf of the largest bookcase in his office was devoted to such enigmas, his favorite of which was Brunswick stew. The Southern favorite typically had a tomato base and included beans, vegetables and meat. Jackson was introduced to it with a version made with chicken and pork, but he had found historical accounts using rabbit, squirrel and even possum. The question looming about the dish wasn't what should go in it, but who invented it.

Both Brunswick County, Virginia and Brunswick, Georgia make that claim. Jackson was reading an article about a similar recipe originating in Germany from the early 1800's when he heard the front door open.

He thought about bursting out of the office, but he knew his wife would come up soon enough. Another minute and he heard her feet on the stairs. Then Audrey walked as far into the room as the clutter would allow.

Jackson immediately stood up. "How could you!?"

She had hoped some time would cool her husband off, but she was wrong.

"You embarrassed me! You embarrassed our family! How dare you put our marital quarrel out there for the world to see?" Blood vessels were starting to push out of his bright red forehead. "You had no business getting involved in my work! And how much did that revenge cost!? Thousands of dollars!?"

Audrey waited until he was out of steam. "What I spent was far less than what you cost that restaurant. I've learned to live with the favors to your father. I've had to. I've stayed silent as you served undue praise, but I won't stay silent for your slander."

"Audrey, I've told you..."

She cut him off and for the first time raised her voice. "It was a petty attempt at revenge! And if you continue to say otherwise, then I'm leaving for good. I will not be married to *that* critic anymore."

"I got suspended because of you!"

"Good."

He thought his wife was done hurting him. "Good?"

"Use the time wisely, Jackson."

"What's that supposed to mean?"

"I want nothing more than you to be happy, and I want to be happy with you. But right now, I'm not. So instead of worrying about the next meal and the next review, worry about us. Take however long you have, however long you need, and decide if where you want to go from here works for us both."

Audrey had never gone this far. She never thought she'd have to. But everything was different after witnessing the end of Chapman's Steakhouse. She didn't want Jackson to end up like James. She couldn't watch her husband wither. And because he seemed blind to the possibility, all of this was worth it in Audrey's mind.

She stepped forward and gently touched his hand. As her foot fell, it knocked over a stack of magazines. "And maybe clean this place up a little too," she said, her smile relieving some of the tension.

Jackson took her hand with both of his. He didn't need time to think about what he wanted. Losing Audrey was his biggest fear, far greater than the panic and dread that arose when he thought about actually quitting his job and writing a book.

He bent down and collected the stack of fallen magazines, being careful not to jar loose any of the colored tabs of paper sticking out of the pages. "These are all about the Caribbean descendants who brought their culture and cuisine to Florida." He found a nook for them at the back of his desk. Then started pointing at other piles around the room. "Those are about the Gullah people in the Lowcountry of South Carolina and Georgia. And this bunch is all about the Scandinavian settlers in the Northeast."

Audrey never paid much attention to the jumble. "Okay."

"I know it doesn't look like anything, but it's all research." Jackson looked his wife directly in the eyes. "For my book."

"You're writing a book?"

"No. But I want to."

"That's great. So, write it."

"It's not that simple. I would have to quit my job."

"Even better!" This all sounded like good news to Audrey.

"I don't have the first clue how to find a publisher, much less convince them to pay me to write a book. I haven't written anything over five hundred words in twenty years. And it would take months on the road to research, then who knows how long to actually write it."

Audrey's eyes were wide with excitement. "Months on the road?"

"Yes, we'd be driving down the entire East Coast, stopping at all these little towns from Maine to Florida."

"That's not just a book, Jackson, that's an adventure." She looked around the office and the heaps finally made sense, but now something new bothered her. "You've been collecting this stuff for as long as I've known you. Why did it have to be a secret?"

"Because it's terrifying. And because I knew you wouldn't stop until the hardcover version was sitting on our coffee table."

"Wouldn't stop? I think you mean support."

"Of course. And I really do want to write it someday, I'm just not sure I'm ready yet."

"You're running out of space to get any more ready. Besides, the fear of the work is harder than the work."

"You always loved that saying."

Jackson had fought enough for one day. He wasn't going to quit his job at the paper, at least not any time soon. But he couldn't tell his wife. They needed to be together again. So instead, he started telling her about the book.

"There is a little town, more of a village, at the top of Maine called Estcourt Station..."

***

"Overnight lows will dip into the high 30's," said the Channel 2 weatherman as he pointed at the map. "You may even sew a few flurries overnight, but there won't be any accumulation."

"Oh please, not yet!" Joan Jones said from the anchor desk a few feet away.

"No, but it's coming sooner this year for sure. We may even have a shot at the record low for the month of September- 28.9 degrees, set back in 1942. And as I send it back to you, I just want to say that I love your new hairdo."

"Why thank you, Gus."

The bouffant was gone. Her blonde hair, and some that wasn't hers, now rested on her shoulders with a side part that not only took years off her look but could actually be considered contemporary. The casu marzu story had changed the Midwestern newswoman's popularity and appearance. It had also given her aspirations for the national spotlight. But the story was starting to lose traction online, and Joan had been grasping at straws to keep it going each day. There was the interview with a Wisconsin cheesemaker that fell completely flat. He had no idea why anyone would put maggots in a wheel of pecorino and couldn't find Sardinia on a map if you spotted him the Mediterranean.

Then there was a pointless three minutes spent talking to a food safety expert, who from a technical standpoint said the illegal cheese was perfectly edible. His comments about there being a greater risk of food-borne illness from raw oysters led to several calls to the station from representatives of the National Shellfisheries Association, and an on-air clarification by the host.

Joan looked over at the weatherman. "And just a quick reminder to bring your furry friends inside tonight, right?"

"Absolutely. If you're cold, they're cold."

"Speaking of cold, I know it's been a few days since we had a real update on the casu marzu illegal cheese case, but it's heating up, Gus."

He stared blankly back at her. They had done thousands of shows together, and it was always the same. He wrapped up the forecast. They exchanged some light banter for twenty seconds. Then the host tossed to a commercial break.

"I'll let you handle that forecast," he said, forcing an uncomfortable smile.

"Well, multiple sources have given us here at Channel 2 the name of the chef who served it."

The producer screamed in her ear, "What are you doing!?"

Joan pressed on. "Patrick Schuler, a Chicago native who is known for his series of underground dinners, and get this, he likes to serve bizarre food."

"That was not confirmed! I told you we weren't putting that on air!" the producer yelled.

Gus did his best interpretation of a statue, so Joan turned back and faced the camera head on.

"Now, we want to be fair to Chef Schuler, so this is an open invitation to come on the show, and you can either confirm or deny your involvement in the case. And if anyone has eaten at one of the chef's strange dinners, please let us know. We definitely want to hear about it."

"Joan, I swear to God if you don't go to commercial!!!" the voice in her ear shouted. But she knew exactly what she was doing. This was what TV movies were made of.

Maybe they would use this exact clip. Or let her play herself in a reenactment. Joan had started making notes for a book. And she planned for it all to lead to anchoring the evening news in New York City.

"And don't forget our tip line. We are still looking for information that will help the authorities catch the person responsible for smuggling the cheese into the city. That is the real big fish and the one we expect will do considerable time in jail for the crime. So, Chef Schuler, the ball is in your court. If you have nothing to hide, then you've got the forum to come on and say as much. And if our sources were incorrect, I will be the first to offer you a full apology."

But the source wasn't wrong. Because the source was Patrick Schuler.

12

Trey woke up to a low beeping noise and didn't recognize the bright white ceiling tiles above his head. He looked down at the light blue gown he was wearing, then at the IV in his arm. As he struggled to figure out how he had ended up in a hospital, a young woman carrying a tablet computer entered the room.

"Mr. Chapman, I'm Doctor Boyce."

"Where am I?"

"Rush University Medical Center. You were brought into the emergency room about forty-five minutes ago. What's the last thing you remember?"

"I was on a run. My legs were burning, but I thought that was because I hadn't exercised in a while. Then they started to go numb."

"Meralgia paresthetica."

Trey's voice went soft. "Is it cancer?"

"No. It was most likely the tight yoga pants."

He lifted the sheet to find he was no longer wearing the bright orange compression pants.

"What?"

"We had to cut them off when you arrived. The numbness you described is consistent with extreme pressure on the nerve in your outer thigh."

"My outer thigh?" Trey asked, sitting up in bed.

"That probably isn't what caused that bump though," she said, pointing to the left side of his head.

Trey reached up and felt the knot.

"Were you aware your cholesterol is dangerously high?"

"I knew it was high, but dangerous?"

She looked down at the tablet screen. "The blood panel also showed an electrolyte imbalance, which explains your abnormal EKG."

"EKG? Can you dumb it all down for me? Why did I pass out?"

"It's unclear if you lost consciousness before you hit your head or after. We could run some more tests. You're very lucky someone saw it and called an ambulance."

"If it wasn't just the tight pants, is it going to happen again?"

"I can't say for sure, Mr. Chapman."

"Well, when can I get out of here?"

"We'd like to monitor you for a few more hours at the very least. The person listed as your emergency contact in your phone should be here shortly."

"Who is that?"

The doctor swiped for a moment on the tablet. "A Mr. Trammel." She locked the screen and tucked the device under her arm. "Try and rest for now," she said and walked out of the room.

Trey laid back down. Of course his emergency contact was Biv. Erica had programmed the phone. The celebrity chef was embarrassed, not just at the pants and ending up in the hospital. He was embarrassed that there wasn't anyone else in his life to call when things went wrong. On top of all that, the run hadn't helped Trey with the looming decision. He stared at the ceiling tiles, and it wasn't long before his eyelids got heavy, and he took the doctor's advice.

***

Patrice LuFont had already put in her paperwork for early retirement. The fact that she had to wait until January was mostly bureaucratic red tape. Although her successor had been chosen, she was still technically the boss, so Andy Truman was her problem.

"You want to take a guess why you're in my office?"

Andy put his hand on his chest and leaned forward. "Was it the office pot luck? Look, if I said something that offended you as an African American..."

"Honey, I'm Black with a capital B. I've never been to Africa. What offends me is you running around the city playing Batman."

He wasn't sure how much she knew. "Batman?"

Patrice clicked the mouse on her computer and Andy's voice started coming out of the speakers.

"It's Anderson Strout. I'm still interested. BEEP. Hey man, it's Anderson again. I'm not sure if I got the time or place wrong, but I still want to meet up. BEEP. It's Anderson. I'll double the amount this time. I really want something *unique* for my girlfriend. Let's make this happen. BEEP."

"You want to tell me what it is you've been up to?" Patrice asked.

"Okay. I heard about this guy who smuggled illegal food into the States, and I was trying to set up a meeting."

"Why? You're a health inspector, Andy. You can't be running around and using fake names."

"I know. But with that maggot cheese all over the news, I thought if I could catch the guy, then..." Andy trailed off, and his head went down.

"You're chasing the casu marzu smuggler?" She put her hand to her forehead. "Now I've got to call the FDA and apologize for you meddling in their investigation."

"I was onto this guy before all that came out. Just give me a few more days to try and set up a meeting."

"No way. There were seven more messages on that recording. I have no idea who sent this email or who else they sent it to. It's damage control time. If this were to get on the news or in the paper, we'd have to fire you." Her voice softened. "You've done a lot of good for this department. For the city, really. I know it's not the most exciting job in the world, but it is important."

Andy knew she was right. As exhilarating as the whole thing had been, it was over.

***

Audrey had barely slept the night before. She laid in bed picturing the fantastic road trip Jackson had begun telling her about. Everything would be a new experience, and more importantly, a shared one. She could envision them huddled together on a rocky coastline trying to avoid the salt spray of the frigid North Atlantic, then retreating to a small roadside cafe for a warm bowl of chowder. It would be so different from the white sand beaches and palm trees welcoming them at the end of their journey. That made Audrey think about a bathing suit, and if they even had enough suitcases to pack all the clothes they would need. It was a minor concern, of course.

There was so much to figure out for such an adventure. Would they drive from Chicago or fly and rent a car? How long would they stay in each place? Would they book everything in advance? Or just find a room as they jaunted from town to town? When Audrey's mind had exhausted all the little questions, she had no choice but to confront the big one. When? When would Jackson actually write the book that it had taken him so long to even tell her about? When would he quit his job? Those were the questions that kept her up, and they were the reason she had skipped her morning run and had just walked through the main entrance to the Chicago Tribune on North Stetson Street.

Although she had been to Martin Easley's office only once, she had no trouble remembering how to get there. Audrey didn't break stride as she knocked and walked right up to his desk.

"You should've called," he said, not getting up.

"You wouldn't have answered," she said, sitting down.

"That's why you should've called."

Audrey leaned back. "Then you wouldn't hear how I've solved our mutual problem."

"The problem exists between you and your husband, and I have nothing to say to you after that stunt you pulled."

"Fine, then just listen. Jackson is interested in writing a book. It's apparently something he's been researching for years. It involves a culinary and historical adventure down the East Coast."

"How does that help me?" Martin asked, cutting to the point.

"The trip alone would take weeks, if not, months. Then there's the actual writing. It would not allow Jackson to continue as the paper's restaurant critic. You would get to hire a new one, someone of your own choosing. It's the fresh start and control over the column that you deserve."

"Great. When is he quitting?"

"He's not."

"Then why are you bothering me with this?"

"Jackson is the most risk averse person I've ever met. There is no way he would not only leave a paycheck, but then spend his hard-earned money on the hopes that someone will buy his book. He needs a publisher. And I'd be a fool to think that he would all the sudden be pursuing one now. That's where you come in."

"What makes you think I can make that happen?"

Audrey glanced at the diplomas on the wall. "You're a smart man, Martin. And resourceful. You also know my husband's work better than anyone. He's a talented writer."

"His talent was never the question."

"Championing him would leave a bitter taste in your mouth. That isn't lost on me. I didn't come here because any of this would be easy. My presence in your office has predestined me for another argument. News of the book was not mine to tell. But I am willing to tolerate more short-term discomfort for the longer gain. And I'm betting you are as well."

"You probably think that you've left me no choice. I want to be clear as you leave that is not the case," Martin said as he motioned towards the door. "Good day, Mrs. Chapman."

Audrey slowly stood up. "I only hope to leave you motivated."

She locked eyes with the editor for several seconds before turning to leave. As she exited the office, Audrey was more confident than ever in her next stop. She needed a new bikini.

***

Biv had been sitting in the chair next to the hospital bed for almost an hour. He had no idea why his client was there. That information, he had been told repeatedly, was for family only. He debated calling Joey or Jackson, but didn't want to alarm them if there wasn't any need.

It was the emergency part of being Trey's emergency contact that had his head spinning. He had no idea if it was food poisoning, a sprained ankle or a massive heart attack. But until he knew more, there was no sense in worrying anyone else. The business manager kept himself busy on his phone scouring the tabloids and social media to see if anyone knew about Trey being in the hospital yet. He was just about to start typing out a press release when his client started to wake up.

Trey blinked his eyes open. It took a second to focus on the ceiling tiles, then it all came rushing back. He looked to his right and saw the familiar spiky white crew cut.

"Do you need me to call the nurse?" Biv asked, rising to stand next to the bed.

"No. Can I get out of here?"

"I don't know. They won't tell me anything. What happened?"

208

Trey tilted his head to show off the golf ball-sized knot. "I was running and apparently fell. I had on these stupid tight orange pants. They started to make my legs go numb. But then the doctor was talking about my cholesterol and an EKG. She said they could do more tests to try and figure out what happened."

"Are you okay?"

"I don't know. I guess."

"Does anyone else know you're here?"

"I don't think so."

Biv pulled out his phone. "Then I'm going to say it was dehydration."

"What are you talking about?"

"We need to put out a press release. People in hospitals talk. There's always someone willing to make a few bucks off leaking celebrity gossip."

"Hold on," Trey said, sitting up. "Dehydration is code for a drug problem."

"We can say it's a private matter."

"Give me a minute." Trey said just as Dr. Boyce walked back into the room. She still had the computer tablet tucked under her arm.

"How are you feeling, Mr. Chapman?" she asked.

"My head hurts a little, but otherwise I'm fine."

"Have you considered the tests we talked about?"

Biv jumped in. "Do they have to be done right now?" He looked at Trey. "I can get you set up with Dr. Nevins as soon as we get back."

Trey had always known that Biv Trammel was his biggest supporter, and a fierce advocate. And up until that moment, he thought that he cared about him too. But Trey was sitting in a hospital bed. Business was the furthest thing from his mind, and the fact that it wasn't for the man standing next to him spoke volumes. He didn't have to guess anymore what Biv would do if he asked to end it all. Would he help? Would he fight it? Would he sue him? He had his answer.

"I just want to get out of here."

"Okay," Dr. Boyce said. "I'll discharge you, and I'll make sure the other tests are in the notes so you can schedule them when you're ready. The nurse will be in shortly."

As she left, Trey flipped the sheet off and looked down at the hospital gown he was wearing. "Have you seen my clothes?"

Biv pulled a plastic bag from behind the bed and handed it over. Trey held up the orange pants and examined the legs, which had been completely cut up both sides.

"There's a store across the street. I'll get you an outfit. Need anything else for the trip?"

Trey shook his head.

"All of this because of some tight pants," Biv said with a chuckle as he walked out of the room.

But it wasn't funny to Trey. He had spent weeks considering the livelihoods and feelings of everyone that would be impacted by walking away, most of all Biv. He struggled with disappointing the man who had helped him build it all. Now he was the one disappointed. And angry. And ready to get arrested, even though he had no idea how.

***

"Don't camels weigh like 500 pounds?"

Patrick Schuler pressed his phone to his ear as he paced in front of the large glass windows that overlooked the river. "All I need is like thirty. You can't get that to me by next week?"

The chef hung up, striking out for the second time that afternoon in his attempt to score camel meat. He had tried the supplier in Nevada that came through with the rattlesnake for his *Crawl, Slither, Run* menu. It was the same story with the California importer though. Camel wasn't illegal, but Schuler didn't have a third connection for the exotic meat. The clock was ticking since

Joan Jones had linked him to the casu marzu story on Channel 2 and he needed to capitalize on it with another dinner. Time was just one of the things going against the underground chef, however. With the spotlight on him, he couldn't risk using any illegal ingredients.

Schuler was daydreaming about how much he could charge per plate when there was a knock at his door. He looked through the peephole. He was both tired of people surprising him at his home, and terrified that the man on the other side knew where it was.

"Merlin," he said, opening the door.

Joey pushed his way in. "Why is your name on the news?"

"Probably somebody from that task force. This guy, Nakara, came here and knew I was the one who served the cheese."

"He came here?" Joey asked.

"Yeah. He had a gun and everything. Said I could get in real trouble."

"Does he have any of the cheese?"

Patrick looked confused. "No."

"Do they have any pictures of you serving it?"

"No."

"Then they've got nothing on you," Joey said, beginning a self-guided tour of the condo. "All you have to do is keep your mouth shut."

That was going to be hard for the chef to do. He had reporters calling him asking for an interview. He even had an agent reach out about getting him on a Food Network reality show. Schuler didn't even know chefs had agents. All he knew was that the buzz was building, and it wouldn't last forever. But he needed to put Merlin's mind at ease.

"I gave that agent a wrong description, just like you said."

Joey stared up at the exposed ductwork at the top of the ceiling. "At least you got that part right."

"Look man, I don't even know your real name. I can't tell them anything if I wanted to."

"That's the point."

"But just so you know, this Nakara seems pretty serious. It's like he's got way more information than he was letting on."

Getting rid of Andy Truman was one thing, but Joey knew he couldn't single-handedly shut down a joint task force. He thought about the bag at the airport a lot, and what it would take to get him to use it. Leaving wasn't about where he could escape to, it was about never being able to return. And some idiot chef getting his name mentioned on TV wasn't enough to make him flee Chicago.

"This should go without saying, but what I've learned from dealing with you, is that everything needs saying." Joey got uncomfortably close. "Don't go on the news."

Schuler retreated until his back was pressing on the cold marble countertop. "Of course." Joey turned for the door, feeling in his gut this would be the last time he needed to see him.

The chef, however, couldn't help himself. "Hey, any chance you can get your hands on some camel meat? I can't find the damn pachyderm anywhere."

Of course he couldn't. He would have to know that camel is an important part of the Somali diet. And he would have to know that the largest population of Somalis in the United States was in the Twin Cities of Minnesota. And he would have to know Bashiir, who made the best camel burger at his grocery & deli in St. Paul. It would help if he even knew what group of animals they belonged to. Of course, Merlin knew all those things.

"They're not pachyderms. They're ungulates," Joey said, opening the door. "And no."

***

Always start with the boss.

Unless, of course, she starts with you. Ken Nakara wasn't even to the email portion of his morning and had just sat down in his office to his morning tea when the phone rang. Why is Patrick Schuler being mentioned on the news? Who leaked his name? The Deputy Director demanded answers the Supervisory Special Agent didn't have. The task force was supposed to be Nakara's launching pad to a promotion. But after a verbal lashing and getting hung up on mid-sentence, he figured that was getting less and less likely despite the team's recent success.

His tea now cold, Nakara walked to the community kitchen and put it in the microwave.

As the mug spun on the turntable inside the machine, one of the rookie ICE agents bounded in.

"Another one of your high fiber meals?"

"Tea," Nakara said.

"I think the sponge looks a little jealous," he whispered.

"I take it your stakeout is over."

The rookie aggressively pulled several paper towels off the roll above the sink. "Yep."

Nakara wanted to put both agents in separate rooms and play the prisoner's dilemma to see if their stories would match up, but he didn't have time for games. Their participation, or lack thereof, would be documented in his final report. But their return did give him an idea on how to exact a little payback. The microwave beeped. Nakara retrieved his mug.

"See you at the briefing then."

When the Supervisory Special Agent was steps from his office, he heard his phone ring again. He raced in, thinking it was his boss, and sloshed hot tea on his hand. Nakara let out a rare expletive as he shook off the hot liquid and answered the phone.

"Hello."

"Is this Ken Nakara?" the voice asked.

"Yes."

"My name is Patrice LuFont. I work at the Department of Public Health."

He sat down. "How may I help you, Ms. LuFont?"

"Actually, I'm calling to apologize. I just found out one of our health inspectors, Andy Truman, has been attempting to catch your smuggler on his own."

"What? Why?"

"Apparently it started before your task force was assembled. Several weeks ago, he bought some illegal cheese off a woman, and he was trying to set a meeting with the man who he believed was in charge. I'm forwarding you an email that was sent to me anonymously. It includes messages he left using a fake name."

Ken Nakara could feel a layer of anger-induced sweat forming on the back of his neck and tugged at his collar. In the past ten minutes, he had been yelled at by his boss, burned the back of his hand, and now found out his investigation may be compromised. But Nakara was not one to shoot the messenger. He took a deep breath.

"I want to meet with him as soon as possible."

"Absolutely," Patrice said. "I'll send him to your office this afternoon. Andy's a good man, Mr. Nakara, just a little excitable."

"Thank you," he said, and hung up.

Nakara picked up his tea, but any chance of a calm start to his day had passed. There was no point in the ritual. The standard issue analog clock on the wall said it was time for his morning briefing anyway.

Inside the conference room, the entire task force was assembled for the first time in over a week. Supervisory Special Agent Ken Nakara marched in and got right to it.

"Which one of you leaked Schuler's name to the news?" he asked.

No one spoke.

"The only people who knew about his involvement are in this room, so don't make me ask again."

"It wasn't us," said the ICE agent who was in the kitchen earlier. "We didn't know anything about the guy until we heard it on Channel 2."

"Because of your stakeout?" the older OCI agent asked, putting the last word in air quotes.

"You got a problem?" the other ICE agent asked.

"Yeah, you guys are supposed to be a part of this team, but you haven't done jack!"

"Quiet!" Nakara yelled.

The younger OCI agent slowly raised his hand.

"What?" Nakara said, gruffly.

"No one has said anything on the tip line about Schuler. So, if it wasn't one of us, then Joan Jones or someone at the station must have more information than they're telling us. She's, like, obsessed with this story."

Nakara thought for a moment.

"Wallin, can you write one of your programs to go back and search for any mention of the chef on social media before Joan outed him?"

"Sure thing."

"We've got another problem. I just found out a health inspector has been running his own rogue investigation into the smuggler. I'm having him come in this afternoon. Wallin, OCI, I want you guys there for the debrief."

"What about us?" asked one of the ICE agents.

"Since you guys like stakeouts so much, I want you to go sit on Channel 2. Note everyone who goes in and out of the building. If Joan Jones or someone else has a secret source, I want to know about it."

The ICE agents grumbled.

He stared them down. "Is there a problem?"

"No, sir," they said simultaneously.

Nakara didn't love that the assignment smelled of retribution, but someone had to put them in their place. And it turned out, the place he was putting them couldn't be more right.

The automatic doors sprung open as Trey walked past the front of the store, but he wasn't ready to go in. He needed to catch his breath after the hurried walk through the neighborhood, so he went around the side of the building into the alley. The celebrity chef had taken more precautions on this outing to go unnoticed. He took off his sunglasses and lowered his hoodie. The knot on the side of his head was still there. The pain was completely gone though. He attributed that to the best night of sleep he'd had in as long as he could remember.

The afternoon in the hospital had given him clarity, and the evening at his high-rise condo had given him confidence. Thanks to Erica's assistance on the phone, Trey had managed to order a movie. By the time he got to the end of *Brewster's Millions*, he understood what Joey meant. What he was about to do wouldn't make sense to anyone, and he was okay with that. Just as Montgomery Brewster got a chance to explain himself, so would Trey. He awoke refreshed and ready to put his plan into action. And now that he was no longer panting, the celebrity chef flipped his hoodie back up and walked into the store. He avoided eye contact with the clerk and disappeared down the first aisle. Before he had a chance to find the section he was looking for, his cell phone rang.

"Hey, Jackson."

"Are you okay? Audrey just read me this crazy story about you being in the hospital."

Trey didn't have to look to know it was Lindsay McKeil. "Yeah."

"It says you passed out while running because your pants were too tight. But Biv called it dehydration."

"Of course he did," Trey muttered to himself. "Look, don't believe everything you read. Especially the tabloids."

This was just more proof that she wouldn't stop. At least jail would be temporary.

"I'm just worried about you," Jackson said.

A little kid had been staring at Trey, which got the attention of her mother, so he quickly walked down the aisle and turned the corner.

"I'm fine. Better than ever, in fact. Did you talk to Dad?"

"Yeah. He's selling the house. And Trey, I think it's the right move."

"Why?"

"It's all too much. Too much house. Too much stuff. Too much mom."

Trey found the section he was looking for. "Where's he going to stay?"

"He doesn't know yet, but he said he'd rather live at the restaurant than lose it."

"Live at the restaurant!?"

"I know. I told him it doesn't make any sense, especially since the bank owns the land, but you know Dad. And I can't really deal with it right now because I've got a lot going on between the paper and Audrey."

Trey picked up a very realistic looking toy handgun off the shelf. "Me too."

13

The gun was not having the effect Trey was hoping for. He had covered the orange tip with an old black marker left over from a book signing, and thought the fake firearm looked very real when he was practicing in the mirror.

But the teller immediately recognized the celebrity chef and pulled her finger away from the silent alarm. The customers in line at TW Bank & Loan looked more bewildered than scared. Some even went back to filling out their deposit slips. One woman slowly raised her phone to take a picture. Even the security guard by the door stood motionless, not sure what to do.

"This is a stickup!" Trey yelled again, this time with more emphasis.

He raised the gun, as if to fire, hoping that his crime would seem more... real. Still, everyone just stared back at him. Trey looked around and instead of panic, he saw smiles starting to spread. They were small at first, but soon wide grins turned into nervous laughter. The hostages had called his bluff. There would be no shots ringing out. That was impossible anyway. Trey let out a sigh and lowered his arm.

The bank manager scurried out of his office to investigate the commotion. He was a rotund man in a sloppy suit who upon seeing Trey Chapman holding a gun in his branch nearly doubled over to the floor with an almost inaudible wheezy laugh.

"Making a withdrawal, Mr. Chapman?" the manager asked, striding right up to the robber and giving him a wink and fake punch to the ribs.

Trey Chapman was now just as confused as everyone watching him. This was not going to plan. The alarms should be ringing.

"I'm robbing the bank," Trey said matter-of-factly.

"How much do you need?" the manager chuckled. "Half the money in here is yours."

Trey looked around, but having never been there before he was unclear as to how that could be possible. "It is?"

"Your whole family has been banking here since before I started."

"Everything okay, boss?" the security guard asked, finally doing something.

"We're fine," the manager said, waving him off. He reached down and grabbed the gun. Trey, still in a daze as to how the situation was backfiring, made no attempt to stop him. He just watched as the fat man admired the toy, then waved it around mockingly.

"Pretty convincing," the manager said.

"I'm robbing the bank," Trey whispered, but no one could hear him. With the bizarre situation seemingly under control everyone went about their affairs and the din of doing business returned. Trey seemed like just another customer waiting his turn.

"You celebrities," the manager said, shaking his head. "Oh, you should've worn those tight orange pants! That would've been hilarious."

This was supposed to be the grand last act of Trey Chapman, the celebrity chef. The shackles on his life were supposed to fall off as the handcuffs went on. The pictures of him being led away in a police car would dominate the news cycle. Lindsay McKeil would get her one last story. He had even been thinking about a quote to give her. But Trey couldn't even get himself arrested, which led him to the most painful conclusion of all.

He looked at the bank manager. "How much money do I have here?"

"Come with me," the fat man said, leading him back towards his office.

Trey had no idea how much it would take. He hadn't read the contracts. He had never hired a lawyer. Someone was about to put a dollar sign on how much his privacy and time were worth. And that person was Biv.

"Here's your gun back," the manager chuckled.

"Keep it," Trey said, pushing it towards him. "Hey, does the bank own the land that Chapman's Steakhouse is on?"

"Yes. I think Alan is gone for the day, but let me introduce you to Sable."

"Sable? Jesus."

Trey needed a drink. Now that he wasn't headed to the police station, that was an option.

***

Jackson got off the elevator and slowly made his way to Martin Easley's office. He had managed a truce at home, albeit a temporary one. There were only two possibilities, in his mind, for this meeting with his editor. Either he was about to strike a second ceasefire or simply be fired. Jackson stopped several feet from the office door and knocked from a distance.

"Please, come in."

Jackson barely crossed the threshold.

Martin was prepared to be annoyed, but not this quickly. "Have a seat."

"If you're terminating me, then I won't stay long enough to need one."

"For God's sake, Jackson, just sit down."

The critic looked at the diplomas on the wall, then angled a chair so that they would be out of view. Then he took a seat.

"You are not being fired. Audrey told me about your desire to write a book."

Jackson's face went flush immediately. "How dare she?!"

"Quit being so damn proud. What has stubbornness ever accomplished?"

"What I do or want to do in my free time is none of your business."

Martin sighed. "Do you honestly think I called you in to tattle on your wife and rile you up? Just listen for a moment. I'm in the process of lining up a publisher for you."

Jackson eyed the editor. "Why would you do that?"

"Because I'll get to hire a new critic."

"So, I have to quit?"

"I'm sure with your vocabulary you can come up with a more pleasant term, but yes," Martin said, flopping back in his chair. "If you want to go on your odyssey and write your book, you have to quit."

Jackson began to feel as though he didn't have a choice in the matter, which made the anger rise back up. The situation seemed decided before he entered the office. The way his editor sat screamed "checkmate." Audrey's involvement only forced his hand more. He couldn't possibly turn this down. The situation at home would become unlivable. Surely there had to be another outcome than the end of his job or the end of his marriage.

Jackson stared at Martin trying to figure out if there was a way to get the upper hand back.

"Chicago has been lucky to have you," the editor continued, "but I'm excited for more people to get to read your work."

Jackson had been looking at it all wrong. He didn't have to like Martin's motivation. He didn't have to like Martin. This was an opportunity. One he'd been too scared to go after alone. One that his biggest supporter and best friend had helped make happen. This wasn't Audrey trying to force him to live up to his potential. It was Audrey trying to help him follow a long-held dream.

"If I do this, I want full autonomy to review whatever I want before I leave."

Martin laughed. "I was under the impression that's what you'd been doing."

"And I have one request for my successor," Jackson said. "This job can do a lot of good. Find someone who will do more than I did. Find someone who will spotlight the deserving; the people who are taking risks and trying to change their lives."

"I couldn't help but already give your replacement some thought, and I've decided that I'm not going to jump right in. I'm going to audition people for a week or two at a time, see who really connects with the city and the readers."

"I think that's wise."

"Do you know Isaiah Williams? He's a copy editor here."

"No, I don't believe so."

"He pops up at random spots on weekends to sell these triple-cut stuffed pork chops that he smokes. They're outrageous. He's got over 150,000 followers on social media. He's going to get first crack, I think."

Jackson smiled. "That's 150,000 more than I've got."

"It's not too late. Maybe you should start an account for your journey."

Jackson stood up, and after a brief pause, stuck out his hand. "Thank you, Martin."

It was the first handshake they'd shared in five years, and even though their business wasn't officially complete, it would be their last.

***

Andy Truman was supposed to be inspecting La Vaca Brava, a fast casual Mexican restaurant in Belmont Gardens, but instead was seated in front of four of the six members of the casu marzu task force. The conference room at the Food and Drug Administration in Lisle was now serving as more of an interrogation room. Andy was both excited to be involved, and terrified at the intensity of the situation.

"Look, man, I was just trying to help."

Ken Nakara sat directly across from him, flanked by the two OCI agents on his left and Wallin on his right. "Well, you didn't, and now my job is to figure out how much you've screwed things up for us."

Nakara was frustrated. Each promising lead kept fizzling out almost immediately.

Wallin's social media scrub for all things Patrick Schuler was a bust. He got a few mentions each time he hosted a dinner, but there was nothing helpful before Joan Jones spilled the beans about his involvement. Now there was too much chatter around the underground chef to even sort through. His team had reached a dead end.

"Did the guy use a code name?" one of the OCI agents asked.

"No," Andy said.

Nakara looked at the agent. "Let me handle the questions."

"Sorry."

Between the morning's call and the time the overzealous health inspector arrived, Supervisory Special Agent Ken Nakara had created a detailed list of questions that he wanted to ask in a certain order. They were typed up and on a clipboard in his lap. There was a method, and everything needed to be well documented. Apparently, he hadn't made that clear enough to his team ahead of the inquisition.

"Before you failed to set up a meeting with the man, you made contact with a woman, correct?"

"Yeah."

"Can you describe her?"

Andy's arms went up and out. "She was enormous."

"Not cool," Wallin said.

"I mean it. She was over six feet tall and built like a powerlifter. She could start for the Bears o-line tomorrow."

"They could use the help," the other OCI agent said, getting the laugh he was looking for from his partner.

Nakara shot them a sideways glance. "What did she sell you?"

"Some sort of unpasteurized cheese. She said it was from France, but I'm not sure. Didn't really seem that illegal to me, that's why I tried to get her to sell me something else. Then the picture of the maggot cheese got on the news, and I get a call from this guy. Like I said, it was before you were even working it."

"And that was your only contact with the woman?"

"Yes."

"What can you tell me about the man who called you?"

"Not much," Andy said, starting to feel a little more comfortable. "We only talked that once. We set up a meet, but he didn't show."

"You probably spooked him," one OCI agent said.

"If he's gone underground, we'll never catch him," added the other.

"Seriously guys!?" Nakara yelled. He looked back down at his list. "Aw, you made me skip a question. Go back to the meeting with the woman. Where did that take place?"

"This sketchy little parking lot off some alley in Near North."

"Was it for a business?"

"Sort of."

"Sort of? What's the name?"

Andy leaned forward. "That's the thing. There isn't one. I even tried to look it up at work, but there's no record of it. The rest of the address is for some bougie hotel, but there's a door back there that definitely goes to something else."

"Could it have been a bar?"

"Sure."

The hair stood up on Nakara's arms. The only tip sent in to Channel 2 that correctly identified Merlin mentioned a nameless bar. He turned to the OCI agents. "You guys check out any places in Near North when you were following up that tip?"

The agents looked at each other. "We went to so many, boss."

"I can take you there!" Andy said, a little too excitedly.

Nakara looked at his list of questions. The rest could wait. "Let me get my keys."

***

224

After leaving TW Bank & Loan, Trey had walked straight to the nameless bar. He was unfamiliar with the entrance policy, so he banged on the door for several minutes. Crete decided to finally let the celebrity chef in, but not before calling his little brother, who agreed to get there as soon as he could.

There was no one else looking to get drunk before lunch, so Trey had the place to himself. He took a seat at the counter, directly in front of the bartender.

"Bourbon, please."

Crete grabbed a bottle of brown liquid and poured a small glass.

"Can we do that thing where you leave the bottle?"

"No."

He downed the drink and motioned for another. "Then you might want to pull up a seat."

She refilled the glass, then looked back at the security feed on the TV behind the bar, wondering how long it would take Merlin to get there.

Trey didn't know what to do next. He had honestly gotten himself a little excited about jail. It would've been a totally new experience. He thought about the types of characters he would be with in the holding cell. Maybe he would even make a new friend. And there would be no commitments. He wouldn't have to give any speeches or sign any cookbooks. Instead, Trey was headed back to a much tinier, sadly familiar prison. This time tomorrow, he and Biv would be in the air. He hadn't even paid enough attention to the calendar on his fridge to remember where they were headed. Trey finished his second glass of bourbon. He hated to fly hungover.

"Another please."

"I'm not sure that's such a good idea."

"It's a great idea. I just robbed a bank."

"You what!?" Crete said, now checking the security feed for cops too.

"Well, I tried. I didn't get any money or anything." Trey held up his left hand. "I thought I was gonna leave in cuffs. Instead, I left with paper cuts. So how about that drink?"

"I don't understand," she said, giving him another small pour, "but this is your last one until your brother shows up."

"Which one?" Trey asked happily.

"Merlin."

"Merlin?"

It never dawned on Crete that the Chapman family may not know about the youngest brother's extracurriculars. It took her a minute to remember his actual name. "Uh, Joey."

Trey was confused but was more interested in the drink.

Crete put the bottle away and just stared at the TV, wondering who would show up first.

***

The seven-year-old Toyota Camry was not exactly the poster vehicle for sting operations. It had no lights or siren, and despite being on a freeway, Ken Nakara had no interest in making it a high-speed endeavor. The twenty-five-mile trip back to the city was going to take a while. Andy Truman was loving it though. Maybe even a little more because he got to ride shotgun. Wallin was not, as he sat sandwiched between the two OCI agents in the back seat.

"How many miles you got on this?" one of them asked.

Nakara looked down at the odometer. "121,723."

"Oh, you can get 200 out of it easy. These things will run forever."

"You know what I like?" the other agent said, leaning across Wallin. "The Sonata."

"Is that a Hyundai?" the first agent asked.

"It is. I was surprised too."

Wallin put his headphones in. He could be deep in the bowels of FBI headquarters in Washington helping extract bitcoin from ransomware hackers. Or at the Pentagon writing code to take over enemy unmanned aerial vehicles.

Instead, he was killing time in the backseat of a family sedan by writing a program to alert him to anything that popped up online relating to a case about a wheel of cheese filled with maggots.

Nakara ignored the banter behind him and focused on the road as he began to merge towards the Eisenhower Expressway.

"You're not taking the Ike, are you?" Andy asked.

"Yes, I am."

"That's a mistake," the health inspector said.

A lengthy debate ensued, which the two OCI agents were more than happy to be a part of. Ken Nakara was not. The only positive so far for the Supervisory Special Agent was that he would be reimbursed for the mileage.

***

Joey finally popped up on the TV behind the bar and Crete couldn't press the button fast enough to let him in. After the loud buzz, he entered and could see that his brother was already half in the bag. Trey looked over and once he saw Joey immediately held his glass up to the bartender.

"Can I have another one now please?"

Crete looked at Joey, who waved her off.

"What's up with the 11am bender?" Joey asked, taking a seat.

"Because the 10am bank robbery didn't go so well."

"Bank robbery?"

"Get arrested, you said. It's the only way, you said. Well guess what? I couldn't even get that part right."

Joey looked underneath his brother's stool. "Wait, if you didn't get arrested, then where's the bag of cash?"

"What bag of cash?"

"Two things can happen when you rob a bank. You leave in cuffs or you leave with cash."

Trey spun to look at his brother directly. "Unless you try and rob the bank that our family, including myself apparently, has been using for decades."

"What?"

"The manager laughed at me. Took the gun right out of my hand."

"Gun!?"

"It was a toy," Trey said, his speech now starting to slur.

"So, what did you do?"

"I bought the restaurant."

Joey was having a hard time following the whole bizarre tale. "You bought Chapman's Steakhouse?"

"Yep. And the land. I bought the restaurant, the land, the dirt, everything."

"Why?"

"Because I could. Turns out I have a *lot* of money. Figured I might as well do something good with it."

"Does Dad know?"

"Nope. Not yet. Maybe I should be like his secret Santa," Trey said. He puffed his cheeks out and used his arms to mimic a fat belly. "Ho ho ho." That refrain eventually turned into laughter and Trey almost fell off the stool before Joey steadied him.

Outside, Ken Nakara eased the car into the tight parking lot. All five men piled out and made their way to the door. Andy Truman couldn't help but smile. Here he was on an operation with an actual task force. It was just what he needed to get his name back in the papers and turn his career around. He stood behind Nakara as the Supervisory Special Agent knocked on the door.

Crete whirled around to look at the security feed on the TV behind the bar and started to panic.

"They've got guns!" she said.

"How did they find me here?" Trey asked.

Joey stood up and leaned across the bar to get a closer look. He saw Andy Truman.

"They're here for me."

The situation started to instantly sober Trey up. "What are you talking about?"

"I'm in trouble."

"What kind of trouble?"

"Like jail trouble," he said, his eyes darting around the room. "And I'm not going. Crete, is there a back way out of here?"

"This way," she said, flipping open the drawbridge-looking section of the bar. Joey hurried through with his brother right behind him.

"I'm coming with you."

"Fine," Joey said.

Crete led them into a small back room and used her impressive strength to push a massive bookcase down the wall a few feet. She unscrewed a metal plate the size of a hotel sheet pan.

"Once you're through, go right," she said. "There will be a door that will take you out near the bathrooms just off the lobby of the hotel. I'll make 'em wait outside as long as I can."

"Thanks, Crete. I owe you," Joey said.

The brothers squeezed through the opening, then the bartender replaced everything behind them.

Trey tried to get some answers as they made their way down the dark hallway.

"She called you Merlin earlier. Does this have anything to do with that?"

"You know that story on the news about casu marzu?"

"That was you!?"

"Yeah."

"Wait, you're some sort of smuggler?"

Joey put up his hand for his brother to be quiet as he opened the door. With no one in sight, they hurried past the bathroom and into the lobby. As soon as they were on the street, Trey went back to asking questions.

"What else have you smuggled?"

"Horse meat. Foie gras. A little absinthe. Some rare birds." He looked around to get his bearings. "I need to get to the airport."

"You're leaving?"

"I kind of have to."

It was too much too fast for Trey to take in. Unfortunately, it didn't look like his little brother had any plans to slow down. He needed as much time with him as possible to try to make sense of it all and figure out what to do.

"My place is only a few minutes away. We can take my car."

"You have a car?"

Several, but Trey didn't need to say that part. His brother would see soon enough.

***

After five minutes of uninterrupted knocking, it was clear the assembly on her unwelcome mat wouldn't go away easily, so Crete finally opened the door.

"Can I help you?"

Nakara and his men looked up at the enormous bartender.

"That's her!" Andy shouted.

"Whoa," said the younger OCI agent.

Even Wallin shook his head. "Damn, you were right."

Crete was savvy though. She knew that it was Andy's word against hers, so she was prepared to let nothing on.

"Do I know you?"

"Yeah, you sold me illegal cheese!"

Nakara put his hand up to silence the bunch. He was tired of them stepping on his authority, and he was already hoping this would be the last task force he ever had to lead.

"I'm Supervisory Special Agent Ken Nakara of the FDAOCI. We're investigating the smuggling of an illegal cheese called casu marzu into the city. May we come in?"

He knew they needed to be invited. She knew that too. "No. I'm the only one here anyway."

From what Nakara could see, that appeared to be the truth. He would have to remain in the doorway, and without a list of questions prepared, he was just going to have to wing it.

***

Trey led Joey around the back of his building into the garage. They walked up to the small booth by the electric gate and tapped on the window. The parking lot attendant looked up from her book and her jaw dropped at the sight of the celebrity chef. She fumbled to open the tiny door and step out.

"Oh my god! Trey Chapman. I can't believe it's true."

He turned to Joey. "I don't drive much."

"That's an understatement," she said. "I've been working here fourteen months. Which car do you want to take?"

"You have more than one?" Joey asked. "Who are you?"

The enthusiastic attendant opened a metal box on the wall and grabbed a handful of keys.

She led them down the ramp and around the corner, stopping in front of three pristine luxury vehicles.

"Take your pick."

Joey was now the one in awe. He walked the line of cars. "Is that a McLaren Senna?!"

Trey shrugged. "Sounds right."

"It's got a 789 horsepower, 4.0 liter twin-turbo V8. This thing tops out at 211 miles per hour."

"If you say so," Trey replied.

Joey's eyes went down the line. "You've got a Lamborghini and Maybach too? You didn't even have a car in high school."

"I did this charity thing with Rowan Atkinson in London. He's all about them."

"Mr. Bean?"

"Yeah. Now that guy's got a collection. Except for Porsches. Don't ask."

The attendant jangled the keys. "I've got to get back to the booth, so which one is it going to be?"

"I would say the McLaren," Joey said, "but I'm not trying to draw that kind of attention. Let's take the Maybach."

The attendant went to hand the keys to Trey, but Joey grabbed them. "He's been drinking. I'll drive."

Trey couldn't argue. Plus, with his brother at the wheel it would let him focus as they drove to the airport. The attendant left and the Chapman boys got into the souped-up Mercedes. Joey revved the engine for a moment before slowly pulling out of the parking space. But as soon as the gate arm lifted, he peeled out of the garage.

"So much for not drawing attention," Trey said. "What's the story behind Merlin?"

"I got a rep for being able to acquire things. This guy messed up sourcer and sorcerer, and the name just stuck."

"I thought Merlin was a magician."

Joey shrugged.

"But how'd you get that cheese and all the other stuff into the country?" Trey asked.

"I used to just bring it in my suitcase, but then I found a guy who ships massive containers of tile from Italy and all over Europe. It's easy to stash stuff in the pallets. They're never going to unload thousands of pounds of marble to check every one."

Joey got to the end of the alley and turned left.

"Aren't you going to the airport?"

"Midway. It's not as busy and I've got a bag there."

The whole point of Trey coming along was to buy time so he could somehow talk his brother out of fleeing. Now he understood that this was not a spur of the moment decision. There was haste, but also a plan. It explained why Joey had been so hard to get in touch with recently and why he seemed so distracted when they were together. His brother was the subject of a city-wide manhunt, one with guns apparently, and since fight was not an option, Joey had prepared for flight.

"What happened this time that you got caught?"

"You heard of Patrick Schuler?"

Trey shook his head.

"He served it at one of his underground dinners. Someone took a picture of the cheese and it went viral. Then your buddy Joan Jones worked it into a national frenzy. She even had an assistant district attorney on asking him about jail time. This type of thing should be a little fine. A slap on the wrist. It's not like it's heroin."

"But if you leave, how are you ever going to be able to come back?"

"I don't know. I can't think about that right now."

"We *need* to think about that right now. What if you turned yourself in? I could get you the best lawyer in the city. In the country even."

The light in front of them turned red and Joey stopped the car. He turned to his brother and made it clear. "I'm not getting arrested."

The word rattled around in Trey's brain as they sat there. He didn't know what else to say and Joey seemed content to ride the rest of the way in silence. The light went green and he eased the pricey black sedan down the block towards the freeway. Trey just watched out the window as the buildings started to go by faster and faster. The ride to the airport started to make him think about his own trip. All the chaos of the last couple weeks had changed nothing. It was about to be status quo again for the Chapman family.

Off in the distance, a tiny rectangle came into view. Trey couldn't read the sign, but it looked familiar. It took another half block before he recognized the building. A solution to both of their problems started to swirl inside his brain. He looked at the clock on the dashboard. It was almost noon. The timing was right. Trey knew it didn't quite make sense yet, but if there was a way for neither him nor Joey to get on a plane, it was worth it.

"Pull over!" he yelled.

Joey slowed a little, but didn't stop. "Why?"

"There's something I gotta do."

"I need to get to the airport, Trey."

"I know. But your bartender friend is going to keep those guys occupied for a while. Ten minutes. I need you to trust me."

Joey whipped the car over to the side of the road. Before he had time to ask any questions, his brother jumped out and hurried down the sidewalk. Joey got out and chased after him, running right by a white van. Inside were two Immigration and Customs Enforcement agents. Even if the rookies had been paying attention, they would never have known that the casu marzu smuggler and his brother had just gone by.

Trey went right through the glass doors, but Joey stopped at the front of the building and looked up at the marquee.

"Channel 2?"

Inside, Trey scanned the lobby and rushed over to the spherical security guard. "Taka!"

"Chef Chapman!" she said. "What's this I hear about you coming to do a demo while I was on vacation?"

"I'm making up for it now, aren't I?"

"I didn't know you were coming today."

"I know. This is sort of a surprise."

She untucked a clipboard from her massive arm, and scanned the paper. "You're not on the list. I can't let you in if you're not on the list."

Trey was worried about that part, but he had gotten to know the former sumo wrestler a little over the years and even once hired her as private security for an event. He pointed to Joey who was still outside staring up at the sign.

"See the guy by the door. That's my little brother."

Taka squinted. "Like Big Brothers Big Sisters?"

They both watched as Joey pushed on the door for a minute before realizing he needed to pull to get in. Trey thought quickly and decided to go with it.

"Yeah,"

"You're his little brother?" she asked Joey as he walked up.

"Yep."

"One sec, Taka," Trey said, pulling Joey off to the side.

"What's going on?" he asked.

"Just wait here." Trey walked back over still formulating a way to get upstairs.

"I thought they were supposed to be like little kids."

"He's only twelve. He's got that disease that makes him look old."

The security guard stared over at Joey. "That's horrible, man."

"I know. I'm just trying to make his day a little brighter."

Taka leaned in and sniffed. "Have you been drinking?"

"Part of the kid's wish," Trey shrugged.

She looked the celebrity chef up and down for a minute before stepping to the side. "If this gets me in trouble, you know I'm coming for you, right?"

"Thanks, Taka!"

He waved Joey over and they got in the elevator. Trey took getting this far as a sign. He closed his eyes on the slow ride upward. The soothing music was the perfect soundtrack for the momentary calm. There was haste, but he too now had a plan, at least for the next few minutes. Trey had no idea what would happen after that.

The doors opened and Trey steered Joey down the hall to the green room.

"Wait here."

"Straight to the airport after whatever this is, right?"

"Yep," Trey lied.

As he continued down the corridor, he wondered how many times he'd been on TV there.

Certainly, more than a dozen, and far more than any other news station. Trey made a quick left past the makeup room and was soon standing in front of the studio door. He saw the red light flashing above it and knew to be quiet as he slipped inside. Joan Jones' voice echoed across the set. She was saying something about kittens, but he was too focused on the tangle of wires that crisscrossed the floor. Trey danced over them and found a place just behind one of the cameras to wait for his chance.

"Talk about a purr-fect ending," Joan said. "Up next, what are the chances of a white weekend in the Windy City. Gus has your forecast right after this."

"Clear!" the stage manager yelled.

Lights came on and people immediately started moving around the set. The hair and makeup pit crew descended upon Joan. Trey used the commotion to make his way over to her.

"I like the new 'do," he said, unleashing his charm.

"Trey Chapman! What are you doing here?"

"This casu marzu story has kind of been your thing, and since we go way back, I thought I'd let you have the breaking news."

The producer jumped in her ear, "No, no, no. Joan, whatever this is, it's not happening. Someone get him off my set!"

Joan reached up and pulled the earpiece out. "Breaking news?"

"I need you to put me on live in the next segment."

"90 seconds back!" the stage manager called out.

The midwestern anchor with the now straight, shoulder-length hair was intrigued. The hometown celebrity chef having some information on the bizarre case would certainly draw some attention. The reward seemed greater than the risk, so Joan patted the chair next to her behind the anchor desk.

"How about a little anti-shine for the chef?" she said to the makeup artist. Trey sat down and closed his eyes for the quick dusting across his face. "This better be good," she said.

The stage door opened and the producer came flying up to the desk. "Don't you ever take your earpiece out when I'm talking to you! And you," he said to Trey. "I don't know what the hell you think you're doing, but you need to leave right now."

"30 seconds back from commercial!" shouted the stage manager.

"In 30 seconds, you're going to be famous," Trey said.

The producer grabbed Trey's arm and tried to pull him off the chair. As he tugged at the celebrity chef, he called up to the production booth. "Larry, you're going straight to a single of Gus for the weather, got it?"

"Larry, Dear," Joan said. "If you want to direct this show ever again, you'll come right to me on a single, then cut to a two shot when I introduce our special guest."

"10 seconds!"

Trey shook off the producer who went flying to the floor. The celebrity chef straightened his shirt and sat back down just as the red light came on.

"Welcome back to Channel 2 news, I'm Joan Jones and the studio is just buzzing with excitement right now. And I'm not talking about Gus's forecast, which I promise is coming up. We have a surprise visit from celebrity chef Trey Chapman! Welcome Trey."

"Thanks so much for having me on, Joan."

"Now just to be clear for our viewers, Chef Chapman was not scheduled to be on today. But he rushed in here and, get this, he says he has breaking news on the casu marzu smuggler!"

Joey's jaw dropped as he watched from the green room couch. He stood up and walked right to the TV.

"Let's have it. What light can you shed on this mystery that has rocked our city, and really captured the nation?"

"I'm the one who smuggled the cheese into the country."

"What?!" Joey said to the empty room.

"Oh Trey, you're hilarious. Is this some sort of prank?" She glanced at the producer who was still sitting on the floor, now looking more upset than ever.

"No. I'm the one who sold the cheese to Patrick Schuler. My street name is Merlin."

"You're serious? Why?"

"Excitement, I guess. It's something I've been doing for years." Trey was trying to remember everything his brother had told him on the ride over, but he felt like he needed to add more to the story. "I was always trying to push the limit with my cooking. It was nice to find chefs who wanted to do that too, even if the ingredients weren't exactly legal."

Joey was now pacing back and forth. "What are you doing?"

The midwestern anchor couldn't process what she was hearing either. "Okay, but then why confess now? I don't think anyone would've ever guessed it was you."

"The whole story was just getting out of hand. I never meant for anything like this to happen. So, I'm taking full responsibility. As soon as we're done, I'll wait in the building until someone from the task force or police arrives."

"Well, I am at a loss. You know I was the first person to ever put you on TV."

Trey managed a slight smile. "And you just might be the last."

He had done what he came to do, and had nothing more to say.

Joan stared at him and shook her head. "Kind of hard to send it over to Gus for the weather after that, huh?"

The producer, who had finally gotten to his feet, whispered, "Just go to break."

"We're going to take a little TV timeout and process this revelation. For those of you just joining us, celebrity chef Trey Chapman has admitted to being the casu marzu smuggler. We'll have much more on that exclusive, breaking news. But when we come back, Gus has the weather."

"Clear," the stage manager said, barely audible.

Then the entire studio went quiet. There was no cacophony of rolling cameras and cables.

No race to reposition for the next segment. No one knew exactly what to do. After an awkward moment, Trey stood up.

"Thanks, Joan. Thanks, everyone." He patted the producer on the shoulder as he made his way back to the green room.

***

Ken Nakara hadn't made much progress outside the nameless bar. In fact, the Supervisory Special Agent had managed to get nothing out of the colossal bartender blocking the door. He couldn't come up with any more questions, so he just leveled with her.

"In a couple hours someone from the Department of Public Health will be here to close this place down. They'll bring the police if they have to. Whatever this is that you've been running, it's over."

Wallin's phone started beeping loudly, and before he could turn off the alert, Nakara shot him a look.

"I'm not sure what type of fines they'll levy," he continued, "but charges are not out of the question either. So, I'm going to ask one last time for..."

"Uh, boss," Walling interrupted.

"Not now!"

"We don't need her anymore. Trey Chapman just confessed on Channel 2 news to being the casu marzu smuggler. It's blowing up on social media."

"Did you say *Trey* Chapman?" Crete asked.

"Yep," Wallin answered.

"He's at Channel 2, right now?" Nakara asked.

239

"Yes sir."

Nakara pulled out his phone and quickly dialed the ICE agents who were positioned outside. He didn't even wait for them to speak. "Get in the building and detain Trey Chapman!"

"The celebrity chef?" one of them asked.

"Yes, he apparently just confessed to being the smuggler. Get in there right now and hold him until I get there."

Nakara hung up and rushed over to his car. The other members of the task force quickly followed, but he stopped them. "You all stay here and just deal with this."

Andy Truman, Wallin and the two OCI agents turned back just as Crete closed the door. They stood there as the lock made a loud click. Then they watched the Toyota Camry pull out of the tiny parking lot.

"Now what do we do?" Andy asked.

***

Trey walked into the green room and found his brother tugging at his hair. "You didn't have to do that. I was ready to leave."

"I want you around, Joey. And I want to be around too. This way we get both."

"But you're going to jail!"

"I was already prepared for it when I walked into that bank," Trey said, sitting down on the couch and propping his feet up on the coffee table. "It's the only way."

"Why here? Why on live TV?"

"If I had told you what I was going to do, you wouldn't have let me."

"No way."

"Exactly."

Joey put his head in his hands. "Dad already thinks I'm a royal fuckup."

"Who says he has to know? Who says anyone has to know? Probably best if no one did, really."

"Patrick Schuler does. How are you going to keep him from talking?"

"I haven't figured that part out. I've only had about 20 minutes to process this whole thing.

One of the ICE agents peeked his head in the green room. "You're Trey Chapman, right?"

The celebrity chef nodded.

The agent yelled down the hall. "He's in here!"

Joey's eyebrows went up. "That was fast."

Both men entered the room. "You're under arrest," the other one said.

"Give me a minute." Trey turned to his brother. "Do me a favor. Call Dad and Jackson. Tell them I'll explain everything."

"You got it."

Trey reached into his pocket and pulled out his phone.

"Hey, what are you doing!?" the first agent asked.

"I'm texting my business manager," he said, without looking up. When he was finished, Trey stood and put it away. He rolled up his sleeves just enough to expose his wrists and held them forward. "I'm ready now."

"I don't think handcuffs are necessary," the other agent said.

"Oh, they're necessary," Trey replied.

The first agent shrugged, then pulled out his cuffs and tightened them on the chef's wrists.

"Let's go."

Joey desperately wanted to say something. Anything. He opened his mouth, but the right words weren't there. The youngest Chapman simply watched as his big brother was led away.

Trey was flanked by both ICE agents as they stepped off the elevator into the lobby of the building that houses Channel 2. As the celebrity chef hoped, there was a crowd of media and other onlookers starting to build outside. The first agent opened the door and the air was instantly filled with shouts and camera clicks. Trey made sure the handcuffs were clearly visible as the trio made their way down the sidewalk. Out of the corner of his eye, he spotted Lindsay McKeil and slowed just enough to make sure she got the perfect tabloid photo. There was no doubt it would go viral before Trey was even fingerprinted.

The Toyota Camry pulled up to the curb and Ken Nakara hopped out. The sight of Chef Chapman being led away immediately set him off.

"I told you guys to wait for me! How hard is that to understand?"

The rookies just looked at each other.

"And why is he in handcuffs? Did you place him under arrest?"

"It was his request," one of the agents answered.

"His request!?" Nakara couldn't take it anymore. "Give him to me!"

Trey smiled as the Supervisory Special Agent took him by the arm and helped him into the back of the car. Nakara fumbled with the seat belt trying to buckle the detainee in.

"Any chance we can switch to a police car?" Trey asked.

"I'm not a cop. I work for the FDA," he said, finally getting the buckle to latch.

"What's with the gun then?"

Nakara sighed deeply, then shut the door. He kept his head down as he walked around the car and got into the driver's seat.

"Quiet type, huh? I get it," Trey said, and leaned back on the headrest.

The Supervisory Special Agent adjusted his rearview mirror. He thought back to the description Patrick Schuler gave of the smuggler. *Maybe fifty. Wavy, blonde hair.* In the underground chef's attempt to describe anyone other than Joey Chapman, he had created a spot-on portrait of Trey. But even though the man in his backseat looked the part, Nakara's gut was telling him something was off. He started the car and had the entire ride to the police station to try and figure out what.

14

Trey walked out of the police station into the frigid night air and immediately saw the familiar hired black sedan idling beneath the streetlights. He knew it was for him even before Biv Trammel opened the door and stepped out. The business manager pulled his wool overcoat tight. He squinted through the cold as Trey bounded down the steps.

"Thanks for bailing me out."

Biv scanned his client's eyes for a moment. "I don't really understand, and maybe I'm not supposed to, but I know this wasn't you."

This was the part where Trey's story differed from Montgomery Brewster. He didn't get to tell anyone the truth. Perceptions of the celebrity chef were forever changed, and he could never change them back.

"We all have our secrets, right?" Trey said. He rubbed both of his arms, then dove into the waiting car, where he almost landed on Erica Tomlin. "What are you doing here?"

"I was at the office when you texted. I can't believe I missed this," she said, holding up a photo of Trey in handcuffs being led out of Channel 2.

"Lindsay McKeil?" he asked.

"Yep."

Biv squeezed in and shut the door. "I've already called your lawyer."

"I have a lawyer?"

"Of course you do. I'll have him contact the district attorney's office and work out a deal- if that's what you really want."

"It is."

"Everything we've built," Biv said, staring out into the night. "It's all gone then, Trey." The celebrity chef had to work hard to keep the smile off his face. He also had to be sure.

He needed to hear Biv say it. "What do you mean?"

"I've spent the entire day on the phone. Everyone knows. Not to mention there's some crazy picture of you in a bank with a gun. I'd ask what that's all about, but I know you won't tell me the truth. They're all pulling out. The publisher wants the advance for your next cookbook back. They're taking your kitchenware off the shelves. And Donnie Byrnes was a real asshole. They're turning every *Trey Chic* into one of their burger joints." The business manager sounded beaten down. "All we've got left...all *you've* got left is the six restaurants. But I'm not sure if they're going to make it through this."

"Then let's close 'em," Trey said, a little too upbeat. "Miami's a train wreck anyway."

"What's going on with you!?" Biv exploded. "You're losing everything! Decades worth of work down the drain and you're practically giddy."

Erica inched as close to the door as she could, but there was no way to escape the awkward scene.

"Biv, I'm not..."

"You are! You've ruined your name and reputation. You want to end it all? Fine. I'll negotiate the lease exits and send you the bill. We're done."

It didn't sound so good put that way. There was so much hurt. Trey had made Biv the bad guy in his mind for the past several weeks. He had painted this narrative of the business manager as the cause of his problems. But Trey was taking away everything Biv had worked for too. It was his tenacity and drive that pushed the Trey Chapman machine forward. It was his sweat on the paperwork. He had shared in every step of the creation, yet was forced to watch its demolition from the side lines.

"I don't want things to end like this," Trey said, his head hanging down. "We've been through too much."

Biv stayed silent, turning ever so slightly farther towards the window. Erica could see his sullen reflection on the glass, and an identical sadness on Trey's face. It was a look of finality.

She wondered if she was witnessing these two men share the same air for the last time. That awareness, however, set off a panic of her own. This was not the mood or setting for the pitch she had been working on, but what if it was her last opportunity? What if it could solve everything? Erica took a deep breath. If nothing else, at least her audience was captive.

"I'm not sure how artsy you guys are, but you know Broadway, right?"

Trey looked over at her. He didn't want to answer, but he couldn't hurt her too. "Like Hamilton?"

"Exactly," she said, peeking over to see if she had Biv's attention. "If a show does well in New York, then they go on a world tour. I've been working on a restaurant concept with a similar model. You take an up-and-coming chef, maybe someone who's only doing pop ups. Someone without a brick and mortar. You give them a place of their own for a month. If they do well, you send them on tour to another city to keep building their rep. Then a new chef takes their place."

"Sort of like a farm system?" Trey asked.

"Yes! And if they're successful, we get to partner with them on a place of their own in whatever city they want."

"That's a great idea, Erica. I'd be happy to invest."

"I don't want your money," she paused, "anymore, that is."

Biv looked over. "You want the restaurants. Instead of closing all the locations of *Trey*, they become the tour stops."

"It's a win win win," she said.

"It's a huge risk," the business manager argued.

"What do lease exits get you? Nothing. Think about it. You've got the framework in place. No one loses their jobs. All you need is the chef."

"That's a pretty big part of the equation, don't you think?"

Trey liked the idea of everyone keeping their jobs, even if he didn't know who they were.

More importantly, Erica's proposal could tie up the remaining loose end.

"What about Patrick Schuler?"

Biv let out a deep sigh. "The guy you sold the illegal cheese to? Allegedly."

"That would turn some heads," Erica said. "And there's no hotter name right now."

"I don't know." Biv looked back out the window. He had gotten into the hired black sedan hoping for a way to fix everything. Then the mission went from save to salvage in an instant. But there was nothing to recover. And now the business manager was being asked to fan the flames of some culinary phoenix out of the ashes of his life's work.

Trey could see the consternation, but he knew Biv Trammel well enough to understand that was only taking up half his mind. Somewhere in the background, he was playing out the Broadway proposition. The *Trey* marquees were coming down. Patrick Schuler's name was going up in fancy script.

"I'll give up my half of the restaurants," Trey offered. "I don't need the money."

Erica's eyes went wide. "Whoa."

But it wasn't his assistant that needed convincing.

"What if I got Schuler to sign with you? You could turn him into a star. Cookbooks, aprons, knives. The whole thing, just like you did for me. And this kid's already got a head start."

Biv thought for a moment. "What makes you think you can convince him?"

Trey smiled. "Just send me the paperwork."

"Is this really happening?" Erica asked.

"If this doesn't get you an A, I'm not sure what will. And if I'm not in prison, I'd really love to come to your graduation."

Trey twisted in his seat so he could extend his right hand towards Biv. The business manager brushed it aside, and instead reached over to give his now former client a hug.

***

Joey balanced a tray of coffees in his left hand while he knocked for the third time on the door of the Gold Coast high-rise condo. The sound of the latch clicking meant he had finally reached the correct volume to rouse his brother out of bed.

"I thought you had a key," Trey said, opening the door.

"Good morning to you, too." Joey slid past and set the cardboard carrier on the counter.

He held out one of the small cups. "Cafecito?"

Trey popped the lid and closed his eyes as he inhaled the steam. "Thanks. Where's it from?"

"Little place off Milwaukee Ave."

"A bit out of the way, isn't it?"

"So's jail."

Trey gave a tight-lipped smile before taking a sip of the dark roasted Cuban coffee. It was intense, just shy of burnt, then came the almost caramel sweetness. Next came the thought of Teresa. The flavor was entwined with his memory of her long before their impromptu morning together in Miami. And the truth was she had been on his mind ever since. Trey didn't know how she fit into his new life or if she fit in or if she even wanted to fit in. He just knew there was now time to find out. Or there would be soon enough.

"Figured the coffee you're about to be drinking will be pretty rotten," Joey said, taking his cup and walking over to the couch.

247

"Probably." Trey leaned against the counter and swirled the light brown foam. "Did you talk to everyone?"

"Yeah."

"Was it bad?"

"What'd you expect?"

Trey downed his last sip. "Hey, is the gas still on at Chapman's?"

"The steakhouse? I think so."

"Is there electricity? Pots and pans?" Trey said, his voice trailing off as he walked into his bedroom.

"Why?"

"Do you think you could get Dad, Jackson and Audrey there tonight?"

Joey sat forward. "You want to do a family dinner?"

"It would be easier to talk to them all at once. And I have no idea when I'm going to get the chance to cook again."

Trey reappeared with a slip of paper and handed it to his brother. "Can you get this stuff?"

Joey scanned it. "When did you make a grocery list?"

"I was in that holding cell for like six hours. I would get everything, but I can't exactly go shopping right now. It's nothing complicated and I'll pay you back."

"Sure," Joey said, folding the paper and putting it in his pocket.

"And I need you to call Patrick Schuler and tell him he has to I.D. me as the smuggler. And he's gotta sign with Biv."

"Why would he do that?"

Trey sat in the chair across from his brother and put his feet up on the coffee table. "Because if he does, he gets his own restaurant."

"Sounds like a pretty good deal."

"Tell him my assistant, Erica, will be in touch to work out all the details."

Joey finished his cafecito and set the cup down. "You got any booze here?"

"It's a little early."

"For tonight. I sold everything from Chapman's."

"Tell Jackson to bring some wine."

"You know how he is," Joey said, walking over and rifling through the cabinets. "He's going to want to pair it with the meal and it's going to be a whole thing."

Trey laughed. "You're right about that. I'm going to hop in the shower. There's something I gotta do while it's still early."

"What time tonight?"

"Let's say seven."

"You got it," Joey said and let himself out.

***

Audrey leaned over from her stool and looped her arm through Jackson's. Everything was perfectly calm inside Chapman's Steakhouse. The restaurant was illuminated only by the lights above the bar where they sat. For the moment, they had the place to themselves and had never looked so content in each other's company.

"I can't believe Trey bought it all," Audrey said.

Jackson put his finger up to his mouth. "Shhh. Dad doesn't know yet."

"This is going to be quite a night full of surprises then."

The swinging door to the kitchen burst open and James came out holding a bottle of liquor.

"I thought you were helping Joey unload things, Dad."

"I helped long enough to find this," James said, making his way around the bar.

He pulled three glasses from a low shelf and gave them a quick dust with his shirt sleeve.

"What should we toast to?" Audrey asked as James poured.

"You know in Scotland, there's a tradition of..."

"Christ," James interrupted. "Can't we just have a simple drink for once?"

Audrey couldn't help but laugh. Jackson just shook his head as he picked up his glass.

Outside, the black McLaren Senna couldn't have looked more out of place pulling into the dusty parking lot. The car door swung open and Trey emerged wearing a brand new chef's coat. He could have been going to a red carpet or cookbook signing or any of the events from his former life where he was more celebrity than chef. But Trey's jacket was no longer part of that costume. It was his uniform again, and he was proud to wear it even if he was just cooking a family dinner. He reached back in the car and pulled a black duffel bag off the passenger seat, then headed towards the large wooden front door.

All three heads at the bar turned as Trey walked in. He was prepared for a comment about his outfit from Jackson. When that didn't come, he knew they were all waiting for him to speak first. He strode over to the bar and nodded at the bottle.

"What are we drinking?"

"Weller," James said.

"Look, I know I owe you all an explanation, and there honestly isn't a lot to say, but can we save it until dinner?"

"It's your party," Jackson said.

"Is Joey here?"

James motioned with his head. "In the kitchen."

Trey walked in to find his youngest brother unloading the last of the food from brown paper bags onto the counter.

"What's with the chef's whites?" Joey asked.

"Right after you left, I went to my restaurant to pick up some knives and a few spices," he said, setting the duffel bag next to the stove. "I saw it hanging there and it just felt right."

Trey turned on the oven, then rummaged through the shelves and drawers.

"What's on the menu?"

"Meat and potatoes."

"I got that much," Joey said, leaning underneath the counter and retrieving a cutting board. He handed it to his brother.

"Thanks. It's all pretty simple and classic stuff. What else do you serve at a steakhouse?"

Joey hopped up on the steel counter. "A shrink would have a field day with you."

"What are you talking about?"

"You're cooking Dad's food. In Dad's old restaurant. Which you now own. Is this like a 'Last Supper' thing before you go all fusion and molecular gastronomy on him?"

"You've never eaten at one of my restaurants, have you? And no, I haven't even thought about the menu. There's a lot more to figure out before we get there."

Trey tossed a head of romaine lettuce at his little brother. "Make yourself useful. Wash this."

As Joey hopped back down, James, Jackson and Audrey came through the swinging doors.

"What can we help with, Trey?" Audrey asked, setting her glass down and lifting an apron from a hook on the wall.

"I need the juice of two limes. Thanks," he said, pulling a small bowl off a shelf and handing it to her. "Jackson, how about you grab a pot and wilt all that spinach?"

"Aye, Aye."

"Dad, you want to help with the potatoes?"

James slid a stool out and took a seat. "I've washed enough spuds in this kitchen for two lifetimes. I think I'll just enjoy my drink."

"Any word from your lawyer?" Joey asked.

"I talked to him this morning," Trey said as he picked up a massive piece of beef and generously coated it with salt. "He's already been in touch with the district attorney's office, but it could take a week or so to work out a deal. I won't go in front of a judge or anything until that's all squared away."

The kitchen went quiet except for the soft swishing sound of Joey cleaning lettuce in the deep wash sink. Trey appeared to be the only one moving in an otherwise frozen scene. Then out of nowhere came the loud clang of James' empty glass on the metal counter. It was punctuated. Purposeful.

He stood up. "You're going to jail, aren't you, son?"

Trey didn't say anything, but his father wasn't waiting for an answer anyway. He walked into the dark hall and down to his office where he closed the door behind him.

"Don't say I didn't warn you about a family dinner," Joey said.

"He'll be fine, especially with the good news about this place," Jackson said, pulling the pot off the burner and showing it to Trey. "How's this look?"

"Oh, I get to review you for once?" he said with a smile.

The mood started to lift and it wasn't long before the Chapman brothers were laughing and running around the kitchen like they were boys again. Trey was at the helm, fully in charge. Jackson got distracted with the spices in the black duffel bag. Joey divided his time equally between sneaking bites, helping, and disappearing to the bar for a refill. Audrey couldn't remember the last time she'd seen them all in the same place and this happy. She eventually slipped away, leaving them to their revelry.

The dinner took quite a bit longer to prepare than it should have and it was almost nine when the family gathered near the front window. There was far more food than needed for the five white plates lining the large rectangular table. Caesar salad nearly overflowed an old wooden bowl and there was a crock of creamed spinach and a full sheet pan of roasted potatoes. Trey came out of the kitchen with the last platter containing two towering bone-in double cut ribeyes. He set them down at the head of the table but remained standing.

"First off, thanks for coming. And thank you for your help. I promise we'll get to eat in just a minute. Look, I know this all doesn't make sense," Trey said, turning towards his father. "And I'm sorry. Not just for the craziness of the past couple days. I'm sorry for not being here. For not really being a part of this family. But that's over. The restaurants, cookbooks, demos- they're all gone. And the silver lining is that I get back all the time those things took from me. And if you're willing, I'd like to spend it with you guys."

Joey slid his chair back and stood up. He locked eyes with his older brother. Trey had no idea what he was about to do, and worried that a confession was coming. All he could do was watch as Joey put his hand on his dad's shoulder. The youngest Chapman scanned the other faces at the table, then finally looked back at Trey. "So can we eat yet or what?"

Trey, who had unknowingly been holding his breath, exhaled deeply and waved his arms at the food. "Dig in."

He shot Joey a look and collapsed back into his chair.

Jackson leaned over and pulled a bottle of white wine from a cooler bag. "I think this Petit Manseng will go nicely with the salad."

"Oh, fuck you Petit Manseng," Joey said.

Jackson didn't understand the offense. "What?"

"Didn't I tell you he would do this, Trey?" Joey turned back to Jackson. "No one drinks Petit Manseng, not even the French."

"This is from Virginia," Jackson argued.

Joey turned and headed to the bar. "I'm getting more bourbon."

"Well, I'd love to try the wine," Audrey said, offering her glass up. "And since you've got the floor, why don't you tell everyone your exciting news?"

Jackson gave his wife a generous pour and then set the bottle down. "I'm leaving the paper and writing a book."

James looked up from slicing a chunk of steak off the bone. "I didn't know you were unhappy at The Tribune."

"It's not that I was unhappy, Dad. This is something I've wanted to do for years, and with Audrey's help, I now have a publisher. We're going to travel the entire East Coast as part of my research."

"A book and a road trip?" Trey said. "That's really great. I can't wait to read it."

Joey lifted his glass as he returned to the table. "Congrats." He suddenly found all eyes on him, which he quickly dismissed. "Don't look at me. I don't have any big news. I'm gonna stick around for a bit though and enjoy this place I'm staying at in the West Loop. Dad, there's plenty of room if you need somewhere to crash after you sell the house."

"I have until the end of the month," James said.

"I'd be happy to help you find an apartment if you want," Audrey offered. "We don't leave for a couple weeks."

"Thank you."

Trey knew there was just one big reveal left and it was his. "Dad, I know you're scared for me and rightfully confused about what I've been doing. But I just figured out that's not why you've been upset all night. You think this is some grand sendoff for the restaurant. And if anyone deserves to host, it's you. But you're not a guest. And this isn't the last dinner here. The restaurant is ours now. I bought it."

"You what?" James set his fork down. "I told you I didn't want your charity."

"It's not charity. I need you in the front of the house with your suit and hat. No one is better with the customers. I'll handle the food. You handle everything else."

It was exactly what James wanted. Or had wanted. That hope, though, had calcified with time, beginning the moment Trey went out on his own. The family patriarch was now too hardened against the idea. He wasn't getting to hand the restaurant down. This felt like a handout. James Chapman Jr. would not be pitied. He rubbed the stubble on his chin with both hands and was planning his exit when he locked eyes with the picture of Josephine across the restaurant. Her lips were sealed, but he could hear her voice.

"Jimmy. That's what your mother would call me if she were here. She knew I hated it. To me, it was a schoolboy nickname that had no class. She only used it when she wanted to make a point. She would say, 'Jimmy, being proud can't make you a dollar, but it sure could lose you a few.' I know that's what she's thinking right now. That I'm being too damn proud. And she's right." James reached over and put his hand on top of Trey's. "And I know she'd love to be able to keep tabs on both of us in one place."

"Yeah, she would," Trey said.

Jackson raised his glass. "To mom."

"To mom," everyone said in unison.

"And to the new Chapman family restaurant," Jackson added.

"That's a terrible name," Joey said.

Jackson scoffed, "Well, I didn't mean that was necessarily the name."

"Chapman and Son? Chapman and Sons?" James suggested, looking over at his youngest.

"Pass. But I do know a good bartender who needs a job," Joey said.

Trey gave a little wink. He was about to say that he was going to have plenty of time to sit and think about the name, but there was no need to remind everyone of what loomed. The night had built to a crescendo of celebration. Trey made sure it stayed there. Jackson produced several more obscure bottles of wine from near his feet. Joey teased him mercilessly. And James took turns embarrassing each of his boys with childhood stories of them at the restaurant, much to Audrey's delight. It was a scene seven years in the making.

***

It took two full days for Jackson and Audrey to recover from the late night, the first of which was spent mostly in bed trying to chase the libations out of their bodies with a proportionate amount of coffee. The next morning, Jackson was spurred into activity upon waking to find his wife had resumed her normal routine. He lumbered down the steps and was greeted by the familiar smell of dark roast and a slice of pecan kringle. Next to the plate, Audrey had unfolded

The Tribune to his final review. Jackson sat down on the lone stool at the counter and took two bites of the flaky, sweet pastry in quick succession. After he had wiped his hands clean, he picked up the paper and rubbed the newsprint between his fingers one last time.

This column marks the official end of my tenure as the food and restaurant critic in these pages. Many thanks are due. To you, the reader, for letting me share my experiences be they plate, bowl, skewer or chopstick. To my editor, Martin Easley, for his grace in dealing with my difficulties. And to my wife, Audrey, for the exact same reason only multiplied.

I am off to live out a culinary travelogue that has been rattling around in my mind for far too long. What I would like to leave you is a bit of encouragement. You don't need to leave your neighborhood to take your taste buds to a new country. Try the food cart that only pops up on the corner on Saturdays. Go to a Farmers Market and buy something you can't identify or pronounce. Visit the hole in the wall that you've walked by for three years without stepping inside. Find yourself a gem, like Patti's Soul Food on W. 87th Street and try every combination of "meat and three" possible. These are the people that deserve your attention and support. It is my sincere hope that the scribe who gets to fill these inches next will do a far better job highlighting them than I have.

With that said, my final review is not of a restaurant, it's about the end of one. Chapman's Steakhouse served its last meal to customers weeks ago after nearly a half century as one of Chicago's landmark eateries. It was started by my father, James Chapman Jr., when he was barely in his twenties. He hosted Presidents and plumbers, movie stars and machinists.

My brothers and I grew up there, our lives and careers molded by what we saw, smelled and tasted.

Recently, my family gathered there for dinner, with Trey back at the stove he first learned to cook at. The now celebrity chef, whose claim to fame was a 10-course tasting masterpiece, prepared a simple meal. The Caesar salad was made with lime juice, honoring the original recipe from Mexico. The roasted potatoes were elevated with a dusting of harissa powder and espresso. Fresh nutmeg added its own warmth to an otherwise pious creamed spinach. Two enormous ribeyes were the centerpiece, and if I'm being honest, as a critic should, they were disappointingly past medium rare. But if that's all the rust my brother needs to knock off after so many red carpets, then I think the new restaurant will do just fine. You see that's what the assembly was all about. This was not a farewell. A proper sendoff for Chapman's Steakhouse would be impossible. This was about the start of something; a joint effort between James Chapman Jr. and James Chapman III. An opening date and menu are still far from determined, but if you do choose to stop by I have no doubt you'll recognize the tufted booths, the laughter and the hospitality.

There is no shortage of mantras about living life to its fullest, but I'll leave you with my favorite, borrowed from a dear friend-find someone that will split an appetizer with you at breakfast.

As Jackson lowered the paper, he heard the front door open and the soft sound of Audrey's footsteps in her running shoes coming down the hall. He took a sip of coffee and made quick work of the remaining kringle. She stopped at the kitchen desk and opened the drawer, removing a small, brown package that was delicately tied with twine.

"I have a little something for you."

"Another sercy?" Jackson said, thoroughly wiping his hands before accepting it.

"No, this is to mark the occasion of your final column, which was lovely."

"You liked it?" he asked.

"I did."

Jackson carefully opened the gift, revealing a journal bound in almost buttery red leather. He admired the front and back cover before turning to the first page. The inscription, in Audrey's perfect handwriting, was not about the end of his time at The Tribune.

"The fear of the work is harder than the work," he read.

She slipped the book from his hands and gently set it on the counter, then took its place in her husband's lap.

"We have 2,118 miles ahead of us, give or take," she said, curling her arms around his neck. "I'll be there when it's fun and I'll be there when it's daunting."

"Audrey Darlington Chapman, you are truly amazing." He kissed her until his legs had fallen asleep and his coffee was cold.

***

Ken Nakara sat in the back row of the sparsely filled courtroom wearing a suit and tie. He fidgeted on the hard wooden bench, physically and mentally discomforted at the proceedings.

"You don't need to be here," the woman on his right said in a low voice as she took off her gloves and set them in a pile with her scarf and overcoat.

"Deputy Director, I'm telling you this isn't right. You think Trey Chapman is showing up at car washes selling ackee fruit? It doesn't make sense."

"What part of 'drop it' was unclear?"

The Supervisory Special Agent turned to implore his boss one final time. "Chapman is a celebrity. His face is everywhere. Yet no one could identify the guy selling to them?"

"Maybe he wore a disguise. Maybe he threatened them not to talk. It doesn't matter. Chapman confessed. Patrick Schuler confirmed it. We're getting a conviction and you're about to be promoted. Try and enjoy it."

That much Nakara was happy about. But the feeling that the real smuggler wasn't being brought to justice wouldn't go away. He stared at Trey Chapman, who was seated next to his lawyer at a table in the front of the room. The Supervisory Special Agent had been in court dozens of times and had never seen someone look so carefree before going to prison. Trey, though, was already aware of his fate. It had taken a week for all the parties involved to reach a satisfactory deal. The sentencing was merely a formality.

The hearing was closed to the public, so the entire right side of the courtroom was empty except for the rest of the Chapman family seated in the front row. Trey turned and whispered, "Thanks for being here."

"Is there always this much paperwork?" Jackson asked.

Trey shrugged. He didn't know what to expect, but there was an awful lot of signing and passing of documents. The judge finally set her reading glasses to the side and looked ready to speak. The assistant district attorney, who was not Glenn Bitman, stood. Trey and his lawyer followed suit.

"It is my understanding that both parties have finally reached a plea agreement satisfactory to everyone. I have reviewed the most recent signed version. Are you ready to proceed with the plea hearing?"

Both the ADA and Trey's lawyer answered, "Yes, Your Honor."

"Mr. Chapman, please come and stand up here at the lectern with your attorney."

Both men complied. Trey had been fully prepped, yet the length of questions from the judge seemed endless. She asked about recent use of drugs and alcohol, prescription medication, being under the care of a doctor, if he was fully alert, if he was nervous, and about a dozen other things before she finally arrived at the actual deal.

"You are pleading guilty to one count of felony smuggling, correct?" she asked.

"Yes, Your Honor," Trey replied.

"And you've discussed it with your attorney?"

"Yes."

"Do you understand that if I accept your plea of guilty it will be the same as though you've been convicted of that felony charge?"

"Yes."

"Are you fully satisfied with how your attorney has represented you in this matter?"

"Yes."

"At this time, I will review the plea agreement with you. It specifies the length of your sentence of incarceration should be 60 days."

The judge paused, letting the number hang in the air for a moment. Trey wasn't about to have a change of heart though. He had studied the calendar on his fridge to know exactly when he would get out. Tracing the days with his finger over and over had smudged the ink. And that's when Trey realized he was already free. There would be no more book signings or cooking demos on the local news. No more private jets to restaurant openings or late-night dinners with investors. He had ripped the calendar down and crumpled it up, leaving an empty and joyous spot on the fridge.

"Additionally," she continued, "no separate charges will be filed in connection with an unrelated incident wherein you possessed a replica firearm inside a bank."

That was news to everyone in the front row except Joey.

"Did she say he had a gun?" James asked.

"At a bank?" Jackson added.

Joey just remained silent.

"Is this your agreement, Mr. Chapman?"

"Yes."

"Then it's my finding that the defendant, James Chapman III, knowingly, voluntarily and intelligently entered a plea of guilty to the felony count of smuggling. The court accepts his plea under the terms of this agreement. Mr. Chapman, I commend you for coming forward in this matter, but I am personally concerned about a sense of entitlement that your celebrity seems to have given you. I hope that you realize it holds no favor with this court and that you use these next 60 days to reflect on how you want to use your fame and considerable means in the future. Is there anything you'd like to say?"

Trey looked over at his family. He had already said everything he needed to.

"No, Your Honor."

"It's my understanding you're prepared to begin serving your sentence immediately. The bailiff will now take you into custody. This court is adjourned."

The Chapman family stood up and Trey looked down the line at them as he waited to be escorted away. James, Jackson and Audrey all wore some version of a brave smile. Joey's face was different though. It was filled with guilt. The reality of what his older brother was doing for him had finally set in. He wanted to jump over the railing and switch places, but he knew it wasn't that simple. As he watched Trey being led away, all he could muster was an almost imperceptible nod.

No one moved until the door closed behind the bailiff.

"He's going to be okay," James said.

"He'll have the whole place wrapped around his finger," Audrey agreed.

Joey wouldn't leave that to chance though. He had gotten to see the name of the correctional facility Trey was headed to on a copy of the plea agreement in the high-rise condo. With Crete's help, and quite a bit of his life savings, Joey had made sure that his older brother already had friends waiting on both sides of the bars.

There was something else waiting for Trey Chapman in prison, something he hadn't gotten to do in decades. The former celebrity chef would get to put his head down on the same pillow every night for 60 days. There was solace in something so normal- a word he hoped would describe everything to come after.

THE END

Want to know what Trey, Joey and the rest of the Chapman family are up to next? The sequel, 86 The Secret, is available now!

Trey Chapman thought his troubles were over when he walked out of Cook County Jail. He was wrong. Meanwhile, Joey trades smuggling for sleuthing in a desperate bid to stay out of prison. But between a new flame, a truck full of illegal fish, and a kidnapping gone sideways, staying free will take a whole new recipe for survival. The Chapmans are back—stirring the pot, dodging bullets, and serving chaos hot.

If you want to be first to know about Adam K. Watson's next book, sign up for our mailing list at woosterstreetpublishing.com

Thank you for reading!